Praise for *Beneath a Peaceful Moon*

"Debby Lee offers a unique voice in the harsh landscape of WWII. She captures the culture and experiences of Navajo Code Talkers and Native Americans in the war with a deft hand in *Beneath a Peaceful Moon*. Lee's well-crafted, heroic characters fight for their county, survival, and love. Readers will cheer at every step of their journey."

—Carmen Peone, award-winning writer
and author of *Captured Secrets*.

"A gripping WWII novel, *Beneath a Peaceful Moon* takes readers to the Pacific Theater where secrets, war, and evil conspire to destroy. Debby Lee has created a page-turning romance and diverse characters with much to lose. You won't want to miss this next book in the Heroines of WWII series."

—Danielle Grandinetti, author of *To Stand in the Breach*,
A Strike to the Heart, and *As Silent as the Night*.

"Debby Lee has beautifully used her love and pride for Native Americans to share the story of the famous Code Talkers—the Navajos instrumental in ending WWII. A sweet romance is creatively interwoven into the nail-biting action and a deeply satisfying conclusion."

—Barbara Tift Blakey, author of *Bertie's War*,
"A Place to Belong" in *The Pony Express
Romance Collection*, and "Emma Underground"
in *The Underground Railroad Brides Collection*.

T0043374

≡ HEROINES OF WWII ≡

BENEATH A PEACEFUL MOON

DEBBY LEE

BARBOUR
PUBLISHING

Beneath a Peaceful Moon ©2023 by Debby Lee

Print ISBN 978-1-63609-571-4
Adobe Digital Edition (.epub) 978-1-63609-572-1

All scripture quotations, unless otherwise noted, are taken from the King James Version of the Bible.

This book is a work of fiction. Names, characters, places, and incidents are either products of the author's imagination or used fictitiously. Any similarity to actual people, organizations, and/or events is purely coincidental.

Cover image © Mark Owen / Trevillion Images

Published by Barbour Publishing, Inc., 1810 Barbour Drive, Uhrichsville, Ohio 44683, www.barbourbooks.com

Our mission is to inspire the world with the life-changing message of the Bible.

ecpa Member of the
Evangelical Christian
Publishers Association

Printed in the United States of America.

DEDICATION

Jesus Christ the same yesterday, and to day, and for ever.
HEBREWS 13:8

Dedicated to the countless servicemen and women who, through the years, have served and sacrificed so much for our great country to safeguard our freedoms and protect our republic. My thankfulness for you, and your families, knows no bounds.

In Memory of Bob Hansen, with gratitude and respect. He was a talented and courageous author, founder and backbone of the Inklings critique group. He helped me sharpen my writing skills and kept me going through the years. I miss him so much. I have no doubt he is regaling the angels with stories of Larsunu and Pancake the Mouse.

ACKNOWLEDGMENTS

Many heartfelt thanks to the museum curators and citizens of the Navajo nation who answered a myriad of questions and offered insights into the Navajo culture. It was an honor to visit your reservation. I did my best to write about your tribe and culture with sensitivity.

To my fellow Yakama Tribal members, it is an honor to be counted among you. I used the original treaty spelling of our tribal name, Yakima, to be more historically accurate. That is how it was spelled at the time this book takes place.

Thank you to my agent Tamela Hancock Murray for being my fabulous agent. I am blessed to have you in my corner.

To the Inklings critique group, Barbara, Carolyn, Heather, Joyce, Julie, Kristie, and Kyle, thank you for being the best critique partners. Your editing skills and support have helped bring this book to fruition. I wouldn't be the writer I am today without your help.

To my children, Michelle, Devon, Toni, David, and Steffen, thank you for all the little things you endured to help support me in my writing career. My love for you is endless and I'm so proud to be your mom.

Thank you, Steven, my husband and my dearest friend, for helping me research this book, and for not laughing too hysterically at all the crazy things I did to get into character. And when the technical aspects of operating my laptop drove me to absolute frustration; thank you for being there to help me through it all. Your encouragement means the world to me. I will love you to the moon and back, forever.

⫸ CHAPTER I ⫷

Camp Pendleton, California
Late October 1944

Private Mary Wishram clenched the dreaded telegram in her hand and dropped into a chair in her small duplex apartment.

WOUNDED.

LEYTE BEACH, PHILIPPINE ISLANDS.

Her heart hammered in her chest, smacked against her ribs with pain-filled thuds that echoed in her ears. He couldn't be.

"Oh, Daniel, no. No!" Not her dear older brother, so proud to serve his country. He had wanted to provide a better life for any children he may have one day.

Though her throat constricted and her fingers trembled, she forced herself to uncrumple the paper and read it again.

Words blurred on the page.

CAPTURED.

PRISONER OF WAR.

Her breath hitched.

There was hope he lived, but being held in a Japanese POW camp must be a horrifying experience.

Mary scrunched her eyes closed. Memories of her friends, the Takahashi family, floated to the surface of her mind. They were being held in the Manzanar internment camp in the California desert. The previous week, on her day off from delivering supplies around Camp Pendleton, she'd taken a bus to visit them.

Barbed wire, armed guards, the dark haunted eyes of those held captive. Conditions there were rudimentary and hope in short supply, yet they were far better than what her brother must be enduring.

If he lived and wasn't—

Mary shook her head, as if to shake the horrible possibility from her mind. With their parents gone, Daniel was her only blood relative. She had just knotted a colored bead to her *Ititamat*, a time ball, to register the death of her father. She couldn't bear the thought of tying something else to it for the loss of her brother. She had to do something, anything.

She leaped from her chair. Someone at the Department of Defense Accounting Agency could help her find out what happened to him. The thought of never knowing his fate was more than her sore heart could bear.

If only this awful war would end. Then, at least to her way of thinking, her brother wouldn't be in any more danger. The government would then see that the Takahashi family, and other Japanese Americans, weren't a threat—and thereby release them.

If Hitler and the Japanese surrendered, she could resume selling produce at Pike Place Market in Seattle. Apples, peaches, and cherries grew abundantly on the Yakima Reservation, which she and Daniel had called home only thirteen months ago, before they enlisted in the service.

Daniel.

Swiping at the wetness on her cheeks, she threw on her pea coat and stuffed the telegram in her pocket. Glancing at the clock as she raced out the door, she realized the agency would soon close. If she ran, she just might make it.

The late afternoon wind blew through her as she sprinted along the sidewalk. She rounded a corner. The heel on her left shoe broke. She stumbled but managed to right herself. The fact that this was her only pair of shoes hardly registered in her mind. There was no time to stop. Not when Daniel's life hung precariously over death's chasm.

Minutes later she hobbled up the concrete steps, gasping for breath. She reached for the door handle and gave it a hard tug. The glass rattled, but the door stayed closed.

"No!" Mary gripped the cold metal handle and shook it so hard her fingers ached. She pressed her face to the glass, hoping to see someone.

When no one appeared, she trudged through the bushes along the side of the building. By standing on her tiptoes and placing her hands on the windowsill, she pulled herself up to peer inside the window.

Not a soul in sight.

Mary dropped to the ground and huffed. The building wouldn't open again until Monday morning, and that was two long days away. Her heart seized, thinking of how much suffering her brother would endure in that time. And if he died, the Japanese wouldn't let her know.

Would Daniel become one of the countless others whose fate was known only to God?

Not if she could help it.

Tears threatened to spill onto her cheeks, but crying would do Daniel no good. She swallowed the rough granite lump in her throat. A gritty residue remained.

She gave the side of the building a good swift kick.

"Ow!" She cried, wobbled. The heel on her right shoe had broken off. Well, if that wasn't just fine and dandy. Two broken shoes. At least now they matched.

"Please, God." Mary gripped the medicine pouch hanging from her neck. At best, she had a lukewarm relationship with the Almighty. Would He even hear her prayers?

Voices in the distance snagged her attention. A Jeep roared to life.

People. Someone to help her.

Kicking off her broken shoes, she raced toward the parking lot on the other side of the building, the pavement cold and damp beneath her nylon stocking–covered feet.

Two officers sat in the Jeep. They stopped talking and stared at her as she ran toward them, waving her arms.

"Wait," she yelled. In a most unlady-like manner, she braced herself against the front of the vehicle. If she could just garner a moment of their time. "My brother—please, you have to help me find out what happened to him."

A short, portly man emerged and gave her shoulder a squeeze. "There, there, Miss. Don't worry your pretty little head. My name is Major Morton. How can I help you?"

She cringed at the man's unsolicited endearment but forged ahead.

"I received this telegram. My brother, Daniel Wishram—he's been captured." She pulled the paper from her pocket and handed it to him.

The major donned a pair of glasses and eyeballed the missive. He then removed his spectacles and smiled.

How could he smile at a time like this? Uneasiness churned in her stomach. She stifled a rebuke, much as she wanted to kick him. Remembering that she had no shoes and Daniel needed her, she pushed aside her indignation.

"With all due respect, sir, if you are unable to check the records for more information, please direct me toward someone who can."

"Ma'am, Lieutenant Henry Brandon has been known to deal with matters like this, but he's unavailable tonight. I, however, will be happy to assist you. Let me give you a ride to the Tiki Lounge where we can discuss things over a drink."

Lieutenant Brandon? The husband of her acquaintance, Catherine? Mary yanked the telegram from the man's hand. "No, thank you, sir. I'll locate the lieutenant myself."

Minus her shoes, she took off down the street toward the base hospital where Catherine worked as head nurse. Mary sucked cold air into her lungs as she ran, praying she wouldn't catch pneumonia from the exertion.

By the time she reached the hospital, she was out of breath but thankful. The front doors were open, and people milled about. Her friend Samuel Acothley said hello. She hardly managed a wave before entering the building, though she wasn't sure if Catherine was even there.

Mary approached the front desk, drawing in a deep breath to steady her nerves.

"Excuse me," Mary said. "Can you direct me to Catherine Brandon, please? I'm her, uh, friend, Mary Wishram."

The nurse, in a crisp white uniform, scrunched her eyebrows and pursed her lips.

"Please," Mary begged. "I need to speak with her. It's urgent, a matter of life or death."

"I'm sorry. Mrs. Brandon is entertaining guests tonight. She won't return until Monday."

Mary's heart dropped like a ship's anchor into the ocean's depths. What was she to do now?

She would fight to bring Daniel home, before it was too late.

———— ≈ ————

Corporal John Painted Horse, a proud Navajo, entered the home of his commanding officer, Lieutenant Henry Brandon. The luxurious conditions of the home shocked him, but the officer and his wife, Catherine, had invited him to dinner. He wasn't about to decline the offer, though he was certain of his CO's motives.

Lieutenant Brandon had worked hard to convince him to become a code talker. So much was at stake, but the government promised it would bring honor to his people.

Despite his hesitation to enter the program, the evening would not be a total waste. By the growling in his stomach, he was sure of it.

All kinds of noise resounded from the kitchen where Catherine Brandon whipped up concoctions that smelled heavenly. At least they smelled better than what was served at the chow hall on base. Likely tasted a whole lot better too.

Henry Brandon handed him a bottle of Coke. "Here's something to wet your whistle until Corporal Samuel Acothley arrives."

"Thank you." John took the bottle and squirmed in his seat on the plush sofa. How could folks live in such luxury? People on his reservation made do with sitting on the ground.

Brandon dropped into a leather wingbacked chair and lifted his own bottle. "Cheers."

"Cheers." John took a sip, hoping the bubbly drink would wash down the uneasiness crawling up his throat. He may not be traipsing through the jungles of Saipan, but this was still an ambush, no matter how he looked at it.

"Did Samuel tell you he signed up for the next class even before the last one finished?"

"I don't know him that well. We attended different boarding schools and only saw each other at Christmas. I've only seen him once on base, briefly at that."

"As I was saying," Brandon continued, "it only takes six weeks to learn the code, eight at most. You and Samuel are smart men. I'm sure you'll pick it up in no time."

John gritted his teeth, swallowed hard, lest he say something stupid that landed him in the brig. "Sir, with all due respect, I haven't agreed to enter the program. Not yet anyway."

Lieutenant Brandon downed the last of his drink and placed the empty bottle on the polished mahogany coffee table. He then scowled for a moment before replying. "And what, pray tell, is holding you back?"

"Sir, I have a widowed mother and two young sisters to care for. What will become of them if, uh, if anything happens to me?" John wanted to do his part for his country. He wasn't afraid of fighting, facing death, or even dying. But leaving his mother and sisters to forever fend for themselves terrified him.

The lieutenant held up his hands. "John, the government will take good care of your family. You have my word."

John bristled. The United States government didn't have a great track record of keeping their promises to the Navajos, or any other tribes for that matter. So, why should he believe the lieutenant?

He couldn't count the number of communities on his reservation that didn't even have running water. This included his family, who were entrenched in desperate poverty. Could he really trust the government to take care of them if he were killed? He didn't think so.

Before John could argue his point, the doorbell rang.

Catherine rushed to open the door, and then Samuel's voice echoed into the living room. John took in a deep breath and blew it out. How was he to argue his points with Brandon and Samuel both pressuring him?

Samuel's voice mingled with the soft tone of a woman's he recognized from somewhere. He rose and moved forward to investigate.

Before him stood a woman with black hair in a long braid. Haunted dark eyes met his as introductions were made.

Samuel said, "Mrs. Brandon, I ran into Mary Wishram at the hospital tonight. She said she needed to speak with you, and I thought she could keep you company in the kitchen while I speak with your husband, so I brought her along."

"That's fine. Mary, I'm so glad you could come," Catherine said.

Mary Wishram.

So, that was her name.

A flash of recognition went through his mind. He'd gone to visit a wounded buddy at the hospital. While there, he'd seen her speaking with Catherine. He was taken with her beauty the first time he saw her but hadn't had the chance to meet her, until now.

And she was on Samuel's arm.

Should he be envious? A needle of jealousy poked him. Samuel said they were just friends, but that could mean anything. Samuel did have a habit of flirting with ladies.

Mary offered him a gloved hand. "Pleased to meet you, Mr. Painted Horse."

He gave it a gentle squeeze. Noting the medicine pouch around her neck, he realized she had Indian blood too. He observed a hint of tears in her eyes and wondered what traumas she might be carrying.

Catherine placed an arm around Miss Wishram and excused themselves to the kitchen. Perhaps, later, he'd have the chance to speak with her more.

For the next thirty minutes he listened to Brandon and Samuel extol the benefits and wonders of code talking.

Samuel held his head high. "The code talkers are heroes."

Lieutenant Brandon pointed at John. "The program is making a huge difference and saving lives, which heightens the need for fresh recruits."

John's shoulders sagged. At that moment, he almost believed the jungles of Saipan would be safer. Then he remembered how spiffy his father had been in his WWI military uniform. Where had that gotten him? A long, slow death from mustard gas poisoning.

Catherine mercifully entered the living room. "Dinner is ready, gentlemen."

Grateful for the respite, John followed Samuel and Brandon to the dining room table. He shifted his thoughts to the meal before him.

The dining table was bigger than any he'd seen, with the exception of the chow hall, and it was crammed with more food than any of the homes—hogans—on his reservation. It was almost too much. If only there was a way to send a portion of this bounty home to his family.

He shifted in his chair as Mary approached. She was lovely in spite of the wan smile and the anxiety in her eyes.

He enjoyed the aromas of pot roast and gravy. As Mary took a seat next to him, he was then greeted by the fragrance of fresh lavender.

He wondered why she wasn't sitting next to Samuel. Perhaps they weren't as cozy as he initially thought.

Catherine said, "Henry, we must remember Mary's brother in prayer tonight. She received a telegram. He's been captured by the Japanese."

Mary sniffled. A small sigh escaped from her lips.

John's breath froze in his lungs. The poor girl. And this was a stark reminder of what his family would go through if *he* were taken prisoner. The image of his mother receiving one of those dreaded telegrams drove into his heart. But he was a tough marine, so how could he not do his duty to his country? Torn between the desire to serve his country and fear for his family, he clenched his fists. Why did the government have to ask so much of him, of his people?

Everyone bowed their heads, and Henry Brandon said the blessing. He asked for God's protection and mercy for Mary's brother.

The pot roast tasted divine. It still didn't go down easy. Not with him worrying over his family, and now Mary.

When dinner was over, Samuel said to Catherine, "I have early KP duty, so I need to cut out and hit the sack."

"That's fine, Mr. Acothley. Thank you for coming." Catherine rose from her seat and cleared a stack of dishes from the table.

Samuel then turned to John and asked, "Do you mind walking Mary home for me?"

John glanced at Mary, who seemed unfazed. She was either a smart girl for not falling for Samuel's charms, or she was too worried about her brother to care about the man.

John thought Samuel should walk her home since he'd brought her here, but the last thing he wanted was trouble with a fellow tribal member. "Mary, are you all right with this?" he asked.

Mary smiled. "I would be delighted for you to walk me home."

Regardless of what might or might not be going on between Mary and his friend, he wasn't about to pass up a chance to spend time with her.

Samuel excused himself, and Brandon stood to see him out.

Catherine stepped back into the dining room. "Mary, would you like to help me with dessert?"

The two women headed into the kitchen, just as Brandon sauntered back into the dining room. He lit a cigar and grinned like a cat who'd just feasted on canary rather than pot roast and potatoes.

"So, John," Brandon quipped while puffing on a cigar, "have we convinced you to enter the code talking program?"

John shifted in his seat, contemplating his words. "Sir, out of curiosity, for the sake of argument, what would happen if I were to refuse?"

⚎ CHAPTER 2 ⚎

Lieutenant Brandon assured Mary he'd check the information in her brother's file and, if possible, see to his welfare.

"Thank you, Lieutenant." Relief seeped into her bones. It lightened her heart knowing the Brandons would try to find him. Worry still enveloped her, though, and she wouldn't rest easy until Daniel was safe.

John donned his Marines cap. "I'll see her home."

A host of butterflies in her middle took flight. Not only was this man handsome, but gallant as well. From what she'd gathered at the meal that evening, he didn't seem the sort to carouse and imbibe like many Marines did. She wanted to become better acquainted with him, learn more about the Navajo way of life and how it compared to her Yakima culture.

John helped her shrug into her coat.

Catherine then embraced her in a warm hug. "Try not to worry about your brother. We will pray for him, and you too."

"Thank you." Mary bade the couple good night and stepped outside.

John shook hands with the lieutenant. "I'll think about our little discussion and let you know my decision first thing in the morning."

The lieutenant nodded and closed the door, leaving Mary with the dark-eyed marine. She aimed a smile at him, hoping he anticipated their time together as much as she did. For a second, she wondered if she'd see him again. A twinge of disappointment niggled within her at the thought, but she chased it away. If they enjoyed each other's company enough, they'd find ways and time to see each other.

"Which way is home?" he asked.

Mary cleared her throat, taking a few seconds to clear her mind as well. "About a half mile from here."

The man merely nodded, stuffed his hands into his pocket, and stared up at the night sky, as if contemplating a major life decision. Maybe he thought it was too far or that it would take too much time.

Why hadn't she thought to discuss it with him beforehand? He stood well over six feet and appeared strong enough. She didn't think a half-mile walk would overexert him, but it might for some people. It certainly wasn't too far for her.

"John, I hope you don't mind if I take my shoes off."

At the hospital earlier that evening, she'd managed to borrow a pair from a candy striper who was friends with Samuel. Then, she and Samuel had taken a cab to the Brandon residence. While the borrowed shoes fit decently enough, she preferred to go barefoot like she did on the reservation back home.

A mirth-filled chuckle rolled from his mouth. "Most women forgo shoes on my reservation. I won't mind a bit if you do too."

Warmth swept over her. This man was so down to earth and practical. He likely ran barefoot as a child, as poverty was a way of life on many reservations and decent footwear wasn't easy to come by. In a way, it seemed he already understood her. Seeds of admiration took root in her heart.

"My place is down this way four blocks, then head west for six blocks. Are you sure you don't mind?"

"I'm sure. I can't leave a lady to walk that far alone. I have two young sisters. I'd certainly want a gentleman to do the same for them, if they were in your shoes."

Mary looked down at her bare feet. John must have noticed the unintended pun as well. They both broke into laughter.

John unlaced his boots and removed them and his socks so that he was barefoot as well.

Mary placed a hand to her lips and walked down the sidewalk with John beside her. It might take a while to reach her place, and she didn't want to keep the man out all night, given he had a meeting with the lieutenant in the morning.

"So," John said, "tell me about your family. I know you have a brother you care very deeply about."

"Daniel is all I have. Our mother died when I was only two—complications from childbirth. My baby sister died hours later. Papa did a splendid job caring for me and Daniel. His mother, my *ala*, helped as much as she could."

Tears blurred her vision. "Papa and Ala are both gone now. Our home didn't have electricity, and it was so cold two winters ago. They got sick, pneumonia."

John paused, stared into her eyes with sincerity. "I'm so sorry. I know how difficult it is to lose a father."

He kicked a rock. It skittered across the street, bounced off the curb. She sensed his father held a tender place in his heart and chose not to pry.

A quiet moment elapsed between them before they proceeded. Mary's toes wiggled with freedom with each step she took. So many of her stockings had developed snags from abandoning shoes that she'd become an expert in sewing them back together. It was a small price to pay for the opportunity to feel the cool, soft earth beneath her feet.

They paused at an intersection then crossed the street.

Mary asked, "How about your family? You mentioned two sisters?"

He smiled brightly enough to rival the moonlight. "My sister, Tooh Lilini, is the oldest. We call her Lini for short. Her name means river, because she's strong, steady, and doesn't yield much. Ho'o neno is the youngest. Her name means butterfly, because she can't sit still for a minute. She's forever driving Ma to distraction. We call her Neno."

His eyes shimmered. Clearly his family meant a lot to him. As Daniel did to her. She wondered about his father. He hadn't mentioned anything more about the man.

"Your family must be proud that you are so fluent in your native language," Mary said.

"Yes, they are." John paused, seemed to study the moon hanging low in the sky. "When I was a child, attending the residential school, the teachers often slapped my fingers with a ruler for speaking Navajo. They told me never to speak of it again or I'd be punished even more severely."

With a shudder, Mary remembered the same kinds of things from her residential school days at Fort Simcoe. Children punished for speaking the Yakima language. She was grateful her grandmother taught it to her, without being found out.

Thinking it best to change the subject, she asked, "So, what is it you do in the Marines?"

He walked faster, his bare feet slapping against the sidewalk. "I'm to be a, uh, radio operator. If I refuse, it won't go well for me."

Mary had to walk considerably faster to keep up with him. It almost seemed like he didn't want to be a radio operator. Deep down, she didn't fully understand his reluctance. She sensed he wasn't telling her everything. She imagined some kind of clandestine, classified mission, the top-secret kind. Like the spy work she wanted to do.

For several minutes they walked in silence, before he slowed his pace.

Somehow, they were only two blocks from her small apartment. Her time with him tonight was limited, and she didn't want to part ways with dissension between them.

"I'm sorry, John. I didn't mean to upset you."

"No," John said, "I didn't mean to snap at you. I'm just. . .I'm having a hard time sorting through everything in my mind. Like Daniel is everything to you, I'm all my mother and sisters have. How can I volunteer for extremely dangerous work that could take me away from them forever? Who would take care of them if I were killed or maimed?"

Mary nodded, swallowed hard. How well she understood. Being alone to fend for herself in this big war-torn world frightened her to pieces. Empathy swept through her. How hard must it be for John's mother and sisters.

She stopped in front of her apartment, one side of a small duplex she rented from an elderly lady named Mrs. Eleanor Drake. Mrs. Drake was a friend of Catherine Brandon and had offered Mary cheap rent. Not that Mary needed cheap rent. She made a good living driving her delivery truck around base delivering supplies to all sorts of places. She wasn't thrilled with the lack of privacy with base housing anyway.

"This is my place. Thanks for walking me home."

John nodded, gave her a playful salute, and said good night. Mary let herself in and plopped onto the threadbare sofa. Would she ever see John Painted Horse again?

———————— ≈ ————————

The morning after he'd dined at the Brandons' house and walked Mary home, John hurried to his meeting with Lieutenant Brandon. The lieutenant's secretary told him to wait in the man's office. That had been more than twenty minutes ago. John paced the floor, contemplating the ways in which the military could sweeten the deal if he agreed to enter the code talker program.

Perhaps if he received a large advance in pay and sent it to his mother, then maybe he wouldn't be so worried about leaving them destitute and penniless if he were killed. He considered requesting an assignment as far away from the front lines as possible, but he waffled between the relief of relative safety and being labeled a coward.

The door opened and Lieutenant Brandon entered, along with a short, portly man in spectacles.

"Good, Painted Horse. You're here." The lieutenant dropped into his chair and opened the cigar box on his desk. "I'd like you to meet Major Morton."

Lieutenant Brandon faced the major. "By the way, Major, thank you for the cigar box. It's lovely."

"My pleasure." Major Morton puffed his chest. "I have a duplicate on my desk. You know how one hand washes the other in the military."

The lieutenant pursed his lips and addressed John. "Major Morton here works at the Office of Strategic Services and has come up with a plan involving the code talkers. Assuming you'll join the program, I thought you should hear it as well."

Lieutenant Brandon offered cigars to him and Major Morton. John declined. The major did not. He bit his lip as the two men lit their freshly rolled tokens from Havana. Seconds later, the smell of tobacco filled the room. He waved a hand in front of his face in a vain attempt to keep from breathing the noxious fumes.

"So, Painted Horse"—Major Morton dropped into a nearby chair and blew a thick cloud of smoke into the air—"once you learn the code, I'd like you to share it with a few trusted spies."

Lieutenant Brandon frowned. "What are you getting at, Major?"

Morton flicked ash onto the carpet, without bothering to aim it toward an ashtray. "That way, information can be shared without the risk of the spies and intelligence officers meeting in person."

John saw the logic, but it also added to risk of the code being compromised.

Major Morton continued. "If we can find a way to relay messages from spies to those on our side, without the Japs finding out, it would certainly give us an advantage."

John shifted from one foot to the other. Although he couldn't put his finger on the reason, he didn't trust the major. The man made him think of a rattlesnake in the desert. Don't get in their way or they'll inflict a painful bite that's deadly, more often than not.

Lieutenant Brandon scrunched his eyebrows together and drummed his fingers on his desk. "I don't like this. I worry about the Japanese discovering the code. And before we proceed any further, we would need approval from the brass upstairs, and I don't see that happening."

"Sir"—John cleared his throat—"I'd like some more time to think about my decision anyway."

"Of course." Major Morton took another long pull from the cigar. "Let's head to the Tiki Lounge and talk about it over a few drinks, maybe pick up a girl or two."

The major's eyebrows waggled.

Lieutenant Brandon glowered. "You two will *not* discuss this in public."

John squared his shoulders and stood to his full height. "Sir, that won't be an issue. Major Morton, I don't imbibe, and I treat women with greater respect than. . .than what you're implying, sir."

The major's eyes narrowed into two slits. He blew out another cloud of smoke as his booted feet tapped the floor.

Major Morton was a snake. John could almost hear him rattling within the confines of the room, which grew stuffier by the minute. What could he say? The last thing he wanted was a mission that put him in more danger than necessary. Communicating with spies who were behind enemy lines was the very definition of dangerous.

What if this bozo had his way? John shuddered, thinking of what might happen.

The major rose and stepped toward him, his balding pate hardly reaching John's chin.

John clenched his fists. He never thought he'd strike an outranking officer, but if this man was spoiling for a fight, he wasn't about to back down.

The man growled. "I never thought I'd see a redskin turn down a drink."

John raised a fist.

"Morton! Painted Horse!" Lieutenant Brandon stepped between them. "You two will keep your personal feelings in check and keep quiet about this idea, at least until I hear from the brass."

John took a step back and stood at attention. "Yes, sir." He respected his commanding officer too much to do otherwise.

Brandon jabbed a finger at Major Morton. "Is that understood?"

The major snubbed his cigar into an ashtray and mimicked a snarky, "Yes, sir."

If John stayed in the room one more minute with this jackwagon, he'd be court-martialed. With a huff, he slapped his Marines cap on his head and stormed from the room.

Seconds later, he was outside, his boots thumping on the pavement as he walked. He needed someone to talk to, but he'd sworn to keep quiet.

He could go target practicing with Samuel, but his friend was pulling guard duty. In the past, he'd taken walks on the beach to help clear his head. A walk alone on the beach wouldn't cut it this time.

John whipped his cap off his head and slapped it against his thigh.

A memory of Mary Wishram's face popped to the forefront of his mind. She was pretty and strong, and a good listener judging by their conversation the previous night. Spending time with her should be fine, as long as he didn't mention Major Morton.

Would she walk with him if he asked? He hoped so. Without wasting another moment, he headed toward her duplex apartment.

A short time later, he knocked on her front door. His throat constricted when she opened it, looking even more radiant than she had the previous evening.

"Hello, John, come in. I was just signing a few delivery forms for the quartermaster at the Base Supply Center."

He stepped inside and was met with the sweet fragrance of burning sage. Quite a contrast to the stink of Major Morton's cigar smoke.

"Would you like a cup of coffee? All I have is instant." She stepped toward the small kitchenette.

"Actually," John stammered, swallowed, adjusted the tie that had suddenly become too tight around his neck. "Actually, I, uh, thought you might like to go for a walk along the beach. The weather is nice enough, and well, I need to get my mind off things."

To his relief, she didn't burst out laughing. Instead, she smiled at him. Her eyes shone like the onyx gemstones he'd collected as a kid.

"Sure, let me grab my jacket. What seems to be troubling you?" She blew out the sage embers in their seashell holder.

His gaze landed on a ball of rolled-up twine with a number of things tied to it. Curious, he asked, "What's that?"

A smile spread across her face. "That's my Ititamat, a time ball. It's a tradition Yakima women begin when they're young. We tie various things to a strand of yarn or twine to commemorate important events in our lives, like weddings, the births of children, and such. What was it you said was troubling you?"

She had abruptly changed the subject, and the light had gone out in her eyes for a moment. He thought it best to let it go.

John swallowed again. How much could he divulge without disobeying a direct order from his superior? He needed advice but had to choose his words carefully.

He breathed deep and prayed he wouldn't say too much. "Aw, nothing really. I. . .have difficulty working with folks who lack scruples and a moral compass."

"And you can't name any names, can you?"

John clenched his jaw shut so hard his teeth ached. He looked at the floor, folded his hands behind his back, and then stared at the ceiling.

A tense silence filled the air between them.

Mary cleared her throat, donned her jacket, and reached for her handbag. "I hear the sunsets are lovely when watching them from the beach."

To his relief, she seemed to understand. He relaxed his grip on his hat. It was a wrinkled wad in his hands. He'd need to iron it before tomorrow.

He was glad she wouldn't be dragged into this mess. He remembered Major Morton's comments about picking up women at the Tiki Lounge. There was no proof that the major even knew Miss Wishram, and it wasn't like he could question her about the man. He had strict orders to keep certain conversations confidential.

Still, if the scoundrel went anywhere near her, he'd make unsolicited advances. John was sure of it.

Her gaze met his. An innocent smile lit up her face.

"Shall we be going now?" She opened her door and stepped out into the night air.

His hands clenched into fists. He'd never get the wrinkles out of his hat now. A wave of protectiveness washed over him. The haunted look in her eyes told him she was keeping secrets, dark secrets.

≣ CHAPTER 3 ≣

Mary clenched her fists to her sides and paced the floor just outside of Major Morton's office. The nerve of that man. Scheming and back-stabbing were rampant on most military bases. Most often they were perpetrated by officers striving for a higher rank.

But this took the proverbial cake.

She'd willingly make any sacrifice necessary to help end the war and bring her brother home safe, but she refused to accompany him to the Tiki Lounge for drinks and. . .fun. A shudder swept through her at his definition of *fun*.

She'd delivered a package to his secretary and needed his signature on the delivery form, but she dared not meet him alone. What if he tried to blackmail her into doing something unscrupulous?

When she'd met with John at the Brandons' house two nights ago, she'd almost mentioned the skunk but didn't wish to taint the sweet atmosphere. John promised to look out for her when they were together, but she considered herself a strong enough lady. She didn't want to depend on a man to rescue her, like some damsel in a romance novel.

That meant she had to be diligent and utilize every effort to avoid potentially dangerous situations.

Hunched over the secretary's desk, and despising the desperation lacing her voice, she said, "I don't trust this man. Is there any way you could come into the room with me?"

The wide-eyed secretary, an innocent-looking blonde who didn't look a day over twenty, shook her head. Mary bit her lower lip. Sympathy radiated through her. The poor girl would likely lose her job if she crossed the man.

As if on cue, he emerged from his office, sporting a menacing leer. "Miss Wishram, it's a pleasure to see you again."

Mary squared her shoulders. "I'd rather not meet with you at all, sir."

To her relief, he waved a hand at her. "If it's any consolation, I'll leave my door open. Miss Yates will hear everything. Won't you, sweetheart?"

Only half placated, Mary shot a glance at the secretary. The girl pressed her lips into a firm line. Major Morton winked at the girl. Mary noted her eyebrows scrunched into a V. Mary hoped she'd found an ally in this spunky lady.

Clutching her handbag to her chest, Mary stepped into the lieutenant's office. The reek of hard alcohol and cigar smoke assaulted her nose. She yanked a handkerchief from her purse and held it to her face. She coughed.

"Miss Wishram, you look a bit green. Are you all right?" he asked. A half-smoked cigar hung from his mouth.

Heaven help her. The temptation to lie rose like a mischievous prairie dog. Would he believe her if she claimed to have a highly contagious disease? If he did, it would be a perfect excuse to wrangle out of a date with him. He might even ask her to leave immediately, a request she certainly wouldn't object to.

"Don't worry about a thing, dearie. I know just what it takes to set a pretty thing like you to rights again." He sidled up to the bar and poured two drinks.

Her knees turned to jelly.

He slithered toward her, giving the door a shove with his booted foot. At the secretary's woeful expression, any flicker of security Mary had was extinguished. Like the painful thud of a nail driven into a coffin, the door slammed shut.

She sucked in a breath.

She could say she was exposed to a highly infectious disease when she last dropped off a shipment of supplies at the hospital. Would he believe her?

A list of infectious diseases streaked through her mind.

Bubonic plague?

No, he'd never believe that one.

Rabies?

Oh, heavens no! If he believed that he'd lock her up for two weeks.

Smallpox?

No, that wouldn't do either. He'd probably ask her how she could be so pretty while suffering from such a disfiguring ailment. The skunk!

He pushed the drink toward her, inches from her nose.

She snorted. This was ridiculous. A manipulative minx she was not.

She dropped her hand to her side, squared her shoulders, and stood tall. "Major, I don't need a drink. It's the stench in this room that makes me queasy. If I'm permitted to leave, I'm sure I'll feel much better, *sir*."

The darkening in his eyes reminded her of storm clouds swirling in the skies right before lightning strikes. The atmosphere choked with tension. She almost expected a tornado to blow through the room, like in the book *The Wizard of Oz*.

"Miss Wishram," Morton snarled, "if you possess any hope of finding your brother, then you will take this vodka, drink it, and hold a civil conversation with me."

Mary's palms sweated so much her handkerchief grew damp. She swallowed, hard, twice and said, "And if I refuse, *sir*?"

An unsettling grin spread across his face. "And which POW camp is your brother stuck in?"

"What is that supposed to mean?"

"It means that I'll put in a word all right, but not to the Department of Defense Accounting Agency. I'll find a way to contact the commander of that POW camp and tell them all sorts of things. Like Daniel Wishram is a spy and his sister is looking to follow in his footsteps."

She clenched her fists so hard her fingernails bit into her palms. "You wouldn't! That's treason! You'd be executed if you were caught."

"Not if I send the letters anonymously." He threw his head back, his maniacal cackle bouncing off the walls.

Now she really felt sick. Dare she throw up on the man?

In seconds his nose was an inch from hers; his eyes emanated with evil. "I work in the spy business, little lady. I know all kinds of ways to get information from one spot to another without anyone finding out."

A tornado really had blown through the room. And landed directly on her.

He shoved the drink toward her again. "Drink up, dearie."

John strode from his barracks, unable to stop thinking about Mary. Had it only been two days since their walk along the beach? How could he not worry about her? All alone in the world, just like his mother. Both were strong, independent women, but that didn't stop consternation from nipping at his bare heels.

He gave his head a quick shake. His appointment with Lieutenant Brandon was in a short while, and he needed to face the man with a clear head. He pulled on a pair of wool socks then shoved his feet into his boots. Reaching for his jacket, he left his barracks. Fresh air would help him sort through the thready issues that tangled in his mind like spiderwebs.

With Camp Pendleton behind him, he paused in front of a small stone chapel he'd seen earlier. He rubbed his hand across his chin. Memories of cruel teachers at the Indian school stirred in the recesses of his mind. Teachers often berated the children, withheld food, and beat those who dared utter a word of Navajo. Himself included.

Sweat broke out on his forehead as his hands trembled. Yet, not all the white people who came to the reservation were cruel. There were the kindhearted missionaries, the ones who'd brought a basket of food to his family two Christmases in a row. There were new dresses for his mother and sisters too.

Regardless of what had happened in the past, spiritual guidance at that moment wouldn't be a bad thing to have.

John strode up the steps, pulled open the heavy solid wood door, and quietly slipped inside. Candles flickering at the altar helped illuminate the interior and filled the air with a sweet fragrance. Sunshine filtered through the stained glass windows. A kaleidoscope of colors danced across the wooden pews.

"May I help you, son?"

John turned and faced a young man with thick black hair. Surprised at how young the guy looked, John stammered for words.

The pastor chuckled as he dipped his head. He then stood straight, placed his hands behind his back, and smiled. "I'm Pastor Ephraim. I know I'm young."

Pastor Ephraim seemed genuine enough, and he was a man of faith, but John didn't want to take any unnecessary risks. "Sir, can you assure me that this conversation will remain confidential?"

The pastor nodded.

Tension in John's shoulders eased. He slumped against a nearby pew, folding his arms across his chest. "I'm about to meet with my CO, about joining a program that is exceedingly dangerous. I'm not sure if I should volunteer, considering how the government has treated my people. I don't trust the government."

The pastor nodded and then sat in the pew near John before continuing. "My grandfather ministered at a mission near the Shoshone Reservation. Things were hard for the people there."

John's frustration mounted. "I was sent to a residential school when I was eight. I made the mistake of saying thank you for a bowl of soup—in my native language. I was slapped, dropped my soup and went to bed hungry that night. And now, *now* the government says it *needs* me to speak my language?"

The pastor grimaced. "I understand your mistrust. I certainly don't blame you for feeling the way you do, but bitterness is a terrible poison. It shreds your heart in ways much worse than enemy bullets."

John swallowed. The truth weighed on him. His grandmother had warned him about carrying hate like some dubious honor. Uneasiness wormed its way through his middle.

He blew out a heavy sigh. "It's not just that. I'm all my family has. I can't trust the government to take care of them if I'm killed. Can I trust the Lord to?"

"Do you know the scripture passage in Proverbs 3, verses 5 and 6?"

John remembered his conversation with the missionaries who'd helped his family all those Christmases ago. "Trust in the Lord with all thine heart; and lean not unto thine own understanding. In all thy ways acknowledge him and he shall direct thy paths."

Pastor Ephraim said, "You wish to care for your family. That's a noble desire." He adjusted his tie, as if contemplating his next words. "I can't tell you to go, or not to go. All I can say is pray, press into the Lord, and seek His will for your life."

"Will you pray with me?"

"Certainly."

John emerged from the stone chapel, hat in hand, and a much lighter heart. Peace had washed over him like gentle waves of the nearby Pacific Ocean.

He headed toward Lieutenant Brandon's office with sure steps. There had to be a list of benefits for the families of deceased code talkers. He'd ask to see the list and, from there, determine if it was worth the risk.

John had given his family's information to Pastor Ephraim, who promised to look in on them. Should anything happen to him, the pastor promised to contact the mission on the Navajo Reservation and do everything he could to see that John's family was provided for.

With his shoulders free of tension, John strolled along at a brisk pace, whistling a Navajo tune as he walked.

He was still whistling as he ascended the steps to Lieutenant Brandon's office building with a spring in his step. Peace enveloped him as he formulated his game plan. He opened the door and entered the lobby.

Arguing echoed down the long corridor. Major Morton stomped toward him, cursing through the scowl on his contorted face.

John stopped short. Peace fled his mind.

Lieutenant Brandon emerged from his office and followed the major. John bristled at the rough language.

Major Morton stormed past him, emitting another string of expletives. The stench of cigar smoke filled the hallway. A young blonde secretary spoke over the phone. Anguish filled her voice.

How the Marines promoted a man like Morton to officer, John would never know. The man was crazy and a danger to the corps. How hard would it be to have him court-martialed?

John grumbled. Intending to wait for the lieutenant in the man's office, he continued down the hallway.

Two steps into the man's office, he collided with Mary. Her eyes smoldered with anger, and she'd folded her arms across her chest.

Feeling protective of her, his hands involuntarily balled into fists. "Miss Wishram, are you all right?"

Her arms dropped to her sides. A weak smile creased her face. "I'm fine, John. Thank you for asking."

"Mary, please," John said. "Tell me what happened."

She shook her head. "You know I can't do that, so please, don't ask."

John suspected that Morton had attempted something vile and that she'd managed to wrangle herself free from his advances. He'd seen Morton's young secretary warily eye the man every time he came near her.

He wished he could drag Morton behind the Tiki Lounge. Once there, he and Samuel could rough him up. See how he liked being targeted by someone stronger.

Major Morton was an officer, and he didn't like John and Samuel. He'd likely report them to the authorities, and then where would they be?

"John, are you all right?" Mary's voice drew him back to the present.

He forced himself to relax. If he were to be thrown into the brig, it would only serve the enemy. Anger bubbled in him. Men like Major Morton most often escaped the consequences of their ungentlemanly conduct, while grunts like him had to toe the line or risk serious consequences.

"I'm so sorry, Mary. I'll speak to the lieutenant about what I've seen and what I've heard Morton say. I don't know if it will do any good, though."

"Thank you." A grin spread across her face.

He couldn't blame any man for being attracted to her. She was as smart as she was beautiful. And strong and patriotic too.

How easy it would be to hug her all day, but he had a meeting with the lieutenant.

She nodded and turned to leave. She gazed at him over her shoulder and said, "See you later."

John fixated on the twinkling in her eyes. He admired her bravery.

Moments later, Lieutenant Brandon returned and handed him the usual bottle of cola. Throughout the meeting, John could hardly focus.

"Painted Horse?"

John dropped back to earth. Water dripped from his hands from the bottle's condensation. He hadn't taken more than two sips. "Uh, yes. I mean yes, sir, Lieutenant." John swallowed, hoping he wasn't in too much trouble.

A sly grin creased his CO's face. "I was explaining in great detail the benefits your family would receive if anything happened to you in battle. You should be safe enough, though. The code talkers are closely guarded."

"Yes, sir, thank you." John chugged the now lukewarm, flat drink and wiped his mouth.

Lieutenant Brandon said, "That will be all for now."

John nodded and hastily exited the office.

On his way home, he stopped to admire the moon, much like he did when he was back on his reservation. He missed home, the wide-open space. He missed the sounds of his mother singing. The cacophony of sheep and goats bleating and wolves howling in the distance brought a wave of homesickness. He even missed the bustle of the nearest community, Tuba City.

He fixed his gaze on the moon and prayed as his mother and grandmother had taught him to do whenever he longed to feel the Creator's presence. He sang two of his favorite hymns, in his native language. Soon, a wave of peace washed over him.

☰ CHAPTER 4 ☰

The previous day, Mary had managed to escape from Major Morton's office by claiming she had to throw up, which wasn't far from the truth. The man made her sick.

Now, here she was again, facing the man again, with another package for delivery and the form for him to sign. Had he phoned the quartermaster and requested she deliver his packages? She wouldn't put it past him.

The major's eyes blazed, indicating his own rage. "You high and mighty little squaw. I'll teach you to throw a drink in my face."

Anger boiled so hot in Mary's heart, it was a wonder the world around her didn't turn a hazy shade of red. Seconds passed. Anger coupled with fear at what she had just done. She'd reacted to his advances without thinking.

And now, this man could destroy her and everyone she loved.

He reached for a towel and then, to her horror, removed his wet tie and shirt. He wore an undershirt beneath his uniform, but that didn't negate the lax in propriety. Heat climbed up her neck all the way to her hairline at the indecency. If anyone were to enter the room and see her in such a compromising situation, she'd be thrown out of the military. At least she thought she would.

"Sir," she began, "gentlemen don't make such propositions toward a lady."

He donned another shirt, to her relief, but neglected to button it. She turned her head to avoid the sight of him and stepped back.

"Don't tell me what I should and shouldn't do. I'm an officer," he sneered.

Her heart lurched when he moved toward her. She retreated until her backside bumped against his desk. She stared longingly at the door, the one he'd kicked shut with his foot when he'd poured her a drink.

Her heart tied itself into knots of fear. Her fingers felt around on his desk, hoping to find a weapon, a letter opener perhaps, or even a paperweight.

"Now where were we? Ah, yes. I was telling you how I'd send anonymous letters to the POW camp your brother is in and tell them he's a spy."

Ice water, rather than blood—or so it seemed—flowed through Mary's veins.

He continued. "How about I send letters to that relocation camp where your Jap friends are staying? Unless, of course, you'd like the opportunity to talk me out of it, say, at the Tiki Lounge."

A wicked leer spread across his jowly face. His cheeks were a deep red.

Gooseflesh prickled over her. She rubbed her hands over her arms. For the twentieth time she wondered how the Navy promoted men like him. "You're a traitor to this country! You know that?"

"Me? You're the traitor, missy. I'm simply trying to get you to comply with what's good for these United States, and you are stubbornly refusing."

Confusion swamped Mary. "How do you figure that?"

The wicked leer came back to his face. "Officers get lonely. We can do our jobs better if we have a little female companionship, somebody to help us unwind so we can focus on more important matters."

Major Morton raised his eyebrows. He downed his drink and wiped the slobber from his double chin.

Sickness swirled in her middle. This man wouldn't stop at one drink. If she gave in to even the slightest whim of his, she'd be chained to him indefinitely. A slave to his demands.

Her fingers wrapped around a square of heavy metal, likely his cigar box. She dared not take her eyes off him to know for sure.

"Sir," she said again, "I will not be drinking with you tonight, or ever."

His face and neck turned an intimidating shade of red. His eyes darkened, sending chills through the room. "You'd probably just as soon throw another drink on me, wouldn't you?"

Her fingers gripped the cigar box. Would the JAG officers believe her if she claimed self-defense? Did she want to take that chance? Did she have a choice?

A commotion erupted from the hallway.

Lieutenant Brandon and John Painted Horse burst into the room.

The lieutenant glanced from the major to her and back again. His eyes narrowed. "What's going on in here?"

"Now, Brandon, it isn't what you think." Major Morton rolled his eyes. "I was offering to find out which POW camp her brother was in and see if I could offer some assistance. She downed a shot of whiskey and when she reached for mine, it spilled down my shirt. You know how these Indians are."

The contents in Mary's stomach curdled at the lies. The stories and rumors she'd heard about this man were true. His Jeep wasn't firing on all six cylinders and was likely to run over innocent folks. He had to be stopped before he killed someone.

John scowled, and his lips twitched. She imagined the slurs angered him. And who could blame him?

John met her gaze. The hard lines on his face softened. The sympathy in his eyes soothed her. He obviously didn't believe the story the major told. It warmed her heart to know he had faith in her.

Lieutenant Brandon scrunched his eyebrows and folded his arms across his chest. "That can be dealt with later. Right now, I need to have a conversation with you about letting John Painted Horse into that, uh, program we were discussing earlier."

Mary understood the meaning of *top secret* without the words having to be said. It was time to go.

"If you'll excuse me." Mary released her hold on the cigar box. "I was just leaving."

She intentionally stomped on Morton's foot and ground the heel of her new shoe on his boot as she brushed past him.

"*Aahh!*" Major Morton hollered.

"Sorry," she muttered over her shoulder as she hurried from the room, not feeling a bit sorry.

———————≈———————

Before John could contemplate his next step, Mary had stomped past him and directly on top of the major's foot. Her shoes smacked the floor tiles with clacking noises that echoed down the corridor.

"That woman," Major Morton hissed. He shook his booted foot and then limped to his desk. He lit a cigar and pointed to the hallway.

John's ears burned with the insults the major spewed about Indians. He wished he could clock the guy but didn't care to see himself court-martialed. Major Morton wasn't the only one who threw insults at him. That didn't make hearing the slurs any easier. Mary had often voiced the same concerns.

His heart seized, noting the anger written across her face when she fled from the room a moment ago. She was a strong woman, but up against the likes of Morton? He didn't want to think what could happen.

"Mary, wait." He hurried down the hallway to catch up with her.

She had reached the lobby by the time he caught her. She turned to him. A mix of emotions clouded her dark eyes.

He held up his hands. "I just wanted to see if you were all right."

She pointed toward the major's office and tapped her foot on the tiles. "That monster told a bunch of lies about me."

He nodded. She didn't have to tell him what he already knew—that she didn't drink and would never behave that way with any man, let alone a creep like Major Morton. Tears pooled in her eyes, likely from both anger and pain. His heart ached for her.

"And he threatened me," she huffed.

John's heart lurched. "What kind of threats?"

"My friends are in the Manzanar War Relocation Center."

John's heart pounded as she told him the extent of the major's threats if she didn't comply with his demands.

"I'm so sorry, Mary." He wished he could do more to comfort her.

She continued. "If that man really has contact with the Japanese, those running the POW camps, heaven only knows what kind of propaganda he will feed them."

John felt sick. "That's treason."

A lot of innocent people will die if someone doesn't take him down a peg."

The heaviness in John's middle sank to the soles of his feet. She was right. Someone had to stop Major Morton before he did any real harm.

"Look, Mary, how would you like to meet me for dinner tonight? We can take in a movie. I hear *None but the Lonely Heart*, with Cary Grant and Ethel Barrymore, is playing."

A smile curved across her pretty face, deepening the pink hue in her cheeks. He gulped and laid a hand over his chest to steady his racing heartbeat.

"And we can talk about how to give the major his comeuppance," Mary replied.

"All right. It sounds like a date. I have business to take care of before then. Are you fine with meeting me at the restaurant?"

"Of course." She pulled a slip of paper from her purse.

He jotted down the name of the place and directions, then tipped his hat to her, and jogged back to his meeting with Lieutenant Brandon and Major Morton.

Later that evening, John sat at a table in a fancy restaurant. The candles burning from their place in the table's centerpiece added to the romantic ambiance. Several times he glanced at the lobby, hoping to see Mary enter.

He checked his watch again. She was only five minutes late, but he yearned to see her again. Had she changed her mind about meeting him for dinner? No, she would have called the restaurant if that were the case.

Then he heard her voice floating in the air. He turned to the sound of it.

She was here.

His pulse accelerated. He quickly wiped his sweaty hands on his pants. Mary was a beautiful woman, but he could hardly believe the effect she had on him. He normally wasn't this flighty around women. What was wrong with him?

As she approached, he swallowed hard and then noted the young woman behind her. At first, John thought the young lady was Mary's friend and a potential third wheel. The second thought was how nice it'd be to escort two lovely young ladies around town. He wasn't so broke that he couldn't afford to take two ladies to the picture show.

His friend Samuel sure would be jealous. He stifled a chuckle so the ladies wouldn't think he was laughing at them.

"John," Mary said. "I'd like you to meet Miss Yates, Major Morton's secretary."

⫶ CHAPTER 5 ⫶

John had enjoyed dining with Mary and Miss Yates last night a little too much. He needed to pull his head out of the clouds or he'd miss something.

Leaning against the tall bookcase in Lieutenant Brandon's office, he accepted the bottle of Coke handed him. He took a slow drink, praying he wasn't in over his head.

He loosened his tie and stood as straight as his six-foot frame allowed. Just how much did he want to share with his commanding officer about the meeting with the ladies? He cleared his throat. There would be a time for that. . .but not today.

A strong desire, a need really, to make a difference hummed through his veins. He needed to focus on the task Lieutenant Brandon set before him.

"Sir"—John swallowed the carbonation fizzing in his throat— "although Morton is determined to stop me, I've decided to enter the code talker program, and I'm determined to finish it."

Lieutenant Brandon perched on the edge of his desk with his own bottle of soda. "Good. Your friend Samuel Acothley will be glad to hear it. What made you change your mind?"

"I received a letter from my youngest sister. Thankfully, my family is well, but she talks about the land and how much it means to her. She worries about what will happen if the Japanese bomb America or, worse, invade the country. She fears we might lose our home and what little else we have."

Brandon visibly squirmed. "God forbid the Japanese invade the

States, but if they do, I don't think they'd get as far as the Navajo Reservation."

"Sir, for the sake of my sisters, for their future, I will do everything I can to ensure my family doesn't lose our home."

"Whatever has motivated you, I'm glad."

"When does the next class begin, sir?" John took another drink of the bubbly concoction. The sooner the war was over, the sooner he could return to his mother and sisters. And he missed his reservation. The buttes and rock formations were a beauty that far outweighed anything he'd seen in the dry Southern California deserts.

The beaches, though, were a sight to behold. Most people on his reservation had never seen the ocean. So, he sent a number of postcards home every chance he had.

The lieutenant tipped his bottle to his lips, emptying it, and wiped his mouth. He paused a moment before answering. John hoped he hadn't missed out or given his CO a reason to doubt his abilities.

"The class begins next week, but you must remember, John, all this is top secret." The man closed the distance between them. "You can't share this information with anyone, and that includes that spunky, dark-haired beauty you've been spending time with."

John stepped back two paces. Heat flooded into his cheeks. "Sir, I assure you I won't be sharing anything with Miss Wishram, or anyone else for that matter." He took another drink of his Coke and met the man's gaze without wavering.

"Good to know." Lieutenant Brandon clapped him on the back and pulled another bottle of soda from the icebox near the wet bar. "Let me take care of Morton."

John nodded and downed the last of his drink. "Where are the classes being held? Do I need to sign up in person?"

Lieutenant Brandon gave him instructions on where to go, and John left the office.

Later, he strode up the walkway to the assigned building, which had no signs or identifying markers. He noticed how inconspicuous it looked. Folks strolling by wouldn't suspect that top-secret things took place there.

He chuckled. That was probably the point.

"Painted Horse."

John turned to see his friend Samuel loitering nearby.

"Hey, pal, good to see you."

"I take it you just came from a meeting with Brandon." A sly grin slid across Samuel's face, and he nodded slowly.

John caught his meaning. They'd be in the same class. He exchanged small talk with his friend for a few moments. Then, he stepped toward the building the lieutenant had instructed him to go to.

John noted the two guards flanking the front door. Those two guards knew nothing about what went on inside. He gripped his hat in his hands and entered.

The officer in charge of the program handed John a thin file folder. It contained documents stating the details of the program. Orders to keep it *top secret* leaped from the page.

This was serious stuff.

Additional pages stated the consequences he'd suffer—jail, fines, execution for treason—should he disobey the orders and reveal any information.

John clenched the pen in his hand. He had never been one to keep secrets, but this was different.

As for Mary, he didn't feel guilty about keeping this information from her. She would understand. It was all for the good of the country, to facilitate the end of the war. She was as desperate as he was to see it end.

A thought struck him.

What secrets might she be harboring, for the good of the country?

———≈———

Mary exited the yellow cab and paid the driver. Once he drove away, she stood before the shady-looking hotel on the rough side of town.

Cursing flowed from open windows, and a rat darted from the back of the building into the bushes nearby. At least, it looked like a rat to Mary. A blinking neon pink sign hung at a crooked angle above the door. It welcomed her to the establishment.

This was where government officials would interview her in the first steps to becoming a spy? What had she gotten herself into?

What if this was the wrong address? What if this was a trap? She looked down one end of the dirt road and back the way she'd come. There were no military vehicles in sight, something she thought odd. If officers were to question her about becoming a spy, wouldn't their vehicles be parked nearby? Perhaps someone at the Office of Secret Services had given her the wrong address.

There was only one way to find out.

Blowing out a slow, shaky breath, she wished she could expel trepidation as easily.

She entered the building and strolled through the lobby in a manner she hoped appeared confident.

A quick glance around the lobby revealed nobody in military attire. She checked again, this time for suspicious characters lurking about. She bit her lower lip. Would she recognize suspicious characters if she saw them? If she was unable to recognize danger, how would she ever succeed in spying for the government?

No. She wouldn't allow herself to think such things. If soldiers like her brother Daniel could face mortal danger on the battlefield and then horrors at a Japanese POW camp, she could brave these circumstances.

Again, she blew out a deep breath and approached the counter.

In a low voice to the front desk clerk, she said, "I'm Mary Smith. I'm here to see John Smith. Please ring him for me."

The desk clerk raised an eyebrow. "You're the third lady today to ask for that man. I hope he isn't committing any, uh, nefarious activities in this hotel. We have a reputation to uphold, you know."

Waves of heat swept over Mary at the suggestion. She could only imagine what kind of reputation this hotel had. She stifled the urge to defend herself. The officers in charge of the interview had ordered her to keep silent regarding the details. And keep silent she would, regardless of the obstacles.

Even if she impressed the officers enough to become a spy, they likely wouldn't allow her to pick where she was sent. Still, she hoped to somehow infiltrate the POW camp where Daniel was being held. She had to help end the war so her brother and other POWs would be free.

She gripped the handles of her handbag, determined to pass any test before her. "Sir, if you would ring the gentleman, please."

The desk clerk eyed her again. A lopsided grin spread across his face, and then he lit up a cigarette. "Sure thing, doll."

Mary cringed at the term but said, "Thank you."

She stepped away from the desk and waited next to a nearby window.

She paced the small area a few times, wishing she could give her interviewers a piece of her mind for ordering her to such a place. She thought better of it, knowing she couldn't give anyone in authority a piece of her mind without risking a stay in the brig.

Instead, she whispered a prayer for protection.

Finally, the desk clerk pointed her to a hallway. "Last door on the left."

"Thank you," she muttered. She could almost feel the man's gaze on her back as she strode down the corridor. She held her head high just the same, thinking, believing, nothing could be worse about the interview.

She stepped into a small, square room, dimly illuminated by candlelight. It reeked of whiskey and cigarette smoke, but that was where the similarity to most government offices ended.

No officers milled about, telling jokes and drinking brandy. No charts or maps decorated the walls. No aides hustled in and out of the room. No fancy desks piled high with thick files.

Nothing but a rickety table in one corner.

Mary sucked in a deep breath. It stuck in her lungs.

What had she gotten herself into?

A woman sat at the table, flanked by two big, rough-looking gentlemen in civilian attire.

The woman was Catherine Brandon.

CHAPTER 6

Of all people, Mary never would have taken Catherine Brandon, the wife of Lieutenant Henry Brandon, for a spy. Then again, she never would have guessed her interview with the Office of Strategic Services would take place in a seedy hotel either.

The woman had always been so gentle and a stickler for following the rules, a skilled head nurse. Had it all been an act, a cover for clandestine activities? If so, she was quite the actress, one who could give Betty Grable a run for an Oscar.

Catherine raised an eyebrow. "I take it you didn't expect to see me here."

"Um, no. I don't know what exactly I expected, but not this."

A slight chuckle escaped Catherine's lips. "You're not the first one to be surprised by your surroundings. Let's get down to business."

A man of medium height and build entered the room and lurked in the shadows. He sat in a chair in the corner, and his features remained obscured. Who was he?

One of Catherine's men produced a rickety folding chair. Mary gingerly lowered herself, half expecting it to collapse under her weight. She adjusted to a more comfortable position, trying to ignore the squeaks and the wobbly, uneven legs. She folded her hands and placed them in her lap.

A thick file appeared from somewhere, and Catherine took several minutes to thumb through it. Mary presumed the woman was intentionally creating an anxiety-filled atmosphere. She reminded herself that spies did have to remain cool under pressure.

"So," Catherine began, "I see you speak some Japanese. Tell me about that."

More at ease now, to speak about her friends, Mary said, "I sold produce at Pike Place Market in Seattle. The Takahashi family sold strawberries in the booth next to mine. I became friends with their daughter, Yoko, because we both came from different cultures. She taught me some of the language."

Catherine visibly bristled.

Mary's heart lurched. Had she said too much? She prayed she hadn't flunked the interview so quickly.

Catherine pursed her lips and scrunched her eyebrows together. "To perform your duties, the first thing you need to learn is to not divulge excess information. Give short succinct answers, especially if being asked by the enemy."

"The enemy?" Mary's heart lurched again.

"Yes, the enemy." Catherine raised her eyebrows. "In the event that you are captured, your friend Yoko won't be able to help you."

A shudder tore through Mary. Of course, spying on the enemy posed a number of risks, but had she realized how dangerous it could be? If she were caught, she'd be held in a place much darker than this hotel. Hence the need to be a good actress.

A stark realization slammed into Mary. This interview wasn't just about answering Catherine's questions. It was mostly to see how well she behaved under scrutiny. Coming into this, she understood the need for subterfuge but never guessed it went this deep.

Catherine continued. "How well do you speak Japanese?"

Mary squared her shoulders. If soldiers could face hails of gunfire, grenades, and starvation, and continue the fight, then she could face this. Without a hitch in her voice, she said, "I don't know it well, but I'm happy to ask Yoko to teach me more next time I visit her."

Catherine rustled a few papers. Her face was an emotionless mask, and her eyes bored into her. Mary squirmed in her seat under the scrutiny. The chair creaked under her weight and shifted to one side.

"Your friends are in the Manzanar War Relocation Center. What do you know about their ties to the homeland?"

"Yoko said her mother's parents immigrated to Seattle in the early 1900s. Her father and his family came here not long after. I don't know if they keep in touch with family in Japan."

"Just how close are you to them, particularly Yoko?"

"I saw her every time I sold peaches and apples at the market." Mary allowed her mind to drift back to those fun, carefree days before Pearl Harbor. "We talked between customers and on our lunch breaks. She shared her teriyaki with me while I gave her a few pieces of fry bread. We even found time to go shopping together. Those were some fun times at the market before—" A wave of anguish swept through her. Yoko and her family had lost everything when they'd been relocated, and they were now destitute.

Catherine's face remained an emotionless mask. Mary had done it again, said too much.

"I don't believe you'll be visiting Yoko and her family anytime soon. I'm sorry, but we can't risk you inadvertently sharing classified information with them."

"Yes, ma'am." Mary ducked her head. She hoped Yoko and her family wouldn't think she'd forgotten about them. Maybe she could send them a letter without compromising or risking the integrity of any missions.

Catherine interrupted her thoughts.

"I understand you've been spending time with Corporal John Painted Horse. How close are you two? What kinds of things do you talk about?"

Careful of her words, she replied, "Not much. The weather, life on our reservations."

Determination welled in Mary's heart. The sooner the war was over, the sooner she'd be reunited with Yoko. She must do her part to end this terrible conflict. Sitting a bit taller in her chair, she asked, "Will someone else be giving me lessons in Japanese?"

"Yes." Catherine nodded to the man in the shadows.

He stood and stepped forward. "*Watashi no namae wa Akira. Watashi wa anata no sensei ni nari masu.*"

The breath went out of Mary. She'd forgotten about him. His name was Akira, and he was to be her teacher.

"*Watashi no namae wa Mary. Dozo Yoroshiku,*" she replied. She was pleased to meet him.

He informed her that she needed to be trained as soon as possible and then ducked back into the shadows.

Mary turned to Catherine and, in English, said, "I thought the process to become a spy took months of training. Just how soon will I be going into the field?"

Catherine pulled a document from the file and held it up for Mary to see. Mary rose from the rickety chair and took a step closer to inspect it. She noted the signature at the bottom of the page. Horror coursed through her.

"I take it you know Major Morton," Catherine said.

She handed Mary the letter. The words blurred on the page, but she recognized Major Morton's name, all right. She waved the paper in the air. "What is this?"

"Morton believes the Takahashis are spies, Yoko to be more specific. He's threatening to alert the camp's directors."

The major's forewarned threats were materializing.

Indignant, Mary spouted, "That's not true. The Takahashis are loyal Americans. Yoko was born and educated here."

Mary sucked in a ragged breath. She had been born and educated in the United States, but that hadn't stopped the government from corralling her and her people on reservations. Something else she had in common with Yoko. Her indignation rose higher.

"Officially," Catherine said, "he's threatening to send letters to the camp's directors about Yoko and her parents. We can't blame someone for turning in Japanese spies, now can we?"

"The Takahashi family doesn't belong in the relocation center. None of them do. Those places are a disgrace!"

Catherine paused, licked her lips, folded her hands, and placed them on the table in front of her. It seemed she was contemplating her next words.

"I know that." Catherine looked serious. "Unofficially, we think this is a bluff, one that has something to do with you. So, I'll ask you again—what kind of relationship do you have with him?"

Heat swept through her at the insinuation. She tightened her grip on her handbag. "I assure you, ma'am, there is nothing going on between Major Morton and me. No matter what he might imply."

After an hour of intense negotiations, Mary hurried from the dingy hotel.

The desk clerk called out, "Come back and see us again."

Mary waved him off and hustled toward a waiting taxicab. She practically leaped into the vehicle in her desire to leave the premises. She gave the driver directions to her apartment, leaned back against the seat, and closed her eyes.

To qualm her uneasiness, she whispered the words over in her mind. "This is all for Daniel, to help end the war."

———— ≋ ————

Though John was several minutes early, he passed the guards and hurried into the square, unmarked building for his first day of class. The last thing he wanted, or needed, was to be late.

"Painted Horse, over here."

John looked past two other classmates and saw Samuel, ever the eager one, waving his hand. He wove around those milling about to reach his friend. Although he recognized a few faces, like Benjamin Soaring Eagle whom he'd met at a Going to War Ceremony, he didn't know the names of anyone else, except Samuel.

"You ready for this?" Samuel asked.

"Ready as I'll ever be. You hear from your family?"

Samuel grinned. "Got a letter last week. They're good. And you?"

John told Samuel of his latest letter from his family and how it had motivated him to join the program.

Samuel nodded and then dropped into a chair. Sensing tension from his friend, John lowered himself into the seat next to his buddy. "What's up?"

Leaning close, Samuel whispered, "You know, we're not supposed to tell our families anything about the program or where we are. That's going to be hard on my mother, not knowing if I'm all right."

"Maybe it's for the best. I hear we're going to be in the thick of the fighting. I'm not sure I want Ma knowing how much danger I'm in." John was about to pray right then for their families, but a hush fell over the atmosphere.

A tall, dark-haired corporal stepped to the front of the room. "Good morning, gentlemen. I'll be your instructor."

John shifted his focus.

Several charts sat on easels at the front of the classroom, along with diagrams of radios, numbers, and frequencies. He recognized the TBX transmitter as well as the TBY radio system but had never operated one before.

The instructor handed each student a thick book. "These are code-books, gentlemen. Under no circumstances are they to be taken from this room. You are to memorize the vocabulary words and are forbidden to share them outside this class. Is that understood?"

John flipped through the pages. "Yes."

Samuel scribbled notes and was the first one to raise his hand and ask a question.

Hours later, they took a break for lunch and hustled to the chow hall. The meal consisted of sausage gravy with chopped eggs on two slices of white bread. It didn't look like much, but it was filling and nutritious. If only it had come with fry bread.

After lunch they hit the classroom again. By the end of the day, his brain struggled to hold all the information from class. How was he to make it another four weeks without washing out? He prayed and asked God for strength. Perhaps he'd have time to visit Pastor Ephraim.

"Good night, Painted Horse," Samuel said. "I'm headed to the hospital."

"Why? Are you sick of class already?" John chuckled at his own joke.

Samuel laughed and then quieted, though his sly grin remained in place. "There's a girl who works there, and *woo-ee*, is she a pretty one."

"I hope you're not talking about Mary Wishram." Mary *had* been spending a lot of time at the hospital with Catherine Brandon for some reason. A needle of jealousy materialized from somewhere and poked him in the ribs.

"The delivery girl? Nah. She's your gal, isn't she?" Samuel raised his eyebrows.

For reasons he didn't care to admit, he steered his thoughts away from his friend's question. As a means of distraction, he instead wondered who the gal might be. A gasp flew from his lips. "You're not referring to Catherine Brandon, are you? She's the lieutenant's wife!"

"No, no!" Samuel's eyes widened and shook his head. "She's married! Besides, she's too much for following regulations to the letter. I wouldn't even think of crossing her."

"Yeah, I don't blame you." John had heard the rumors of her especially tight but strange bond with the nurses and other ladies in the area.

But those were just rumors.

Samuel continued. "I have my eye on Susanna, and get this—she's from Phoenix, not too far from the reservation."

"Have fun." John waved as his friend hurried toward the hospital. His thoughts drifted to Mary. He hadn't seen her for a few days. She was busy with whatever task the Navy had assigned to her.

A streak of worry ricocheted through him. He should check on her and see if she was all right.

He walked faster toward her apartment. Maybe they could go for another walk along the beach. She'd often said how much she loved the Puget Sound area and how much she missed it.

John knocked on her door several times and even called her name. He wondered if she had a telephone. He'd have to ask for her number.

An elderly lady, with gray hair and wide-rimmed spectacles, poked her head out of the duplex next to Mary's. "What's all that racket?"

John cleared his throat. "I'm looking for Mary Wishram. I'm her, uh, friend, John Painted Horse."

"Well, I'm her landlord, Mrs. Drake." She adjusted her spectacles and pulled her lips into a pout, eying him from crew cut to combat boots. "She's not here. Left early this morning and hasn't been back since."

If he wanted to see more of Mary, it behooved him to be kind to this lady. In his kindest tone, he said, "Thank you, ma'am. Will you tell her I stopped by, please?"

She harrumphed. "If I see her, I'll tell her you stopped by." Then she stepped back into her apartment and shut the door.

"Uh, thank you," John called. This wasn't the end of it, by a long shot. Something in him believed Mary was in trouble. Maybe she wasn't. Maybe she'd simply gone to the beach for the day. Either way, he intended to find out.

John left and headed to see Major Morton's young secretary. Maybe she'd seen Mary.

Minutes later, he stepped into the office building. He hurried down the hallway and around several corners before approaching the major's office.

Miss Yates was not at her desk. The last thing he wanted was to knock on Morton's door and ask about the young girl's whereabouts. Perhaps someone at the front desk knew something.

John turned and hurried back down the corridor. He'd almost reached Lieutenant Brandon's office when he passed a supply closet. Familiar voices from behind the closed door reached his ears.

A sigh of exasperation rolled out of him as he pushed the storage closet door open. There, on the floor behind a row of spare desks, sat Mary and Miss Yates, Morton's young blonde secretary. A myriad of cables and wires sat between them, along with a film recorder.

≡ CHAPTER 7 ≡

Mary sat beside Miss Yates on the supply room floor and nearly jumped out of her skin when John entered. She tried to hide the stethoscope and drill behind her back, though he'd surely seen them. Miss Yates looked sheepish, holding the film camera she'd borrowed from her photojournalist friend.

Catherine Brandon had fine-tuned the plan that Mary and Miss Yates had shared with her. Catherine had also ordered them to keep the details top secret.

Mary turned her gaze to John's, hoping to find compassion. He frowned and tilted his head to one side. Her mind spun in high gear, trying to assess how much he might suspect and what he might do about it. Would he report their suspicious activity to Lieutenant Brandon, or worse, Major Morton?

"What's going on in here?" His voice was low and serious. He folded his arms over his chest.

Mary chewed her lower lip, knowing full well she couldn't reveal anything about her meeting with Catherine Brandon. But she had to say something or he'd know something was up.

"We, uh," Mary stammered. "We have someone else, um, someone higher up, who is helping us with something that's top secret." She cringed the moment the words left her mouth.

Miss Yates aimed a wide-eyed stare at her. Mary chewed her lip, and cold heaviness settled around her heart. Later, once she and the young lady were in private, she'd remind her of the need for secrecy.

Mary ducked her head. She'd been warned about saying too much.

Miss Yates piped, "It's not all as bad as you think, Mr. Painted Horse."

The lead weight in Mary's chest grew heavier. For the hundredth time since this plan had been concocted, she'd wondered what she'd gotten herself into.

Mary squirmed as John eyed Miss Yates. He then locked eyes with her, and she wished the floor would swallow her. He leaned against the doorframe and scrunched his eyebrows together.

"I hope you ladies will be careful."

Mary sensed he knew something. She didn't know what he knew, or how much, but he wasn't stupid. It frightened her to think of what would happen if he guessed what she and Miss Yates were up to.

"Of course, we'll be careful. Everything will be fine." She pasted on a smile and hoped that placated him. She hated keeping this from him. If anything went wrong, she'd feel terrible for implicating him. She'd hate for him to suffer any consequences from her actions.

There were plenty of things that could go wrong, but John didn't need to know that. Plus, she liked him and wanted to protect him from any negative ramifications if their plan went horribly awry.

John threw his hands in the air. "I hope you ladies are following your superior's orders and not going rogue. You could be charged with treason. If you are, don't come crying to me if you end up in the brig."

Mary's heart jerked a bit. Being a soldier, he had to understand classified and clandestine activity. The military demanded secrecy on such matters, especially since military careers, and lives, were at stake.

Still, her words had probably wounded him, as if she didn't trust him. She couldn't blame him, though, for being worried. She herself worried.

Once Major Morton was exposed, she'd explain to him what she could and reiterate the need for secrecy.

Miss Yates rose from the floor. "We're just finishing up in here." She gave Mary a wink, which meant they'd meet elsewhere later that evening.

"Fine," John said. "But Mary, I'm walking you and Miss Yates home."

Miss Yates waved a hand at him. "You don't have to do that, sir. My friend is picking me up from work today. He's the one who loaned us this camera. He's such a dreamboat."

Seemingly unmoved, John leaned in and said, "Okay, but I'm waiting with you until he arrives."

Mary hid their equipment in the bottom of a file cabinet. John stepped from the storage room first and then gave a low whistle when the coast was clear. Mary all but shoved Miss Yates from the stuffy room and then quickly pulled the door closed behind her.

Later, Miss Yates' friend arrived. She hopped into his vehicle without a glance back. Mary detected a hint of romance between the two.

"Let's go." John placed a hand at the small of her back and walked with her down the street. She hoped her overprotective landlady wouldn't question her if she allowed John to come inside for a while. Though she hadn't known him long, she cared for him and wanted to spend more time with him.

"So, have you heard from your family?" Mary asked.

A twinkle shone in his eyes. "Yes, I have. My sister wrote to me not long ago. She told me all about what's happening on our reservation, and she's doing very well in her studies."

"She's getting an education. That's wonderful. I haven't heard anything about Daniel."

"I'm sorry, Mary." He rubbed his hand in circles at the small of her back. The gesture sent waves of warmth and comfort through her. He made her feel safe. Her trust in him grew deeper and stronger.

Though she trusted him, it worried her to think what she'd say if he asked too many questions. Impatience rose within her. The sooner they exposed Major Morton, the better. Part of her hated keeping secrets from John, though she knew he'd not hold it against her.

They reached her apartment. Mary said hello to Mrs. Drake, who was planting daffodil bulbs in her flower garden out front.

"You be nice to her, young man, you hear?"

"Yes, ma'am." John aimed a playful salute at her.

Mary chuckled and invited him in. She lit her sage, and soon the sweet aroma filled her apartment. Together they cooked fry bread. She told him the story of learning to prepare it as a child. In Mary's opinion, making fry bread was a skill that took practice to perfect.

They enjoyed bottles of Coke with their dinner. Afterward, he invited her to walk with him along the beach.

"That would be lovely," she replied. "Let me grab a jacket." Soon they strolled along the shore, watching the waves crash. The smell of salt water tickled her nose and reminded her of Pike Place Market back in Seattle. She choked back a tear, not wanting her homesickness to spoil her time with John.

She gazed into his dark eyes. It seemed they knew what each other was thinking. They dropped onto a nearby log and pulled off their shoes. Mary loved the feeling of warm, dry sand between her toes. There was plenty of warm, dry dirt on the Yakima Reservation. Much as she loved her homeland, it didn't contain a view of the Pacific Ocean.

Her heart hummed with electricity just being near him. She hadn't mentioned Major Morton over dinner, and he hadn't broached the subject of finding her and Miss Yates in the storage closet. She prayed he wouldn't. The moment was too special for the mention of those things.

As darkness settled, she gazed at the stars above, much like she'd done on her reservation. Stars had always held special meaning to her.

John paused a moment and seemed to study the moon. Mary paused as well, and looked at the shining orb. He looked serious, lost in thought. Mary wondered what he might be thinking. Did he care for her the way she cared for him?

She choked back a bit of emotion. As soon as Major Morton was out of the way, she'd complete her spy training. From there, Catherine Brandon would assign her a mission, and then she'd be gone.

A lump formed in her throat so big it nearly cut off her airway. Her mission would transfer her far away from Camp Pendleton. . .and John.

The moon seemed closer to earth tonight, John thought. On the way back to Mary's duplex apartment, it illuminated the sidewalk before them. Their bare feet padded along the dry pavement.

John almost wished he could forgo his combat boots while traipsing through the jungles of the South Pacific. Swamp grass was a far cry from the sands of his reservation. The sharp blades would cut his feet to ribbons. Therefore, he'd be stuck wearing his boots the whole time as he hopped from island to island on his way to Tokyo.

In the meantime, he'd enjoy walking barefoot as much as he could. He allowed himself a moment to reflect on what he'd face when he shipped out.

The beaches along the South Pacific had been combat zones. They wouldn't resemble the shores of Southern California. War was an ugly business, and he hated the thought of lovely landscapes created by God destroyed by artillery shells, mortars, and grenades. He couldn't fathom how many years it would take for war-torn lands to recover from bombings.

He broke the silence between them. "Mary, before you do something crazy, please go over everything with your superiors."

She chewed her lower lip for a few seconds. Then she nodded but lifted her head to the heavens then down to where her feet wiggled in the sand, anywhere but into his eyes. It was nearly his undoing, knowing she was keeping secrets and not knowing if she'd be safe.

"Okay." She stepped toward the water.

A groan rolled from his lips. "I don't mean to upset you. I just don't want to see you or Miss Yates get in any trouble."

"I understand, John. Thank you for your concern." She looked up at him, as if she was contemplating telling him something more. She was hiding something. Should he speak to the lieutenant about it?

They walked for a few minutes in silence.

"Mrs. Drake really likes you," Mary said. "She said you were a kind gentleman."

Waves of heat swept over John. Part of him wanted to develop a romance with Mary, but war held danger and death. He understood he might not come back to her, but did she?

Already, she'd lost both her parents and possibly her brother. Did he want to draw her into a romance, only for him to get killed? Losing her parents and possibly her brother had already cut her to the bone. The last thing he wanted was for her to lose someone else she cared about.

Another part of him said that people couldn't lock themselves away from love forever. Life without love wasn't much of a life at all. His head ached with thoughts that ran through his mind like a runaway string of railroad cars. He rubbed his temple. He had certainly grown to care deeply for Mary, but could he call it love?

"John," Mary said, "are you all right?"

"Uh, yeah." He loosened the tie around his neck. "Tell her I said thank you."

Mary continued. "She's very protective. That's one of the things I like about her. So, you must have really impressed her last time you saw her."

He reached for her hand, held her back as a Jeep full of rowdy soldiers barreled through the intersection. He still needed to act the gentleman and keep her safe.

"Well," Mary said, "here we are."

Memories invaded his thoughts. He'd first walked her home from the Brandon residence at the end of October and had lost count of the times he'd done so since then. Now, here he was, standing in front of her apartment once again. He decided right then, no matter how far away the war took him, he'd do everything he could to come home to her.

Her hand nestled in his. He lifted it to his lips and placed a kiss upon her knuckles. She gasped and gazed at him with eyes as dark as onyx. His heart galloped like a runaway mustang. Did she see as much longing in his eyes as he saw in hers? She made no move to pull her hand away from his.

Mrs. Drake emerged from her side of the duplex. "You kids can come in for a cup of hot English tea. I don't want to see you catch your death of a cold from the freezing night air."

A smile lifted the corners of Mary's mouth. "Give us a moment, please."

The sweet voice did funny things to his heart. Much as he wanted to spend more time with her, he understood that Morton must be handled first.

To Mrs. Drake he said, "Thank you for the invitation, ma'am, but I really must be going. I have a meeting with my CO early in the morning."

Mary slowly pulled her fingers from his grasp. Her smile faded.

The fact that he'd upset her became evident when she placed her hands on his chest and whispered, "John, I beg you, please don't say anything to anyone about what you saw in the storage room today." Her eyes beseeched his.

He wanted to promise her that he wouldn't, unless the lives of her and Miss Yates were at stake, but how would he know if they were or not? Everything in him wanted to know the details, but he guessed that was privileged information.

John whistled between his teeth. All the secrets and clandestine meetings were beginning to grate on him. He almost didn't know who to trust anymore.

"I'll do my best to keep quiet, but if I even think there's trouble, I'll sing like the proverbial canary." To his surprise, she agreed. They said their good nights, and he left.

He had to hurry to reach his barracks before curfew. Samuel arrived minutes later, sweating and out of breath.

"Boy, that was close." Samuel panted. "I'll have to be more careful next time."

John laughed at his friend, but when he dropped into his bunk that night, he tossed fitfully and lost count of the times he refluffed his pillow. When the sun climbed over the eastern horizon and tried valiantly to shine despite the cloudy sky, he was still bone weary.

Once he was showered and shaved, he exited his barracks and proceeded to the lieutenant's office. John plopped into a stuffed chair.

The lieutenant paced in front of his desk.

John shifted in his seat, seeking a more comfortable position, which would not be easy considering the way Lieutenant Brandon eyed him. For a moment he wondered if the man already knew about Mary Wishram, Miss Yates, and the goings-on in the storage closet. And if the lieutenant did know, he likely wondered if John knew as well.

John gritted his teeth. He was up to his crew cut in all this subterfuge. It was only a matter of time before he drowned in it.

Finally, Lieutenant Brandon sat at the corner of his desk. He pulled a cigar from the box that Major Morton had given him. But rather than light the thing, he simply rolled it between his fingers.

"Corporal Painted Horse," Brandon said, "I've spoken to the brass. We believe Morton is a disgrace and a threat to the United States service."

John scoffed. As if any grunt couldn't figure that out.

Brandon said, "Sweetheart, there you are."

John swiveled in his seat. Catherine Brandon, the lieutenant's wife, stepped from the shadows.

⚡ CHAPTER 8 ⚡

John stared at Catherine Brandon. He'd met her only twice at the hospital before the lieutenant invited him to dinner a few weeks ago. How could she possibly be involved in the effort to expose Major Morton? And why would she want to?

Unless...

Unless the major had made unscrupulous advances toward her.

A frigid chill swept over him, followed by a burning anger at the thought.

John shook his head. He must be mistaken. If Morton had tried anything with Catherine Brandon, the lady wouldn't have waited for her husband to redeem her honor. She would have clobbered the scoundrel herself.

As far as he knew, Major Morton was still very much alive.

He hated to wish ill upon anyone, but if Morton was no longer in the military, the women on base would be much safer. Not to mention any soldiers who might fall under his command. If only the brass would court-martial the clown, but they needed evidence to do that. If all they had was the lady's word, well, it wouldn't amount to much against an officer.

There was safety in numbers, though. If several women banded together to testify against him? No, he couldn't imagine subjecting any more ladies to Morton's illicit treatment.

"Corporal Painted Horse?" Catherine Brandon leaned closer and eyed him like she wanted to check his pulse.

"Yeah, yeah, I'm fine. With all due respect, Lieutenant Brandon, sir, why did you call me here? What is this meeting about?"

The lieutenant ran his fingers over the gold rectangular cigar box from Major Morton. Then Lieutenant Brandon sucked in a deep breath. "I'm sure you've heard the rumors, John. Major Morton is engaging in conduct unbecoming an officer."

"Do you mean his unscrupulous behavior with young ladies, or is there more to this?" John folded his arms over his chest and thought back to his time at Camp Pendleton. He'd never thought much of Morton. The man was a blowhard, and the way he treated women was shameful.

John suspected Morton had made advances toward Mary Wishram, but every time he asked her about it, she clammed up. The mere thought of Morton touching her sent John's heart thudding in his chest. His blood heated by several degrees.

Catherine interrupted his thoughts. "Corporal Painted Horse, are you willing to help us prove the major needs to be disciplined?"

Confused, John asked, "How much help could I be? He's a major, and I'm just a corporal."

Lieutenant Brandon replaced the cigar box back on his desk. "You were present in my office the day Morton spouted off his dangerous idea of sharing the code with spies."

John nodded. Major Morton had made a lousy first impression that hadn't changed with the passage of time.

"Colonel Goldman will accompany us to Morton's office for a meeting. You'll be a witness," Lieutenant Brandon elaborated. "The colonel isn't happy with Morton's behavior or his idea to toss the code around like candy at a parade, and he wants to inform Morton himself that he is on thin ice."

"But, what good will a butt-chewing do?" John adjusted in his chair. "I don't think that will be enough to have him tossed from the corps."

"Colonel Goldman is a deeply religious man with three daughters, and he's been faithful to his wife of more than forty years. When he hears how Morton treats women—"

Catherine implored, "You have to trust me on this, John. Can you do that?"

John nodded and allowed the lieutenant to continue.

"I'll inform Morton that the meeting is about the code talking program, which won't exactly be a lie. That way we can be sure he'll be in his office. I'll even imply that Goldman might want more information from Morton."

John shook his head, even more confused than he was a moment ago. "How is this going to expose his rotten behavior, let alone get him court-martialed? And what have you got to do with this, Mrs. Brandon? It can't be safe for you to be implicated in anything regarding Morton."

A smile curved across her face. "Don't worry about me, Mr. Painted Horse. If it helps put your mind at ease, I'm a black belt in karate."

"That's my girl." Lieutenant Brandon grinned. "John, look at this like you would code talking. You don't need to know every small detail about the mission. Just focus on the task in front of you."

"Okay," he said. But he really wondered if it was okay. He thought Mary was also involved, but, of course, she'd never admit to it. That was probably why she was being so secretive.

His heart jerked. His insides had twisted themselves into knots. *God, please keep her safe.* He wiped the sweat from his forehead with the back of his sleeve.

As if sensing his thoughts, Lieutenant Brandon said, "And, John, you are not to say a word about this to anyone, especially that Indian girl who's got you so moony-eyed."

John's cheeks heated. He gulped. His face was probably the shade of a ripe tomato. Both the lieutenant and his wife placed their fingers over their mouths and chuckled. Had the lieutenant's desk been any closer, John would have gladly crawled under it.

"Tomorrow, at 1325," Lieutenant Brandon added, "you and I and the colonel are taking a leisurely stroll to Major Morton's office for a meeting."

"And that's it? Wait, isn't the meeting supposed to be at 1330?"

"Yes, but we'll arrive a bit early." Lieutenant Brandon pointed a finger at him. "And you'll keep your mouth zipped. That's an order."

"Yes, sir." John slowly rose to his feet. His hand shook as he saluted.

"That will be all. You are excused, Corporal Painted Horse."

John left the room, knowing deep in his soul there was more to this than what the Brandons were telling him. He prayed that Mary wasn't involved, but his gut told him otherwise.

He marched out the building and toward her apartment. They were to have dinner that evening. That, he hoped, would give him ample opportunity to warn her to steer clear of Major Morton. The man was a snake.

John also thought about how to allude to the fact that something very dangerous was going down. Something that could get him, and the Brandons, all court-martialed. What if plans went awry? So horribly awry that Morton somehow came out the victor? Would he then finagle his way into a promotion?

———— ≈ ————

Darkness brought a measure of tranquility over Camp Pendleton.

Mary raced to the hospital for another secret meeting with Catherine Brandon. Due to hiccups with a supply delivery, she was ten minutes late and running as fast as she could in her new shoes. The things weren't broken in yet. Both her feet ached. Her heart ached as badly at having to tiptoe through a minefield—the plan she hoped ousted Major Morton from the Navy.

Her dinner date with John was only an hour away. She hoped the meeting would be a short one. She sensed it had something to do with the plan to expose Major Morton. She made a mental note to warn John, as subtly as possible without spilling the whole kettle of beans, that he needed to avoid Major Morton tomorrow, at all costs.

She hated keeping secrets from him. After bursting in on her and Miss Yates in the supply closet, he had to suspect something. All day she'd thought about how to tell Catherine about what John had seen. Mrs. Brandon would not be pleased.

Mary rushed past Samuel Acothley flirting with Susanna, a candy striper.

"Hello, Mary. What brings you here tonight?" Susanna asked.

"Not much." Mary waved and hurried on her way.

Her breath came in gasps by the time she reached the head nurse's station. Catherine scowled at her.

"Sorry I'm late." Mary wrung her hands.

Catherine motioned her toward the linen closet.

Mary followed.

Once inside, Catherine said, "I have another job for you. One that's tied to the first one."

Anxiety swirled in Mary's middle like a whirlpool. "Something else besides catching the snake on film doing awful things?"

"Yes."

"Like what? I'm already acting as bait so Miss Yates can film him through a hole she's drilled in the wall. By the way, how will we keep Morton from seeing the gaping hole next to his bookcase?"

"Don't worry about that. The less you know the better. Just focus on your tasks and leave the rest to me."

Mary nodded. "What else do you want me to do?"

Catherine leaned closer. "I need you to sneak into his office and set his clock back by ten minutes. That way, he'll think it's 1320, when in reality, it'll be 1330. It must be done while he's on his lunch hour."

"But," Mary stammered, "how am I supposed to do that without anyone seeing me going into his office? Why can't I just sneak in tonight when nobody is around?"

"Because we can't risk him figuring out the time difference before lunch hour. If he did, he'd adjust his clock to the correct time, and the plan would be shot. You will receive a stack of, um, *vital* documents that must be delivered to his office while he's on lunch."

"Yes, I'm supposed to arrive and then act as bait. Sneaking in there early and turning the clock back ten minutes is a whole new monkey wrench thrown into the get-along, though. It worries me."

Catherine Brandon tilted her head to the side and said, "Don't worry. You'll do fine."

A widening pool of anxiety swirled faster in Mary's middle. Would she be all right? Could she be court-martialed for this? Could she trust the Brandons to have her back? John's words about the government not keeping promises flitted through her mind.

Mary gulped. "Will Miss Yates be there to help me? To make sure the coast is clear?"

"Only when you enter Morton's office." Catherine shook her head and looked to the floor. "I'm sorry, but I really can't tell you more than that."

Mary tried to swallow the lump in her throat. "I'm still scared."

Catherine placed her hands on Mary's shoulders. "I know, but you'll be all right. I'll be praying for you during that time. You want to be a spy. Consider this a training exercise."

"Yeah, I guess you're right. This won't be half as dangerous as wading into a troop of Japanese soldiers." At least, Mary hoped it wouldn't be as dangerous. Being bait was scary enough, but changing his clock, for whatever reason, was something else altogether. She hoped it would be a simple clock to reset.

"Is there something else?" Catherine asked.

"Yes," Mary said. "Yesterday when Miss Yates and I were in the storage closet at the Office of Strategic Services building, John Painted Horse burst into the room and saw us with the film camera."

Catherine raised her eyebrows. "And what did you tell him?"

"That it was nothing. Miss Yates said something about borrowing the film camera from a journalist friend and we were just putting it away."

Catherine rocked back and forth on her heels. "Do you think he bought it?"

Mary shook her head. "I don't know, but he has to suspect we're up to something. I hope that's not a bad thing."

If she were in John's shoes, without a doubt she'd suspect something. John was a street-smart guy. She hoped he wouldn't act upon any suspicions he had. That could potentially cause the plan to go haywire.

"Don't worry. I'll take care of it. You're free to go." Catherine grabbed a stack of sheets and exited the linen closet.

A minute later, Mary hustled out the hospital's front doors. Samuel and Susanna were nowhere in sight. Relief flooded through her.

Her date with John was only twenty minutes away. Was that enough time to get home and put herself to rights before he arrived?

≣ CHAPTER 9 ≣

Mary released a thankful breath. Mrs. Drake was nowhere to be seen. She hurried into her apartment and stepped into the shower. She washed her long, dark hair and combed through it. Rather than braid it, she swept up the sides with bobby pins. The rest hung down her back. She applied red lipstick and sprayed on a fine mist of perfume.

John arrived the moment she replaced the bottle on her dresser. She hurried to the door and clutched the knob before opening it. What was the best way to warn him to stay away from Major Morton's office the next day without compromising confidentiality?

She blew out a breath.

She flung the door open and there he stood, hair freshly trimmed and combed, sporting casual civilian clothes and a single pink rose. While it was nice to see him out of uniform, she wondered why he was dressed as he was. Where had he obtained such a gorgeous flower in November?

She'd sensed the relationship growing deeper, the way they'd looked at each other every time they had taken walks along the beach. The long conversations they had about their cultures and traditions. He had even held her hand.

"Hello, Mary. This is for you." He handed her the flower.

Delighted at such a warm display of affection, admiration for him ratcheted up another notch. His eyes held a yearning she'd never seen in any man before. If his heart was a magnet, then hers was made of steel. She couldn't deny the attraction, the drawing together of their souls. How could she say goodbye to this man once she was transferred to parts unknown?

"It's lovely, John. Thank you." She brought the bloom to her nose and savored the fragrance. It would be hard to say goodbye. She tried to convince herself the separation was only temporary. Once this awful war ended, they would be free to enjoy every day together.

She must finish her training soon, and that included doing the mission assigned to her with Major Morton tomorrow. She must not fail.

John scuffed his boots back and forth across her doormat. "I'm dressed like this because I, uh, want tonight to be a relaxing evening, to make us more comfortable for casual conversation."

A ribbon of worry coursed through her. He'd mentioned finishing his training in another month. He would be leaving then too. That didn't explain why he'd dressed in his civvies.

Oh heavens.

Was he going to propose tonight?

Mary gripped her flower so tight a thorn pricked her finger.

"Ouch!" She pressed her stinging finger to her lips. "Come inside for a moment while I put this in water and grab my coat, purse, and hat."

She ducked back into her apartment, and he followed. Two minutes later, she reappeared, snagging her purse strap on the doorknob and nearly tripping over the doormat. There was good reason for her clumsiness, considering her suspicions that John would propose.

If he asked her to marry him, what could she say? She had already lost Mama, then Papa, and now maybe Daniel. Did she want to allow herself to love again if it meant her heart would be crushed? The thought of being abandoned and bereft, yet again, frightened her.

Her mind was a whirlwind of activity, like the dust storms on her reservation. She needed to calm her mind.

Catherine's words penetrated the murkiness clouding her mind. Just do her job. She had to pretend everything was all right between them, and pray he wouldn't ask questions, especially about yesterday with Miss Yates in the storage closet.

She untangled her purse from the door just as he pulled her into his embrace. He held her like he never wanted to let her go, and if she were honest, she enjoyed the feeling. She gazed into his eyes. The longing there was as clear as the cloudless night sky.

"Shall we go? I borrowed a Jeep so we can have dinner at the Seaside Palace. It's a restaurant on the beach. I hear it's a nice place, great seafood that I know you love so much."

She'd bet he had matrimony in mind. Best not think about it now or she'd stumble on the doormat again.

"That sounds lovely," Mary said. "But I bet they don't serve salmon or fry bread." She laughed at her own joke, though she did miss feasting on salmon.

John chuckled. "I bet they don't, but it'll be nice all the same."

He escorted her to the Jeep. Her feet still weren't used to the new shoes. She used that as an excuse to lean into him. The smell of his aftershave wafted in the air, a woodsy aroma that reminded her of the pine forests in Washington State. Her pulse raced. Her breath hitched in her lungs.

Should she say something to him, warn him to avoid Major Morton tomorrow? Her heart ached to do so, but she had to follow orders.

"So, how was work today?" She didn't know exactly what he did. He was very hush-hush about his training. Considering how little they talked about their occupations, she suspected he kept secrets like she did. If she was lucky, he'd mention the major. From there she hoped to express her disdain for the skunk. That wasn't exactly going against orders.

A long silence elapsed. Even in the twilight, she noted how he gripped the steering wheel until his knuckles turned white.

He shrugged. "Training. A meeting with Brandon."

"Oh," Mary said. Should she push for more information? How many questions could she ask without prying or raising suspicions?

"And you? Anything exciting today?" He clipped the curb while steering around a corner.

Mary held on as he sped up. He was nervous, but why? Should she ask? She cursed the secrecy she struggled to maintain.

"Yeah, I dropped off six pallets of chow today. There was so much Spam. You know the stuff is being produced in mass quantity. It made me late for a meeting with—" Mary stopped herself just before the words *Catherine Brandon* flew from her lips.

For a moment, neither of them spoke. She scrambled for words. "I was. . .late to see. . .a friend at the hospital."

"Did you see Samuel? He's sweet on a candy striper."

"Yes, I saw them. Susanna is a nice girl. She's good for him." Mary prayed he wouldn't ask his friend about her. Samuel would tell John that she breezed right past them. That would increase his suspicions. She didn't know anyone else at the hospital. What excuse could she give him for being there? She could say she was delivering medical supplies, but that would be a lie.

"Are you making any deliveries tomorrow?" He pulled into the parking lot of the Seaside Palace.

"Uh, no." She hadn't told him that Catherine Brandon had asked her to curtail deliveries so she could focus on her covert training. She racked her brain to come up with other topics that would steer them away from conversation about top-secret activity.

"Well, here we are." John parked the Jeep in a spot in the back of the parking lot. He helped her down from the vehicle. They were in close proximity, and his presence, being in his arms, discombobulated her.

John cleared his throat and pulled away. He was acting strange tonight. Marriage obviously wasn't on his mind. Something else had his thoughts in a tangle. But what?

John escorted Mary toward the restaurant. Tomorrow he'd execute a mission that could possibly land him in military jail for a long time, possibly forever, if the plan backfired. In his opinion, how could it *not* backfire?

Therefore, he wanted this night to be special.

Even if things went accordingly and Morton was exposed, with the war in full swing, soldiers never knew if or when they'd be transferred. Or to which location.

He wanted to make beautiful memories with her, give her a wonderful night to remember.

"Good evening, sir, ma'am," the doorman said.

"Thank you." They spoke in unison. He paused. They looked at one another.

Mary smiled. The brightness in her eyes did funny things to his pulse. He wished he could spend every waking moment with her until it came time for him to ship out.

Everyone in class, including him, had picked up the code quickly. Private Soaring Eagle had struggled with learning to operate the radio, but another week or two of practice and he should be ready. They were needed in the field. So, it was hard to say how much time they had left.

And so, they'd cherish every minute.

Once inside, the aromas of fine Italian cooking wafted through the air. Although in John's mind, they didn't compete with Mary's rosy perfume.

A large part of him wanted to walk along the beach with her and kiss her under a thousand twinkling stars. He loosened the tie around his neck. No sense in succumbing to dreamy fanfare just yet.

The host greeted them and led them to a table by the fireplace. They placed their order and, later, the waiter brought them their meal.

"Hello there, Painted Horse."

The voice sent icy chills pumping through John's veins.

Major Morton.

"Mighty fine-looking dame you got with you tonight." The major chewed on a cigar.

John noted that Mary's eyes were as big around as his mother's pie tins. Though his jaw clenched, he managed a reply. "If you'll excuse us, sir, we're enjoying a nice dinner."

The major roared with laughter, gaining the attention and glares of patrons at the next table. "I'll leave you kids to it. I just finished my dinner, and now I'm headed to the Tiki Lounge."

"Well, you best get going, sir." John released an exasperated sigh and wished the man would leave.

Major Morton added, "Stop by when you're done here, and bring your date."

A thought struck John. Lieutenant Brandon had decided against informing Morton that the brass was showing up in his office tomorrow. Lieutenant Brandon likely concealed that information, thereby giving the major less time to come up with excuses for his ill behavior or to cover his tracks.

Morton walked away, and Mary blew out an audible breath. John wished he could ask her about the major, but his orders were to maintain radio silence.

Mary chatted about cargo deliveries and how hard it was to learn to drive a big GMC truck, known by some as a deuce-and-a-half. John barely heard the conversation. In spite of his best efforts, his mind wandered. The secrets were chewing a hole in his gut.

When they finished dinner, John asked, "Would you like to walk along the beach? It's right out the front door."

"Yeah, I'd like that."

He paid the bill, took her hand, and led her out a side door. They sat on a beach chair and removed their shoes. They strolled along the surf, the cold waves lapping at their toes. He dug his feet into the sand.

Her hand fit perfectly in his. The smell of salt water filled his nostrils, and the sound of the waves crashing against the shore brought peace to his troubled soul. It transitioned his heart rate into a regular rhythm. There was nothing like this in Arizona.

"I wish my mother and sisters could see this." He chucked a piece of driftwood into the water.

"I've been to Puget Sound a number of times, and even to the Washington coastline, but I haven't seen anything like this." She motioned toward the sand. "It isn't gray."

Perplexed, he said, "The sand is gray along the Washington coast?"

She nodded. "In many places, yes. I heard it's because the sky is always cloudy. There isn't enough sun to bleach the sand white. I've also heard it's because the rocks that create the sand are gray. I think it's a little bit of both."

He paused, unable to take his eyes off her. She allowed the waves to sweep over her feet, nearly up to her knees. The sound of her laughter floated in the air. He really was moony-eyed over her, just like the lieutenant said.

She picked up a piece of driftwood and tossed it into the water. "Tell me about your reservation, John. I just shared a bit about where I'm from."

John closed his eyes, playing in his mind's eye the scene of his family's home the morning he left for boot camp. "The rock formations are so spectacular they take your breath away. They're tall, as if they're trying to reach up and touch the sun. Some are flat on top, and most are created in various shades of red, orange, and brown. The desert stretches from one end of the horizon to the other. On a quiet night, when the wind isn't blowing, you can hear the coyotes howling in the distance."

"Wow. That sounds beautiful. There are rolling brown hills on my reservation but nothing like what you describe. We have a lot of orchards, and rivers running through Yakima Valley. We have lots of coyotes too."

Her chuckles sent his heart into a fit of hammering beats. He grinned and rubbed his chest. "Maybe we can visit each other's reservations after the war."

She tilted her head from one shoulder to the other. "Yeah, maybe. If we can afford it."

John's shoulders sagged a bit. Poverty had dug a deep trench through most reservations. Finding money for shoes posed a challenge. Finding money to travel several states away seemed almost an impossible task.

They walked another half mile in silence, her hand nestled in his.

Then, John spied the Tiki Lounge. He'd never been there, and he didn't care to become a customer now.

"Let's go back." He squeezed Mary's hand and pointed. "That's the Tiki Lounge up there, and I don't want to run into Morton."

A groan escaped from her. She swiveled around. "I don't either."

He placed his hands on her shoulders and turned her to face him. "Look, Mary, if that man bothers you, I want to know about it."

She chewed her lower lip and didn't say a word for what seemed like eternity. "He..."

"Mary," John said slowly, leaning closer to her. She was hiding something. He sensed it, but what?

He was reminded of the meeting with Major Morton tomorrow. How could he tell her to stay away from the man's office without raising suspicions?

"Mary," John said again. "Uh, are you stopping by the Office of Strategic Services tomorrow? I mean, to ask about your brother? Have you heard anything about him?"

She sighed and dropped her head. "No. I haven't heard anything. The uncertainty is tearing me to pieces."

John blew out a breath. He needed to tread carefully. "I, uh, heard Major Morton handles a few cases regarding POWs. Has he been able to shed any light on your brother's whereabouts?"

She stopped. Froze. Even in the darkness he saw her wide eyes shift from the stars above to the sand beneath their feet. Indignation bubbled in him. Why wouldn't she look at him?

She was keeping secrets from him and hiding something that involved Major Morton. Could she be in cahoots with this man? Was he blackmailing her?

John didn't know what was happening, but he was determined to find out.

⧳ CHAPTER 10 ⧳

Mary's palms were sweaty. She struggled to hang on to the files filled with the supposedly vital documents to deliver to Major Morton's office. She breathed in deep and then slowly blew the air out of her mouth. Heaven forbid she hyperventilate in the middle of her assignment.

She tried to keep the heels of her shoes from clacking too loudly on the floor tiles. The less attention she drew to herself the better. A host of willies swam from the outer reaches of her body and headed straight to her heart. She repeated a mantra in her head.

Don't walk too fast.

Don't lollygag.

Don't raise suspicion.

She rounded the corner and spotted Miss Yates at her desk. Right where Catherine Brandon said she'd be when it came time to deliver the files.

Miss Yates must be as nervous as Mary. The girl's hands trembled.

The poor girl swallowed twice before muttering a shaky, "Hello. The major is out to lunch now, but you can go in and leave those on his desk. Watch out for his new desk clock, though. The one on the wall is broken and is being repaired."

So that explained how there would be a clock on Morton's desk and the hole on the wall where someone could film the goings-on.

Mary managed a quivering smile. "Thank you, Miss Yates. Do you know when he'll return? I need him to sign these forms stating that he received the files."

"He should be back by thirteen hundred."

"Thank you again, Miss Yates." Mary slipped into the office. She prayed the ruse had worked, that anyone nearby would know she wasn't in the man's office for nefarious reasons. She shut the door and sucked in air. The stench of alcohol and cigar smoke permeated the atmosphere, and she regretted breathing deeply.

A lump stuck in her throat. She forced it down and dropped the files on the major's desk. Before reaching for the clock sitting next to a heavy cigar box, she walked around the desk and sat in the major's chair.

Then, she reached for the desk clock.

She stared at the spot where the wall clock used to be. Wires hung from a hole about three inches across. Miss Yates wasn't supposed to begin filming until Major Morton arrived back from lunch. Would she have time enough to enter the room next door and start the camera before the evil side of Morton's personality appeared?

Mary hoped the camera captured enough, clearly. But now was not the time to worry about that.

I hope Morton doesn't catch me doing this.

She shifted her focus to the task at hand. The clock was heavy in her hands, but she'd fixed her delivery truck a few times. She was familiar with knobs and levers that twisted this way and that.

She pulled an Allen wrench and a screwdriver from her pocket and fiddled with the piece until she had successfully set the clock back by ten minutes.

Were those heavy footsteps she heard coming down the hallway?

Breath froze in her lungs.

Funny how five seconds could pass in what seemed more like five hours.

When the footsteps faded, the breath slowly leaked out of her.

Quickly, she refocused on her task. Thankfully, it hadn't taken long. She tried not to puff her chest out too much. There would be opportunity for that later, providing the plan succeeded.

She pulled a handkerchief from her pocket and wiped her fingerprints from the clock and then replaced it on the major's desk.

When she was certain it was positioned exactly how she'd found it, she stood. Before she could walk across the room, the major's voice boomed in the hallway. Through the thin walls, she heard him telling a crude joke to another man.

She scrambled from behind the desk and stood like a statue in the center of the room. She glanced at the clock. Although it was set ten minutes back, she adjusted the time in her mind and realized it was still not yet 1300. Had Miss Yates made it safely to the neighboring room? Was she ready with the camera? Mary prayed, hoped the thing operated properly and quietly!

Major Morton slunk into the room. "Well, hello there, dearie. What are you doing in here?" He slithered to his desk and pulled a cigar from the gold box.

As long as he didn't look at his clock, she was relatively safe. A quick glance to his left forearm told her he wore no wristwatch.

Mary stammered, "I brought in a stack of documents that need your signature. If you'll be kind enough to read and sign them, I'll deliver them to the proper people."

Morton lit the cigar. He dropped his colossal rump onto the corner of the desk, blowing puffs of stinky smoke into the air. It took seconds before the room was filled with the awful stench. His smarmy leer sent icy fingers inching along her spine. She shifted her weight from foot to foot.

Morton yanked a pen from his shirt pocket and signed, barely reading anything. When he set his pen down, he said, "Done. Now, what do you say about having some fun, eh?"

Was the camera rolling?

Dare she glance that direction?

"Sir, with all due respect, I'm not interested in that kind of so-called fun." She squared her shoulders and moved to the desk to retrieve the files. He stepped in front of her. The contents in her stomach churned at the smell of cigar smoke mingling with the alcohol on his breath.

She dodged around him and maneuvered to the other side of his desk. She grabbed the files and tried to hightail it away from him, but for a portly man, he was quick.

Mary pivoted, and the heel broke off her new shoe. Stifling a grumble, she hobbled away from the desk and darted behind a stuffed wingback chair. Morton placed his body between her and the door.

His face glowered, dark and angry. He pointed a finger at her. "You've escaped twice now. You're not going to be that lucky again."

"Sir," Mary reiterated, "I have no intention of being your post-lunch dessert."

He quipped, "That's what you think. Third time's a charm, right, dearie?"

He moved toward her faster than she thought possible. She scrambled behind his desk and clambered over two boxes of files on the floor, grasped the desk to keep from falling.

Memories of playing tag as a child swept through her mind.

"Ah!" she yelped. There went the heel to her other shoe. What was she to do now with another pair of broken shoes? She hobbled behind the stuffed chair.

She yanked off her shoes. He chased her away from the chair.

Desperate, she threw them at him. His cursing indicated she'd angered him.

He backed her up against his desk. Her backside bumped into the edge.

She was trapped.

She glanced at the clock on his desk. Catherine promised help would arrive no later than 1330. It was that time now. Where was the cavalry?

Morton stepped closer. His hand snaked out and grabbed her wrist. "You're not getting away from me this time. Third time really is a charm." He threw back his head and cackled.

Mary felt around the desk for something to use as a weapon. Her fingers grasped the cigar box.

Memories flew into her mind of all the unsolicited advances this scoundrel made toward her, Miss Yates, and heaven only knew how many other women.

Enough!

She raised the cigar box and slammed it against the vile man's head.

To her shock, horror, and slight satisfaction, he dropped to the floor like a sack of potatoes.

Blood oozed from his forehead.

Unconscious?

Dead?

John leaned against the wall next to the men's room and checked his watch for the third time in less than three minutes—1330.

Although the meeting with Major Morton was scheduled for 1330,

Lieutenant Brandon had wanted to be there by 1325, along with John and Colonel Goldman. That time had come and gone.

Lieutenant Brandon paced in front of the men's room like an expectant father. They waited, not so patiently, for Colonel Goldman to exit.

The lieutenant clenched his fists and groaned. "What's taking that man so long? He's been in there for twenty minutes."

John shrugged. "I don't know." Tension seeping from his CO clouded the air like a cold, moist fog on an eerie winter morning. Lieutenant Brandon didn't care for sloppiness where military protocol was concerned, but this seemed a bit much. Not something that equaled a devastating loss in battle, or so John thought.

"Maybe he's sick," John added.

Lieutenant Brandon scowled, opened his mouth, and then clamped it shut again. Then he resumed pacing the hallway.

This was unusual. The lieutenant was antsy about something, and John had no idea what or why. John checked his watch again. They were only two minutes behind schedule. Did the fate of the entire mission really depend on two minutes?

The colonel emerged from the facilities with watery eyes and a red face that dripped sweat. "Sorry for the delay, gentlemen. My wife is from Mexico. She prepared a dinner last night that was delicious but packed with jalapeno peppers. Had me running for the men's room all day. Whoo-ee."

John stifled a chuckle.

Lieutenant Brandon rolled his eyes at the ceiling. "Shall we proceed?"

"Yes, yes." Colonel Goldman pulled a handkerchief from his pocket and mopped the perspiration pouring from his brow. He followed the lieutenant down the hallway.

John followed them, glad to finally be underway, if nothing else than to ease Lieutenant Brandon's anxiety. He shoved his hands in his pockets, wondering if Major Morton knew they were coming for him.

They rounded a corner in time for John to see Mary Wishram bolt from the major's office.

Was that blood spatter all over the front of her dress?

Alarm shot through him.

Was she injured? Had Major Morton harmed her? If so, he was having it out with the man, no matter the consequences.

What on earth was she doing in there, anyway? To his knowledge, she wasn't supposed to be at the meeting. If she was snooping around in Morton's office, she couldn't have chosen a worse time to do so.

John started after her. He had to find out if she was all right.

Lieutenant Brandon stepped in his way, pointed a finger at him, and ordered, "You stay put, Painted Horse."

"But sir!" John exclaimed.

Lieutenant Brandon jabbed a finger at him. "That's an order."

John clenched his fists. He didn't like it one bit that his superior officer was preventing him from checking on her. Mary didn't appear hurt, but she had to be shaken by whatever had transpired in the major's office. He prayed she was all right. That was all he could do at the moment. His frustration escalated.

A clanking sound echoed from the storage closet adjacent to the major's office. Lieutenant Brandon shoved the door open. There stood Miss Yates, sobbing on the shoulder of her photojournalist friend. A film camera lay on the floor between the two.

"What in tarnation?" Colonel Goldman grumbled.

The colonel wasn't the only one struggling to connect the dots. John remembered the night he'd caught Mary in there with Miss Yates, and the flimsy excuse they'd given him for being there. His palms grew clammy. What had these two ladies done? And how badly had it interfered with the mission?

The pale journalist whispered, "Somebody needs to check on Major Morton."

Colonel Goldman, apparently growing angrier and more confused, bellowed, "What is going on?"

Lieutenant Brandon said, "I'll take care of things here. Painted Horse, you check on Morton."

John obeyed and stepped into the major's office. The room looked like a tornado had blown through it. A wingback chair lay on its side. Files were scattered across the desk. A lit cigar sat atop a stack of papers on the floor, burning a hole in them.

He stomped on the cigar to extinguish the small flame.

His heart turned into an ice block.

Next to the squashed cigar sat the blood-coated cigar box.

One hinge was broken.

Hearing a groan, John hustled behind Morton's desk. The man leaned against the wall gripping his forehead. Blood seeped through his fingers.

⫸ CHAPTER II ⫷

John yanked a towel from the wet bar in Major Morton's office, rushed to where the man lay sprawled against the wall, and knelt beside him. He was sure Mary had done this to him, and he could certainly guess why. Fear slithered through him. What would happen to her now?

He placed the towel to the major's bleeding forehead with trembling hands. As a man of faith, he should pray for the major, that God would grant him recovery, except no words came to mind.

Prayers for Mary did, though. *Lord, wherever she is, please help her.*

Lucidity descended upon Major Morton. His eyes filled with clarity. He glared at John.

"See what that crazy dame of yours did to me? Wait until I get my hands on her."

Fright turned to indignation. John rose to his feet, huffing. *Lord, help me harness my tongue. Don't let me say something that lands me in the brig.* "Sir, I mean no disrespect, but if I know Miss Wishram, I'm sure she was acting in self-defense."

The major sneered. Another wave of terror pooled in John's middle.

Major Morton staggered to his feet. "Why, you crazy—"

Lieutenant Brandon and Colonel Goldman burst into the room, angry scowls etched on their faces. John gulped, then stood at attention and saluted for good measure. He prayed they weren't angry with Mary, or with him.

How could this plan have gone so horribly awry? His stomach roiled. It didn't bode well for his future missions.

Colonel Goldman placed his fists on his hips. His eyes blazed with fury as he glared at Major Morton. "Sir, I've spoken with your secretary and her journalist friend. They have you on film, and if those reels reveal what I think they will, you're looking at serious charges."

John dropped his salute but continued to stand at attention. Flak seemed to fly around the room. The last thing he needed was to be struck by it.

"What reels?" Morton asked.

"Why don't you ask your secretary?" Lieutenant Brandon asked. "The ladies in the military aren't the scatterbrained idiots you take them for."

Morton snorted. "You'd believe a young bubble-headed broad over me? I'm an officer!"

Colonel Goldman bristled. His face turned the color of a shiny new fire engine.

John remembered what Lieutenant Brandon had said about the colonel. He was a deeply religious man, faithful to his wife, and the father of three young daughters. A number of times, Colonel Goldman had gone on record and voiced his disdain for men who disrespected young ladies.

"I've heard very disturbing rumors about you, Morton." Colonel Goldman's eyebrows scrunched together. He glowered at the major.

"With all due respect, sir"—Major Morton puffed his chest, hooked his thumbs into his belt—"I believe officers have earned a few, uh, *unauthorized* benefits. You can't blame a man for admiring his, uh, *surroundings*, if you get my meaning." Major Morton had the nerve to wag his eyebrows.

Colonel Goldman closed the distance between him and Major Morton with his hands clenched into fists at his sides.

Sweat beaded at John's temples. In that moment he'd give anything for a flak jacket.

"I never thought much of your unauthorized schemes of sharing the Navajo code with every Tom, Dick, and Harry in the corps," Colonel Goldman roared. "How dare you even think of jeopardizing the lives of countless Marines? If I have my way, you'll be court-martialed!"

John pieced the scenario together. He suspected Miss Yates had filmed Major Morton making unsolicited advances toward Mary. And Mary clobbered him.

He stepped forward. "Lieutenant Brandon, may I check on the

well-being of Miss Wishram?"

The lieutenant nodded. "I'm sure she's with my wife at the hospital, but go ahead and see if she's all right. We'll need her testimony anyway."

"Thank you, sir." He turned to leave.

Lieutenant Brandon added, "And tell my wife I'll meet her there soon."

"Yes, sir." He forced himself to walk when he really wanted to sprint.

From the hallway, he heard Colonel Goldman berate Major Morton in a tone he didn't expect to hear from a superior officer devoted to his faith. He shuddered and reminded himself to never cross Colonel Goldman.

John hurried to the hospital. He strode to the front desk and asked the clerk where he could find Catherine Brandon's office.

Down a hallway and around a corner, he found the room. He knocked and then entered, feeling a smidgen guilty for not waiting to be invited in.

Catherine Brandon sat at her desk, shuffling through a stack of papers. Mary sat in a straight-backed chair. There wasn't a tear in her eyes, but her hands were shaking. Admiration and respect for her soared. That was his brave, strong girl.

Wait, *his* girl?

Yes, my girl.

His pulse lurched to a stop then surged forward as if driven by electricity.

He gulped, wiped a bead of sweat from his temple. Blood colored the front of her dress. Emotion weakened his knees, and he knelt beside her. "Are you all right?"

She ran her fingers over the stained fabric and nodded.

He wrapped his arms around her trembling frame. She laid her head on his shoulder.

"I twisted my ankle running up the front steps of the hospital, but otherwise I'm fine. I'm terribly afraid, though, of what will happen to me for assaulting a superior officer."

"The reels?" Catherine Brandon asked. "Did Miss Yates catch all this on film?"

John nodded. "I believe so."

"Thank the Lord," Catherine said.

John squeezed Mary's shoulders, hoping his gesture conveyed concern and a measure of comfort. "Everything should be all right. Colonel Goldman is furious at Morton, not only for how he treats women but for, well, things I'm not at liberty to disclose."

Catherine interjected, "My husband wants to see that man thrown out of the corps."

"So does Colonel Goldman—and me!" John added. In spite of his determination to bring Morton to justice and make him pay for what he'd done, he understood the process was difficult, even with the evidence on film. Major Morton had friends who, sadly, behaved the same way he did. The major wouldn't sit back and allow anyone to take away what he believed he was entitled to.

Mary bit her lower lip. "Mrs. Brandon, I'm sorry things didn't go as planned." Just how this would affect the mission, she didn't know, but she hoped they could iron the wrinkles.

Catherine Brandon looked up and pushed her papers aside. "We'll have to see what my husband says. Until then, I won't know what our next step is."

The throbbing in Mary's ankle increased. She rubbed it and winced. Her mind was a swirl of activity. Had her dreams of being a spy ended? No, they couldn't have. She wasn't giving up yet.

Catherine folded her hands and locked eyes with Mary. The scrutiny sent a host of imaginary ants crawling over her. She squirmed, vowing to take anything her boss dished out as long as her dream remained intact. She believed she'd make a good spy if given the chance.

"Mary, I—" John stammered. "I saw you fleeing Major Morton's office. I was afraid he'd, uh, harmed you."

Mary steadied her breathing. Now was a perfect opportunity to prove herself. She had remained calm, strong while under pressure. She hoped her composure impressed the Brandons enough to let her be part of the next operation.

Mary tilted her head sideways and smiled at John. In the steadiest tone she could muster, she said, "Thank you for coming to check on me. As you can see, I'm in good hands." His gallantry always stirred her adoration for him.

He dropped into the chair next to hers. Then he pulled his hat off his head and cleared his throat twice. "I'm glad to hear that. Morton is an unscrupulous cad. I was worried about you."

She wasn't batting her eyelashes at him, or was she? What would her brother Daniel say if he could see her now, practically throwing herself at a man? Her cheeks heated. She placed her hands there to cool them.

She dropped her gaze to the floor. The mission should be her main focus. Not setting her cap for a handsome marine.

John Painted Horse was, indeed, a handsome marine.

John cleared his throat again. He turned to Catherine. "Mrs. Brandon, your husband asked me to tell you he'd be along shortly."

"Thank you." Catherine rose from her desk. "I'll see that Mary's taken care of. My husband and I will do everything we can to protect her from the consequences."

"Thank you, ma'am." John jumped to his feet. "I take that as my cue to leave."

Mary would have stood as well if she believed her knees would support her, and if her sprained ankle didn't ache so much.

The phone on Catherine's desk rang.

John reached for her hands. His strong grip drew her attention away from Catherine's phone call. That was likely his intention.

He met her gaze and said, "Can I see you tomorrow? Perhaps we can go shopping in town or to a movie."

She shifted in her chair. How was she to go shopping with her injured ankle? She had deliveries to make on the other side of Camp Pendleton, but how was she to do that?

"I'm sorry, but I can't. Maybe this weekend we can get together."

"All right." John crumpled his hat in his hands, as if he were nervous. "How does Saturday morning at 1000 sound?"

"That would be lovely." Mary's cheeks warmed again.

John flashed a mischievous grin.

"If you'll excuse us," Mary said, "Mrs. Brandon and I have business to discuss. I need to uh, go over the next delivery schedule with her." That wasn't exactly a lie. Catherine wanted to know when the reels of film would be delivered to her office.

He left, closing the door behind him.

Catherine quietly, somberly warned, "We need to tread carefully with Morton. My husband said he's already filed charges against you."

⊒ CHAPTER 12 ⊒

Mary was grateful John had joined her in this meeting with Colonel Goldman. They had gathered in the colonel's office to discuss the case against Major Morton, along with the Brandons, Miss Yates, and her photojournalist friend who had finished viewing the reels and given their testimonies to Colonel Goldman.

Her hands trembled with anxiety. John reached out and entwined her hands in his. She gazed into his dark eyes and found warmth and comfort there.

Colonel Goldman sighed. "I've filed formal charges against Major Morton. They will be heard at the next office hours session. Personally, I find the major's behavior reprehensible."

Lieutenant Brandon added, "Definitely a case of conduct unbecoming an officer, in my opinion, but I don't know if the JAG office can make the charges stick."

Her nerves prickled at the thought of Major Morton evading the consequences of his actions. How difficult would it be for him to seek revenge against them? How could she go on without reaping a whirlwind of consequences?

"Will there be a court-martial hearing?" Miss Yates asked.

Colonel Goldman shook his head. "I'm sorry, miss, I'm afraid not. He agreed to drop the assault charges against Mary in exchange for weaseling out of a hearing for himself. Besides, the brass doesn't want to waste time on that. We have an enemy to subdue and we need men in the field, not squabbling in a courtroom."

Mary swallowed. She understood. But all of this couldn't be for naught. "Will he at least be demoted? Maybe reassigned to a place where he can't do any more harm?"

"I sure hope so. The lieutenant and I will do everything we can to see that he's reprimanded, but there are no guarantees."

"That will be all for now." The colonel ended the meeting. Miss Yates and her friend exited the room.

John squeezed her hand. "I'm glad you're not being reprimanded. I wish I could stay, but I have to go."

The lieutenant turned to John and raised an eyebrow. John cleared his throat and hurried from the room.

Lieutenant Brandon hung back for a moment to speak with his wife, leaving Mary contemplating what had transpired. John's work was classified and for the good of the country, so she chose not to dwell on it.

The charges against Major Morton weren't what she'd hoped for, but they were something. At least she wasn't facing a court-martial of her own. She hoped to never deal with the scoundrel ever again, but a niggling in her middle told her she hadn't seen the last of him.

Catherine pulled Mary aside. "I'm picking up a case file and then headed to my office. Meet me there in fifteen minutes."

"Yes, ma'am."

Catherine hurried from the room but not before casting a glance at the lieutenant. The slight nods of their heads, the sly smiles that slid across their faces indicated clandestine activity was afoot.

Now that Major Morton was no longer an issue, would Mary be assigned to the next secret operative mission? She hoped this was the opportunity to finally be sent into the field, her chance to find her missing brother. Could she be face-to-face with him, perhaps in a matter of days?

Excitement and wariness coursed through her veins. The stakes in spy work couldn't be higher, and there was no room for errors.

"That will be all," Colonel Goldman said with a raised voice.

Mary turned. Colonel Goldman and Lieutenant Brandon stared at her.

Blood rushed to her cheeks. They had caught her daydreaming. She saluted and rushed from the room.

Once outside, she leaned against the building and sucked air into her lungs.

How could she have acted so scatterbrained in front of those officers?

Daniel had always joked that she walked around with her head in the clouds, but it wasn't like her flighty ways had endangered a mission. She wouldn't let that happen. She *couldn't* let that happen.

Resolve replaced doubt. She pushed away from the building, vowing to do her job.

Later at the hospital, Catherine said, "This is official business. What I am about to tell you will go no further, or you could be executed for treason. Do you understand?"

Treason?

Executed?

What was she walking into?

Did it matter?

Not one bit. She would do everything in her power to end the war, face any risk to bring her brother home. Fear nipped at her heels. She stomped it down. A mix of elation and pride swept through her. "Yes, ma'am."

"How familiar are you with the Catholic faith?"

"There was a Catholic mission on my reservation. I attended Mass there every week, but I stopped going after my father and my grandmother died." Mary sucked her lower lip between her teeth, lest she say too much. She didn't care to elaborate on how she'd lost her faith in God. It didn't matter. She wouldn't let it interfere with her duty.

Catherine said, "There are a number of Catholic missions in the Philippine Islands. A convent is located close to the fighting. You will be assigned there."

A sliver of anxiety needled its way between elation and pride. How close to the front lines would she actually be? Visions of engaging in hand-to-hand combat rushed into her mind. Much as she had longed for a job like this, trepidation crawled across her skin. She rubbed her hands over her arms to chase away the chill.

"Yes, ma'am," she said. "Will I be issued a firearm?"

"Not exactly." Catherine's eyebrows drew together, forming a V. "I'm communicating with the head nun there. This convent will be used as a field hospital if necessary. You'll work undercover as a nun but serve as a candy striper if the need arises."

"I don't have any experience with that, but you can count on me." She bit her lip, hoping she wouldn't encounter anything gruesome. The sight of blood made her sick. When she and Daniel had been children and he'd been bitten by a snake, she'd screamed and fainted. From fear of the creature or the blood that oozed from Daniel's ankle, she wasn't sure.

How was she to tend to soldiers who had suffered horrendous battle wounds?

Again, it didn't matter. She straightened her spine, determined to work through any problems that arose.

Catherine, as if sensing Mary's trepidation, said, "I believe it's imperative that you learn some nursing skills."

"Yes, ma'am," Mary repeated. The minute her meeting ended, she would hunt for Susanna. The girl was just a candy striper, but she was smart and could teach her a lot.

She added, "If the convent becomes a field hospital, I imagine Japanese soldiers will be brought there for medical care. Shall I listen to their conversations?"

Catherine nodded. "Yes. Pay attention to where they're planning their battles and how many soldiers there are. By all means, don't let them know you speak their language."

Memories of Daniel flooded Mary's mind. She cleared her throat, thinking of all the ways she could search for her brother in the local POW camps. She could pose as a nurse looking to treat the men imprisoned there.

Catherine's gaze bore into Mary. "I know your brother is a POW. Can I trust you not to run off half-cocked looking for him?"

A lump lodged in her throat. No matter how many times she swallowed, it stuck there.

Hope sank like a rock. Catherine wasn't lax about protocol. She wouldn't tolerate her orders being disobeyed.

Mary wouldn't give up. After a while, once she'd proven herself, maybe Catherine would give her permission to search.

"Miss Wishram!"

"Yes, ma'am."

"Don't get any funny ideas. You'll be watched the whole time you're at the convent."

"Yes, ma'am." Determination took root in her heart. The military couldn't keep an eye on her every waking moment. Somehow, she'd sneak away, if only for a short time, and find her brother.

John removed his hat and stepped into Lieutenant Brandon's office.

"John," Lieutenant Brandon said, "the missus and I are inviting a group of Marines and their dates to our house for Christmas. You, Miss Wishram, Samuel Acothley and his gal Susanna, maybe a few others from the class."

"Thank you, sir. I'm sure Mary would love to go." John stared at the floor. This would be his last Christmas in the States, at least for a while.

For a moment his lungs couldn't draw breath.

He needed to fill out the necessary paperwork and send it to his family before he shipped out. He made a mental note to send them a care package for Christmas. He needed to send them as many supplies as possible. It wouldn't be enough to feed and clothe them until he returned, but it was something. His mother and sisters would appreciate it.

Maybe Mary would help him pick out a few things. The thought of shipping out to a remote island in the South Pacific, and possibly not coming back, sent a rivulet of worry through him. His family wouldn't be the only ones to suffer if he died in combat.

"Painted Horse?"

John skidded back to the present. "Yeah—I mean yes. Yes, sir."

Lieutenant Brandon's lips formed a thin, straight line. His left eyebrow lifted. "Going moony again for that girl?"

The man knew how much he and Mary cared for each other. "You have my full attention, sir."

Lieutenant Brandon scoffed. "You know my address. Be there at noon on Christmas Day. Catherine is preparing dinner. Afterward, we can open a present or two and then sing a few Christmas carols."

John nodded. His tribe hadn't celebrated Christmas until white folks had come along. It had been a different but nice holiday to get used to. Especially when the local missionary family delivered presents for his sisters and brought food for the table.

"Shall I bring anything, sir? I can pick up a few bottles of Coke and talk Mary into bringing fry bread."

"Fry bread, huh?" Lieutenant Brandon chuckled. "Sure, Catherine and I would love to try it. Maybe Mary can teach her how to make it."

John smiled. Only his mother and Mary had perfected the art of making fry bread to his satisfaction.

"Anything else, sir?"

"Yes," Lieutenant Brandon said. "By then I hope to have news about what will happen to Major Morton."

"That would be nice, sir."

Lieutenant Brandon excused him. John left the room and went to find Mary. He found her at the hospital unloading a truck full of medical supplies. She was delivering a lot of supplies to the hospital as of late.

"Hello, Mary. Let me help you with that." He took the box and shifted it in his arms. It was heavy. How on earth did she manage?

"Thank you." She reached for a smaller box. "We can put these in the supply closet, and then I have to find Catherine."

John suspected she was as deep into secret operations as he was. He'd have to pray for her more often than what he did already. She was a capable woman, though, and he admired her spunk, but bullets didn't discriminate between spunk and cowardice.

A heart-wrenching thought sliced through him. His mind grappled with the frightening possibility. For a moment his knees threatened to give out on him.

What would his life be like if Mary didn't come home?

⟨ CHAPTER 13 ⟩

Christmas Day 1944

Mary adjusted the heavy crate in her arms. Inside, she'd tucked twelve pieces of fry bread and a jar of strawberry jam that she and Mrs. Drake had preserved. It was how they'd kept busy during the tension-filled hours on D-Day. Mary wiped sweat from her brow as she stirred the bubbly preserves. Her landlady prayed and placed lids on the filled jars.

She followed slightly behind John, her medicine pouch bouncing against her chest as she hurried along. Her feet ached, and already she looked forward to yanking her shoes off and going barefoot.

Determined to make what might be her last Christmas in California a joyful one, she lifted her chin and strode with purposeful steps. Twice that morning Major Morton invaded her thoughts, but she'd given them a swift kick to the curb.

"You keeping up all right?" John had paused.

"I'm fine. Thank you." He offered to carry her crate, but his arms were weighed down with two boxes, so she'd declined. She could carry her own stuff anyway.

"I like your medicine pouch, by the way. What do you keep in it?"

She stopped, ran her fingers over the small leather bag. "I brought with me a part of the home I love so much. Two rocks and a handful of dirt."

"They say great minds think alike." His eyes brightened. "I keep a handful of sand in mine and sage my mother dried for me."

John had a medicine pouch? She'd never seen him wear it, but she didn't always wear hers either. "I only wear mine for special occasions."

John chuckled. "I keep mine in my footlocker."

The crate grew heavy in her arms. "We better get going."

John started out again. "We're almost there."

"Yes, I remember." Had it been only six short weeks since she'd received the telegram regarding her brother, Daniel's capture? What kind of Christmas was he having? He obviously wasn't receiving brightly wrapped presents adorned with bows and ribbons. Did he have enough food, a blanket to keep him warm? Had he given up hope? Her heart rent in two at the possibility.

Memories of Christmas on the reservation before Papa and her grandmother, Ala, had died seeped into her mind. A heavy blanket of snow had covered the ground that Christmas. Papa helped her and Daniel build a snow family. Daniel had placed their mother's scarf around the snow mama's neck. The gesture had warmed her heart and made her smile.

It hardly seemed like Christmas without any snow. Most years they had been graced with a white Christmas on the Yakima Reservation. She'd often wondered how her ancestors had survived the bitter-cold months with no shelter other than the longhouses constructed from cedar planks and tule reeds. Would she and Daniel ever see their homeland again?

No tears today, she vowed, increasing her pace.

She blinked twice and the Brandons' house came into view. The warm sunshine shone on the green, well-manicured lawn, complete with a birdbath and a colorful set of wind chimes. A Christmas tree adorned with a shimmering angel and bright lights sat in the front window. The scene was a startling juxtaposition.

John adjusted the boxes in his arms and rang the doorbell.

A moment later, Catherine answered the door. "John, Mary, hello. Merry Christmas."

"Merry Christmas," they replied in unison. He locked eyes with her, and she grinned. She liked it when they replied to questions in unison and finished each other's sentences. That had been happening more often lately.

"Well, come on in." Catherine ushered them inside.

Savory aromas of roasting turkey and stuffing greeted Mary's nose. Bing Crosby's "I'll Be Home for Christmas" played softly in the background.

Laughter filled the air as she followed John into the living room. Samuel and Susanna had already arrived. John and Mary wished them a Merry Christmas and then deposited their boxes under the tree. Lieutenant Brandon offered John a bottle of Coke.

Mary removed her foodstuffs from the crate and hurried to the kitchen. On the way, she saw Lieutenant Brandon pull John and Samuel aside and speak in hushed tones. She picked up on the words *code* and *classified* before mentally shutting her ears. She didn't need to inadvertently overhear anything she wasn't supposed to.

In the kitchen, two pumpkin pies cooled on a rack on the counter. A Bundt cake sat next to them. She added her fry bread to the rest of the desserts.

"Shall I mash the potatoes for you?" Mary asked.

"Yes, please. The masher is in the drawer by the stove." Catherine stirred a pan of bubbling gravy.

Fifteen minutes later, Lieutenant Brandon entered the kitchen and carved the turkey. Mary finished the potatoes and scooped them into a bowl. Catherine pulled a pan of steaming sweet potatoes from the oven. Melted marshmallows oozed on top. Mary had never tried sweet potatoes before and wasn't sure if she wanted to try them now, but she kept that to herself. Susanna opened a jar of homemade cranberry sauce and dumped the contents into a glass bowl.

The Brandons must have been saving ration coupons for months for a feast like this. She had never remembered such lavish meals prepared on the reservation. If the tribal elders could see her now, they'd think she had married a rich man.

A needle of guilt pierced her heart. She rubbed her chest at the ache. Daniel wasn't feasting on anything like this. If the rumors she'd heard were true, he'd be lucky to eat a handful of rice today.

Anger at the Japanese Empire heated her blood. How hard their hearts must be to torture fellow human beings.

She believed in a Creator of the universe, but she hadn't fully accepted the God that John worshipped just yet. If He were as real as John proclaimed, He had to be full of rage as well.

Poor Daniel.

Regardless of Catherine's instructions to the contrary, she'd find a way to locate her brother. Once he was found, she'd figure out how to rescue him without jeopardizing any orders she'd been given.

Her mind swirled with grandiose ideas of freeing the POWs. Marching into the festering camps with swords that slashed the barbed wire to pieces and leading all the men safely to tables laden with food.

Lieutenant Brandon drew her from the jungles of the Philippines back to the present.

"Time to eat, folks."

When they were seated, Lieutenant Brandon clinked his fork on the side of his glass. "Attention everyone, let's bow our heads and pray."

With the prayer complete, the food was passed around the table. Mary heaped her plate full, grateful it wasn't from the mess hall. John made a comment how this fare was much tastier than anything he'd ever eaten. Samuel, ever the hungry one, agreed.

Conversation revolved around the fighting on the European front. Though the Allies advanced toward Germany, the progress was slow. The Battle of the Bulge had everyone on edge. Soldiers starved for warm clothes and ammo as much as for food.

Mary was so angry she squirmed in her seat. Hitler heated her blood as much as the Japanese Empire. Such greed and lust for power. It had never been the way of her people. She struggled to wrap her mind around the concept.

The next bite of turkey tasted like sawdust. Unable to eat any more, she placed her fork beside her plate. She hoped her hosts weren't offended by her actions. She wasn't ungrateful, just unwilling to stuff herself when so many around the world were hungry.

After the meal, they gathered in the living room. Lieutenant Brandon played the Bing Crosby record again while they opened presents. Catherine pulled out a camera and snapped pictures of Samuel and Susanna by the fireplace. She took another of John and Mary sitting in front of the Christmas tree. The flash bulb was brighter than the lights on the tree. For several seconds, Mary's vision blurred before it cleared.

"I promise to give each of you copies as soon as they're developed." She turned and snapped one of her husband holding a bottle of Coke.

Lieutenant Brandon finished his drink, lit a cigar, and announced,

"There will be a New Year's Eve party at the local grange hall. A big band has been hired."

Susanna's eyes brightened. "Will there be lots of dancing?"

"And lots of food?" Samuel asked.

Susanna jabbed him with her elbow.

Lieutenant Brandon blew out a puff of smoke and laughed so hard he coughed. "There will be plenty of both."

Samuel wrapped an arm around Susanna and leaned in to whisper in her ear. The girl's cheeks turned a dark shade of pink, and she nodded.

Mary noted John's gaze on her from across the room. He winked at her. A school of fish swam circles in her middle. He swaggered across the room like a Hollywood star and took her hand in his.

"Mary," he crooned, "would you go with me, please?"

"Yes, of course. I'd like that." Her fingers traced along his calloused palm. "It will be a special night to remember."

His eyes twinkled again. "A special night, huh? I'll tell you what, I'll wear my medicine pouch if you wear yours."

"Agreed."

The fact that either one or both of them could be shipped off at any time poked deep into her heart. Rather than allow fear to quash the feelings blossoming between them, she chose to cherish every moment with these kind people, people whom she'd grown to love.

She gazed into his dark eyes, full of mystery and hope for a better future.

Noise in the room faded.

Not a sprig of mistletoe hung from anywhere in the room, but still, for a moment, she thought he might kiss her.

Did she want him to kiss her?

Of course she did!

But. . .right here. . .in front of everyone?

Thankfully, Catherine interrupted her thoughts. "Mary, will you and Susanna help me with dessert in the kitchen please?"

The romance of the moment dissipated. Mary swallowed her disappointment and pulled herself away from John. She followed Susanna and Catherine.

"Susanna, will you please get the ice cream from the icebox? Mary, you can slice the cake. You know where the utensils are." Catherine pulled a stack of small plates from the cupboard and placed them on the counter. Mary sliced the confection. Catherine's expression was filled with tension. Her eyes implied something serious.

Susanna chattered like a chipmunk about the goings-on at the hospital as she placed a carton of vanilla ice cream on the counter. Catherine scooped it onto plates beside the slices of cake and sent the girl to the living room with the dishes of dessert for the men.

Catherine reached for Mary's hand. "The Office of Strategic Services has arranged everything with the Mother Superior at the convent I told you about on the Philippine Islands. All we're waiting on now is clearance. The office isn't famous for being speedy, but I hope they can have your orders done in a month."

"I have a month, at most, before I ship out?" Mary swallowed. She had completed her training with her Japanese instructor, so she should have guessed it was only a matter of time.

Catherine raised her eyebrows and shrugged.

Mary wasn't sure how to process this bittersweet information. "So I best enjoy the days I have, right?"

"I'm afraid so," Catherine said.

Passion to help her country flamed hot within her. The thought of being transferred away from John left her as cold as the vanilla ice cream on the counter.

Catherine nodded and leaned closer. "And I don't have to remind you, this is top secret. You can't tell a soul. That's an order."

―――――≈―――――

John couldn't take his eyes off Mary when she walked back into the room. Her eyes shone as bright as the lights on the Christmas tree. He wanted to believe she was excited to spend time with him, but they hadn't exactly professed their undying love for each other.

She sidled up to him and placed her hand in his.

For the second time that night, Lieutenant Brandon clinked his fork against his glass. "I have some bittersweet news for you all. Morton has been officially reprimanded for his behavior."

Samuel stuck two fingers in his mouth and whistled. Susanna clapped. John wanted to hoot and holler, but he was content to hold Mary's hand.

Lieutenant Brandon held up his hand. "Not so fast. The charges were for sharing classified information with Colonel Goldman, not for his treatment of women."

Samuel snorted. "For what he's done, give me five minutes alone with him and I'll give him a reprimanding he won't soon forget!" Susanna rubbed his back, and he wrapped his arm around her.

"Morton is friends with a few officers who think like he does." The lieutenant shook his head. "They watched the first few minutes of the reels and actually laughed."

Mary's hand trembled in his. He ran the pad of his thumb over her knuckles and index finger and then squeezed. He wished he could ball his hands into fists and punch the major. For Mary's sake, he forced himself to remain calm.

Catherine's face was as white as the snowcapped mountains near his reservation. "Is there anything else? I mean, what's going to happen to him?"

Lieutenant Brandon continued. "He's taken a voluntary reduction in rank and has been transferred to the front lines, where heavy fighting is going on from what I hear."

John didn't wish harm on anyone, but if Morton were killed or taken prisoner, at least he wouldn't be compromising vital missions. A cold shudder prickled the gooseflesh on the back of his neck. He quickly reconsidered his stance. If tortured, the man wouldn't hesitate to share classified information with the enemy.

He blew out a heavy sigh.

At least Morton was out of John and the lieutenant's closely cropped hair for now.

He set his empty dessert plate on an end table and downed the last of his Coke. "It's getting late. I think it's time I walked Mary home."

John had hoped to take a detour along the beach. The Seaside Palace was likely closed, but it didn't matter. He wasn't taking her out for a meal. He hoped for a Christmas kiss, in spite of the lack of mistletoe. The palm trees would have to suffice.

John helped Mary into her coat. He handed her the crate she had carried with her earlier. He picked up his box of presents that he'd received from everyone.

"Thank you, Mrs. Brandon, for a lovely day." John placed a hand at the small of Mary's back as they stepped toward the door.

He overheard Samuel in the next room.

"Any idea where Morton has been sent?"

Lieutenant Brandon sighed. "It's a small island that's part of the Philippines."

Mary nearly dropped her crate of presents.

☰ CHAPTER 14 ☰

December 31, 1944

For a whole week, Mary had wondered if her brother had the misfortune of coming across Morton. Morton wouldn't last long if he were tortured by the enemy. He'd spill enough secrets to write a book. And then where would her brother and the other POWs be? She tried not to worry, knowing she'd be in the Philippines soon enough.

She shut off the GMC delivery truck and hopped out. The four boxes she hefted from the back didn't weigh much, but they were awkward. Nonetheless, she lugged them into the grange hall for the dance that night.

Though it was only noon, preparations were already underway. A group of red-faced enlisted men were blowing up balloons with such gusto, she feared they'd hyperventilate.

"Over here, Mary." Susanna waved from the kitchen.

She hurried to place the boxes on the nearest counter. "Here are the linen napkins and tablecloths."

"Thanks. Is that the last of them?" Susanna ripped open a box and arranged the napkins on the table next to the punch bowl.

"I think so. I'll bring in the last of the streamers and balloons." Mary strode to the truck and retrieved the remaining boxes. These were just as awkward but thankfully not as heavy. She placed them on a table near the enlisted men.

Susanna approached. "You're still okay with me coming to your apartment and changing into my dress there?"

"Yes, of course. I wouldn't want you to keep your roommates up late, knowing what early risers they are."

"It's a shame they have to miss the party, but they volunteered to work the early shift at the hospital. Their husbands are overseas, and they said they didn't feel like celebrating anyway."

Like she and John and Samuel would be soon. Did Susanna realize that? Mary placed her discomfort at the back of her mind.

"Not everyone enjoys being up all night. My grandmother went to bed with the chickens and got up with them too."

Susanna beamed. "Thanks, Mary. You're the bee's knees."

Mary returned Susanna's embrace. "I'll see you by 1800."

Her friend nodded and bounded toward the kitchen. Mary hustled back to the truck to finish her deliveries.

The excitement of seeing John hummed in her veins. Strolling along the beach was their favorite thing to do. They had planned to do so on Christmas night, until news of Morton dampened their spirits. John walked her straight home. The week had been a busy one that hadn't afforded them the opportunity to return to the sandy shores they loved.

She hoped tonight would be different.

Was it so wrong to want a kiss before she left on her assignment? Her orders weren't supposed to come through for another few weeks, but anything could happen in the military and usually, it did.

Later that evening, Mary braided silver ribbons into her long, dark hair and sang a song her grandmother had taught her. Thankfully Susanna's head was covered with the plastic bonnet of her portable hair dryer, which created a racket throughout the apartment.

Earlier, she'd seen a busload of musicians and their crew enter the base camp. The festive mood was contagious. Would 1945 bring an end to the war? Freedom for her brother and the rest of the world?

That would be something to celebrate!

Susanna pulled herself from under the hair dryer and shut it off. With the contraption silenced, Mary tuned her radio to a station that played a lively tune by the Andrews Sisters. Clad in naught but their stockings and underthings, Mary and Susanna danced around the bedroom singing "Don't Sit under the Apple Tree." They were loud and off-key but joyous in their excitement.

When the song ended, they collapsed on the bed and giggled like giddy schoolgirls. If having a sister was like this, Mary wouldn't have minded having several. She hated the thought of leaving Susanna. Being apart would be hard on both of them.

Her heart jerked for a few beats. Samuel and John were shipping out soon. Susanna wouldn't have anyone then. If only she could send her new friend a letter or a postcard once she reached her destination, but she doubted Catherine would allow it. Not when she was working undercover, spying for the US government.

She shoved the troublesome thoughts aside. Tonight was a night for fun. She jumped up from the bed, tugging Susanna to her feet.

Soon, every curl was combed and sprayed in place. Faces were powdered and lips coated with the latest shade of lipstick. Mary shimmied into her gown and turned for Susanna to zip her up. Mary did the same for her friend. Lastly, she hung her medicine pouch around her neck.

With preparations complete, and surprisingly on time, Mary plopped onto the sofa next to Susanna and waited for Samuel and John to arrive.

Frank Sinatra sang a love ballad over the radio. Mary's mood turned somber. Her heart gave a small jerk. Far too many people in the world were alone and celebrating at the bottom of a bottle.

Her thoughts turned to the Takahashi family in the internment camp. How were they celebrating the New Year? Mary hoped that next year, everyone would be home safe and celebrating the end of the war.

There was still no word about when she was leaving for the Catholic convent. Catherine said completion of transfer would take two weeks. Mary pushed the thought from her mind.

"Susanna, would you like a bottle of Coke while we wait?"

"Yes, thank you. Although we'll have to reapply our lipstick."

With a spring in her step, Mary proceeded to the icebox for the sodas.

While waiting, they listened to the radio and talked about a variety of topics. According to General Patton, he had *rescued* the 101st Airborne in the Ardennes Forest. The men of Easy Company heartily disagreed. Regardless, men had been maimed and killed. Her heart ached for their families. Some of whom were about to receive an awful telegram, if they hadn't already.

She chewed her lower lip. If anything happened to her, who would the government send a telegram to? Besides Daniel, her friends were all she had in the world. When the time came for her to leave, she'd be saying goodbye to them all.

The bottles of soda were soon gone, and Mary painted another layer of red onto her lips and checked her reflection in the mirror beside her front door.

Susanna wore a glossy pink shade. Mary noted that her friend and Samuel had grown closer. There was something enchanting about witnessing two young people doing the dance of courtship. Watching love blossom tugged at the heartstrings.

The last thing she wanted was to see her new friend hurt. "Susanna, do you ever worry about falling deep in love with Samuel, only to have him, uh, not come home?"

Susanna's cheeks blushed as pink as her lipstick. "Yes, I do, but there's an old saying. 'It's better to have loved and lost than to have never loved at all.' Or something like that."

"Well," Mary said, "it'll be easier for you and Samuel to be together after the war. You two live relatively close to each other." Distance wasn't the only thing that worried her in regard her relationship with John. Samuel and Susanna weren't responsible for taking care of others like she and John were. And yet, she was growing to love him more with each day.

She laid a hand across her chest to calm her racing heart.

Susanna pursed her lips and raised her eyebrows at Mary. "John said he's taking you for another walk along the beach after the party tonight."

"Yes, he is." Her cheeks heated. Those moonlit walks were their special time together. Hopefully, they always would be.

A knock resounded from the front door, and Susanna bounded to answer it. John and Samuel had arrived in their dress blues. Mary noted that John had remembered to wear his medicine pouch. It hung around his neck but had less fringe than hers did.

Never before had she seen a man so devoted to his country and proud of his culture. Her heart lurched before picking up speed.

Each man carried a bouquet of flowers. Just where they had found fresh-cut flowers in the middle of winter, in the middle of a war, Mary didn't know. One thing was certain, though, they weren't cheap.

Mary reached for the proffered blooms and held them to her nose, breathing in the intoxicating fragrance. Mrs. Drake emerged from her apartment.

"I thought I heard you kids out here. Let me take your pictures." She ducked inside and then re-emerged with an ancient-looking camera.

The four of them posed as she clicked the button. Then she snapped a shot of each couple and promised copies to everyone.

Mary thanked her, ducked inside, and quickly placed the flowers in a vase of water and left them on the table. There was no time to pause and admire the effect. A New Year's Eve party awaited them.

Tomorrow, she thought. Tomorrow she'd press them in a book for safekeeping.

They piled into the Jeep and headed to the grange hall for the party. Even though midnight was still several hours away, the streets were filled with people laughing, singing, and dancing. Excitement hummed through the air like electricity.

Mary felt it in her core—this would be a New Year's Eve she'd always remember.

———≈———

John turned the Jeep wide to avoid a group of intoxicated enlisted men bellowing the Marines' Hymn while staggering, kitty-corner through an intersection.

He wondered how much time he had left with his friends, with Mary, before shipping out to some forsaken island in the middle of the South Pacific. He didn't want to think of that now. Tonight was a night for making memories.

He parked the vehicle and hopped out. He reached for Mary's hand and gave it a squeeze. The Marines' Hymn was being sung as they entered the building.

John and Samuel grabbed bottles of Coke and sang the lyrics with gusto. "From the halls of Montezuma to the shores of Tripoli. . ."

He noted Mary and Susanna grinning. Though his heart swelled with pride, he continued singing without missing a note.

"If the Army and the Navy ever look on Heaven's scenes, they will find the streets are guarded by United States Marines."

Whooping and hollering commenced as though it were already midnight. He gazed at Mary. And suddenly, he had another reason to go to war. To provide for his family and save the land that had been in his family for generations, yes. Preserving freedom for Mary and every other American like her—that solidified his motivation for defeating the enemy. And he would do it with honor, or die.

A spider seemed to skitter up his spine. He shivered and adjusted his shirt.

The band struck up a snappy dance tune. Saxophonists blasted their horns, and then a singer stepped to the microphone and belted out a number by George Gershwin.

He grabbed Mary's hand and led to the crowded dance floor. He held her close, twirled her around, and as the song wound down, he dipped her. Her eyes held surprise and excitement. His heart pounded like a jackhammer. He committed to memory the sound of her laughter, how the silver ribbon in her hair glistened under the lights, and the way her face lit up when she was happy.

The band slowed things down with the next song. The lights grew dimmer. The singer crooned a melancholy number that reverberated through the atmosphere.

The air hitched in John's throat. He pulled her close and breathed in the intoxicating fragrance of her perfume. He nuzzled her neck and placed a featherlight kiss there. Their cheeks touched and her breath grazed his ears.

Someone stepped on his foot, and he bit back an expletive. He glared at the intoxicated sailor next to him who was drooling over a young redhead who looked like she'd rather be anywhere than in the sailor's arms.

He shifted his attention to the girl in his own arms. Mary. Now where had he left off? Her fragrance wafted up to greet him. Flowers, but what kind? His mind was in such a tizzy he couldn't think.

He ran his fingers over the nape of her neck and was about to place a kiss there when the song ended. The lights flashed on, nearly blinding him.

Dismayed at the lost opportunity for a kiss, he escorted Mary to their table with Samuel and Susanna.

Unable to take his eyes off her, he asked, "Would you like a glass of punch?"

"Yes, please." Mary gazed at him. His heart, fluttered again. Susanna said she'd like a glass too.

John and Samuel strode to the punch bowl. Though his mouth was a dry as cotton, he refused to guzzle his own drink until his gal had been taken care of. They returned to the table, and he placed the glass before her.

Mary said, "John, if you don't mind, I'd like to sit out for a few numbers. My feet are killing me."

"Sounds all right to me," he said. "We can sit for a while and talk."

For the next hour, it seemed as though no one else was in the room.

When the band took a break, she asked, "Have you read the recent article in the *Stars and Stripes*, about the 101st Airborne's terrible fight in the Ardennes Forest?"

"You mean the Battle of the Bulge? Yes, I have. I pray for them every day, that God gives them the strength to defeat the enemy."

"Yes." Mary tipped her glass to her lips.

He noticed how she changed the subject every time he mentioned his faith. She'd said she struggled with her faith but had chosen not to elaborate. He blew out a sigh. She wouldn't be the first person to lose faith in God while evil ran rampant through the world.

She tilted her face to the ceiling. "I can't wait for things to go back to the way they were before the war. Daniel can come home and tend the farm in Toppenish, and I can once again visit the Takahashi family at Pike Place Market."

For a few moments she seemed to look past him into her own world. She had to be wondering about her brother. What kind of wounds would he come home with? Would he come home at all? These things must frighten her.

John hated to admit it, but Mary's ideas of how everything would be as it was before Pearl Harbor were a bit altruistic. Puncturing her dreams would be cruel. He'd pray she would find the strength to face the realities.

His heart squeezed until his chest ached. He sucked down the last of his punch and prayed they'd survive the war without being wounded too badly, in body or soul.

Her soft voice interrupted his thoughts. "If you'll excuse me, please, John, I need to, uh, powder my nose."

He rose from his chair and offered his hand. He couldn't allow her to wander off alone. Jealousy ignited at the thought of a rowdy soldier flirting with her. A green-eyed monster roared in his ears. He reminded himself of the brig and tamped his feelings into submission.

A smile curved across her face. "Thank you."

She placed her hand in his, and he led her to the ladies room. She grimaced. He noticed the way she walked, almost limped. Anger heated his blood to such a degree, he half expected it to boil in his veins.

Had the demoted, now second lieutenant, Morton not chased her around his office, she wouldn't have broken the heels off her last pair of shoes. And she wouldn't be wearing stiff new ones at a time when she should be dancing the night away.

He leaned against the wall outside the ladies room, breathing deep to cool his anger.

A moment later, she stepped into the hallway. Her lips, coated in a delicate shade of red, begged to be kissed. A thick lump stuck in the middle of his throat, and he had to swallow twice before it went down. Her presence stirred something in his soul. He wanted to pull her into his arms and kiss her senseless.

Had they not been surrounded by people he might have done just that. Instead he placed her tiny hand in the crook of his elbow and escorted her to their table.

Before they knew it, a group of squealing, energetic nurses passed out confetti and glasses of champagne.

Samuel and Susanna were already kissing. For a second he wondered how Susanna would deal with Samuel shipping out. She was young and sensitive, and John feared she would struggle with the separation. Thankfully that wouldn't be for another few weeks yet.

A breeze from somewhere blew across his neck. He scrubbed a hand under his collar to ease the prickly feeling. He glanced at his friends. Strangely, they didn't seem affected by a breeze.

Drawing his thoughts to the present, he made a mental note to ask Mary to look after Susanna while he and Samuel were away.

The countdown began.

"Three...two...one! Happy New Year!"

John pulled Mary close and stared into her eyes. A blind man could see the fire burning in those dark orbs. Fireworks exploded in the night air. Horns blew, and the air was thick with confetti.

Samuel appeared and slapped him on the back. "Let's celebrate while we can. I get the feeling our days here are numbered."

The breeze skimmed across his neck again. His heart hammered. "I thought we weren't leaving for at least two weeks. Have you heard something different?" He wanted to shake his friend for saying confidential things like this.

Samuel dragged him to the side. "I met with Brandon today and signed the last-minute paperwork. We're shipping out, soon."

The air in his lungs grew so frigid he almost couldn't speak. "How soon?"

"I don't know, but I'm making sure, tonight, that my ducks are in a row. I suggest you do the same." Samuel wove around two loud soldiers to reach Susanna.

The party continued, but John was ready to leave. "Mary, would you like to go?"

"For a chance to take these shoes off and stick my toes in the sand, yes."

John fished the keys out of his pocket and turned to his friend. "Sam, please take the Jeep back to HQ. I'm walking Mary home tonight."

Samuel grabbed the keys and waved.

John led Mary outside where they both immediately removed their shoes. Hand in hand, they walked down to the beach. John had a driving need to kiss her before the night was over. And he needed to tell her that he loved her.

CHAPTER 15

Mary wiggled her toes in the cool sand as she and John strolled along the moonlit beach. Then she unraveled her long braid and allowed her hair to dance in the gentle breeze. The roar of the Pacific Ocean echoed in her ears. She loved the smell of salt water, though sometimes it made her sneeze.

Would the beaches be this beautiful in the Philippines? She hoped so. She needed something to remind her of John.

She hadn't heard another word from Catherine, so she assumed the plan for shipping out in two weeks remained in place. Still, two weeks wasn't a lot of time, and she was compelled to tell him how much she cared.

Silence hung between them as time elapsed, but it wasn't the least bit awkward. She gave his hand a squeeze, hoping it conveyed her feelings for him.

First thing Tuesday morning, she'd head to the Office of Accounting Services one last time to see if they had news about her brother. Discovering his location and possibly infiltrating the POW camp stirred both hope and excitement in her. She'd find him and do what she could to free him, no matter the danger.

She was a smart girl. She could rescue her brother without compromising her mission.

Much as she loved and worried about her brother, she shifted her focus to the man in front of her. The thought of being separated from him drove needles into her heart. At that moment she was grateful Catherine Brandon hadn't told her the particulars of her assignment.

If Catherine had outlined the intricate details, Mary might have been tempted to share something with John. She wanted no secrets between them, but how could that happen when sharing everything could be deadly?

She paused, staring at John as he held his face to the moon. She turned and gazed that direction. The moon was almost full tonight. The bright milky white orb hung low in the sky, casting a romantic glow around them.

A jolt of electricity hummed through her. Lately that seemed to happen every time she and John were alone. "You must like staring at the moon as much as I do."

He wrapped his arm around her waist, pulled her close, and placed the side of his head against hers. "Yes, I do, for lots of reasons."

"What are they? If you don't mind sharing." Mary leaned into him.

He turned his face to hers, their foreheads touching. The scent of his woodsy aftershave lingered between them. She rubbed her fingers across the back of his knuckles, noticing how calloused and strong his hands were. For a moment she wondered if he would kiss her rather than answer her question.

Instead, he pulled away, ducked his head, and kicked a piece of driftwood. "Aw, you'll think I'm silly if I tell you."

A hint of disappointment swooped toward her like a vulture, but she batted it away. Something was troubling John. He needed someone to confide in. She wanted to be that person, to be his friend, his trusted ally at a time when evil forces were tearing the world apart.

He rolled his eyes and nodded. A boyish grin spread across his face. "The moon—every time I look at it, I think of God."

Warmth cascaded over her. She placed her hands on her still warm cheeks. This was a poetic side of him that she hadn't seen before. It was no small thing to be trusted with sweet nothings from a tough marine. The intimacy between them humbled her.

She gulped. "Tell me more."

"Well, since the days of creation, the moon has risen in the east, moved across an inky black sky, and set in the west. Just like the scriptures say. The Lord is the same, yesterday, today, and forever. The moon, like our Lord, was the same last night, is tonight, and will be, forever and ever, until the end of time."

"Oh my, that is so romantic."

He gave her chin a playful pinch. "Oh, there's more."

"There is?" Could he see her blushing? Did she want him to?

To her relief, he continued.

"Yeah. Like, no matter what storms are raging in the heavens, no matter how many dark clouds obscure its presence, even if I can't see the moon, I know it's always there."

"Oh," she sighed. She had never thought of the moon, or the Lord, like this before. He *had* been spending a lot of time with Pastor Ephraim this week. If the man spoke such words of wisdom, perhaps she herself should pay him a visit.

He glanced toward her, chuckled, then turned his face toward the sky. "No matter how small a sliver is showing, it's still there. Always a beacon of light in a dark place. It's so big, so mysterious, I can't comprehend the enormity of it all. Sometimes. . ."

Jesus, light in darkness. She gulped. Knowing in her head he was right, she struggled to wrap the truths around her heart. "Sometimes what, John?"

"Sometimes, it feels like the moon is so close, I could reach out and touch it, touch Him, with my fingertips."

For several long moments, the only sound between them was the gentle lapping of the waves over the sand. He stepped toward her, closing the distance between them. Her heart skipped once more when he wrapped his muscled arms around her, pulled her to his chest.

There was that captivating fragrance of his aftershave again. A lock of his hair fell over his forehead, reminding her of a wild renegade. Their gazes fixed, neither of them blinking. His lips parted. How desperately she wanted to feel those lips on hers.

And then, his mouth touched hers in a passionate kiss.

Her senses reeled, floated in the heavens among the stars and the moon he spoke so eloquently of. She raked her fingers through his hair, deepening the kiss. She wanted it to go on forever, until the world ceased to exist.

Then, with a need for a breath and the rushing sound in her ears. . . she broke the kiss and stared deep into his eyes, into his soul.

And then she knew, without a shred of doubt, she loved him.

———————≈———————

That roaring sound in his ears. Was it the waves crashing nearby or his emotions running amok? He blinked, breathed in the rosy fragrance of her perfume. There weren't that many roses on the Navajo Reservation, but if there were, they couldn't possibly smell this intoxicating.

The tide swept in and washed over their feet.

Mary squealed. "It's a good thing we're not wearing our shoes."

He laughed. This barefooted Yakima woman was good for his soul. "Would you like to go to the Seaside Palace again sometime?"

"I'd love to." Her cheeks flushed an enchanting shade of pink, noticeable even in the semidarkness. Her laughter filled the air. The sound shifted his heart rate into high gear.

Unfortunately, there wouldn't be much to laugh at when he was shipped out. If Samuel was right, he could be leaving sometime in the next few days. He wished he could tell her that.

Tonight had been nothing short of magic, and it would kill him to spoil the memory. He couldn't do that to the woman he loved. Now if only he could muster the courage to tell her how he felt.

At his first opportunity, he would march into Lieutenant Brandon's office and ask a few pointed questions. He didn't know if he'd receive answers, but he had to try. Until then, he'd cherish every moment he had with her.

"It's getting late," he said. "Should I get you home?"

She walked over and sat on a boulder lodged in the sand. "I don't want this night to end. I worry about us being separated and not coming home to each other."

Did he see a tear glisten in her eyes? He had already considered as much. Either one or both of them could be killed. What could he do to give them hope of returning to each other?

"I have a crazy idea," he said. "Take off your medicine pouch." He pulled his from around his neck. She handed him hers.

"What are you going to do with these?"

He dropped both medicine pouches in a small hole he'd dug beside the boulder she sat on. Then he buried the pouches and moved the rock over the spot.

"There." He huffed for breath. "Now there are pieces of us that will be together forever, if we don't come back. And if we survive, we'll meet here after the war and retrieve our pouches."

She laughed. "You're right, that does sound crazy. But okay. Right here, after the war."

"Now I better get you home before Mrs. Drake sends out a search party."

"Yeah, she'll be worried if I'm out any later, if she's not already." She gathered her shoes and purse. Neither of them donned their footwear, though.

He kissed her forehead and took her hand in his. They left the sandy beach. The pavement was cool beneath his feet. He'd have to get used to wearing his combat boots all the time. If the jungle grass didn't cut his feet to ribbons, a snake could sink its teeth into him.

John wasn't surprised to see the light emanating from Mrs. Drake's living room, and then she emerged from her apartment.

"Glad you brought Miss Wishram home safe. I knew you were a nice gentleman." She smiled, waved at them, and disappeared back inside.

When he held his arms out for her, she leaned into his embrace. How was it that, in spite of all the upheaval in the world, there was nothing but security with her in his arms? He closed his eyes, brushed his fingers through her long tresses, inhaled her fragrance, tried to commit everything about her to memory.

"Tomorrow," he whispered. "I'm picking you up and taking you to the Seaside Palace for a New Year's dinner."

She placed her head on his chest, directly over his heart.

Could she hear the steady beat?

She twirled his tie around her fingers. "I want to spend every moment with you."

"Great. I'll pick you up at noon." Desperation to savor every minute with her slammed into him.

And so, he kissed her again, recklessly, longingly, as if it would be their last.

≡ CHAPTER 16 ≡

Mary stepped inside her apartment and raised her fingers to touch her lips. They still hummed at the memory of John's kiss. Like a giddy schoolgirl, she giggled and fanned her heated cheeks. To calm herself, she fixed a cup of herbal tea.

While it steeped, she changed into her nightgown and hung her dress in the closet. She caressed the delicate fabric. This would be a night she'd always remember. John loved her, and she loved him. As soon as the war ended, they'd be together—forever.

The certainty of it created peace within her.

She strolled into the kitchen. Did John's mother and sisters like tea as much as she did? Her stomach did a little flip at the thought of being part of his family. She sipped her drink, glanced at her clock, and counted the hours until she'd see him again.

A knock at the door jolted her to the present. It was probably Mrs. Drake, wanting to ask her how her night went. In spite of the late hour, she'd welcome the chance to chat.

"Be there in a moment." Mary rushed to her bedroom, donned a bathrobe, and hurried to the front door with a smile. She threw it open, and stood, frozen, in shock.

A private first class, holding a sealed packet?

A Jeep sat at the curb, its engine rumbling loudly. How had she not heard it drive up?

Mary eyed the packet in the private's hand. Could this be another telegram, or information about her brother? Had they found him and brought him home, or was it something much worse?

No!

This night had been perfect, and she refused to consider her brother's possible demise.

She managed a croaky, "Can I help you?"

"Are you Private Mary Wishram?"

"Yes." The word came out slowly. If this man pulled a telegram from his pocket, she'd ball her fists and scream at the heavens.

"These papers are for you. Once you read them, I have orders to bring you to HQ." He handed her the packet and strode back to the Jeep.

Her fingers trembled so much she nearly dropped the sealed envelope.

Orders to report to HQ?

Had Daniel been rescued and brought home?

Oh, let it be so.

Mary tore open the packet, praying it was hopeful information about Daniel. What a blessed relief it would be if he was home safe before she had to ship out. Perhaps he could accompany her to dinner with John tomorrow night. Could life get any more perfect?

She yanked the papers from the envelope.

Scanned them.

Breath came in short gasps.

This had nothing to do with Daniel.

These were her orders to ship out—now! In fifteen minutes she must meet up with Catherine Brandon. From there she was headed for the convent in the Philippines.

This wasn't supposed to happen. She was having dinner with John tomorrow.

John!

Anger at the military rolled through her. To not give her a chance to say goodbye to the man she loved? How cruel! Why would they do this?

An invisible blade sank into her heart and twisted.

She shoved the questions to the back of her mind. There was no time. She yanked a piece of fragranced stationery from her desk drawer and scribbled a note to John. Her tears wet the letter's surface. Then she sealed it in an envelope. Holding it as if it were precious treasure, she placed a kiss over the flap.

Then, she scrambled into her uniform and grabbed her duffel bag. She shoved the necessary items into it, including her Ititamat, and slung it over her shoulder.

With one last look into her apartment, her gaze landed on the flowers John had brought her earlier. A sob rose from the depths of her soul and the anguish spilled forth.

The Jeep's horn blasted.

She sprinted to her landlady's apartment and banged on the door. For a panic-stricken moment she feared the lady was sleeping like the dead. What if she didn't answer?

Mrs. Drake poked her head out her front door.

Mary gasped, "Will you please give this to John? I have orders to leave, now! I wish I could say more, but I can't."

Mrs. Drake, bless her heart, nodded. "I will, and I'll pack up your stuff and keep it safe until you return."

Mary allowed the slew of tears to fall as she embraced the dear woman. "Thank you. I promise I'll write to you." She handed her the envelope and prayed that John would understand.

The private beeped the horn again. She bolted to the waiting vehicle and hopped in. The driver stomped on the gas pedal. She held her hat in place and clung to the dashboard as he sped along the roads. She struggled to wrap her head around the events of the past twenty-four hours.

A mix of emotions swirled around her with the speed and intensity of a hungry tornado. The contents in her stomach churned. She fought to keep her dinner where it belonged.

This wonderful country that she loved so much—would she ever see it again? The brown rolling hills of the Yakima Reservation? The rivers teeming with salmon? The acres and acres of peach and apple trees? These places might be lost to her forever. Tears threatened to spill onto her cheeks at the thought.

One thing stuck fast in her mind: It didn't matter if she was ready for the Philippines or not. Her boots would be on the ground in a matter of hours.

John could have skipped the last block to his barracks but chose not to. If he were caught, Samuel would never let him forget it. Even that didn't dampen his mood. He loved Mary, and she felt way the same about him.

He had never been more sure of it than now.

The memory of her kiss lingered on his lips.

Tomorrow night, after their New Year's Day dinner, he'd take her for another walk along the beach and tell her again how much he loved her. He considered proposing but wasn't sure if he could go through with it. Samuel would call him a coward.

At least he could ask her to wait for him.

He rounded the corner and skidded to an abrupt stop.

Soldiers buzzed around the barracks like a horde of bees before the first frost. A large canvas-covered truck sat in front of the structure.

Was the war over?

Lord, let it be so.

Samuel emerged from the building and sprinted toward him.

"What's going on?" John asked, praying it was good news.

His friend stood before him, his chest heaving. "I heard a rumor they worked the final kinks out of a top-secret mission. As soon as that plane is green-lighted for takeoff, we're headed to the ship anchored at the docks. We're shipping out in one hour."

"But—" John sputtered. "One hour?"

An invisible sledgehammer swung down and punched him square in the stomach.

Mary!

He couldn't leave without telling her goodbye.

"Samuel," he croaked, "can you pack my things for me, please? I need to tell Mary goodbye."

His friend nodded. "Sure, I'll do that. Lucky for you, I already said goodbye to Susanna and got her address."

"Thanks, buddy. I owe you." John turned and sprinted toward Mary's apartment. Though he was in good shape, twice he had to stop to catch his breath.

Finally he approached her apartment. He rushed to the door and banged on it.

"Mary, Mary," he called, not caring if he woke Mrs. Drake. "Please open up. I need to talk to you. It's important."

No answer.

He paced the walkway in front of her apartment for a minute and then pounded on her door again.

Still no answer.

She'd had ample time to don a bathrobe and stumble to the door. Where could she be?

He didn't have all night. He needed to return to his barracks or Lieutenant Brandon would have his head. His hands clenched as he prayed.

Mrs. Drake emerged from her apartment. He was about to apologize for waking her, but she didn't look like he'd dragged her from slumber. She held a plain white envelope.

The fine hairs on his neck stood at attention. His voice was raspy. "Ma'am, where is Mary?"

The woman handed him the missive. He recognized Mary's handwriting. Was that a faint trace of her lipstick on the envelope? He tore the flap open. Her rosy fragrance emanated from the paper.

His heart jerked to a stop and refused to beat again for what seemed like minutes.

My dearest John,

Hundreds of soldiers had received Dear John letters every day. Jokes about them abounded. Yet he never expected to receive one himself, let alone one from the lady who'd kissed him so passionately earlier that evening. He read further.

I've been assigned to another post, and I'm shipping out tonight. I had no forewarning of this or, I swear, I would have told you. When this war is over, I'll meet you in our special place on the beach, under the moonlight. I must go. I love you. Mary

She was gone?

Gone!

He held the note to his nose and breathed in her scent. It was all he had of her until she returned.

If she returned.

His heartbeat slowed to a crawl. How was he to live without her?

He turned to Mrs. Drake, who continued to stand in her doorway. "Thank you, ma'am. Can I write to you? I'd like to have one of the pictures you took tonight."

"Yes, of course." She stepped inside and a moment later returned with the information scrawled on an index card.

"Thank you." His throat threatened to close. "Please, ma'am, if you hear from her, will you let me know?"

"Yes." She shuffled forward and placed a hand on his cheek. "I'll pray for her and you too, young man, that God brings you both home safe." Then she disappeared into her apartment.

He stuffed the note back into the envelope, along with this woman's address, and sprinted to his barracks. He glanced at his watch. He and his comrades were due at the docks in fifteen minutes.

⋛ CHAPTER 17 ⋚

Mary stepped away from the *San Jose Honey* and descended the rolling staircase into a muggy atmosphere. Fat raindrops descended from the heavens. She pulled her coat tighter around her middle. What she'd give right then for a good rain slicker. Catherine Brandon tugged her into a nearby airplane hangar.

"Get in the Jeep," Catherine said.

Mary tossed her duffel in the back, grateful for the canvas top covering the vehicle as she hopped into the passenger seat.

"Did you bring that rolled-up ball of Indian stuff with you?" Catherine started the engine and steered across the tarmac.

"You mean my Ititamat? Yes, I couldn't leave it behind."

"I thought you would. Let me hold it for you, for your safety. The Japanese have been known to torture the Indians they capture."

The woman drove so fast Mary could have easily fallen out, and not just because of the vehicle's speed. Though curiosity needled her as to why the Japanese would torture Indians, she let it pass. Grudgingly, she fished the precious object from her bag and placed it in the space between the Jeep's seats.

"What's the rush?" Mary asked. She prayed they wouldn't skid across the slick, wet pavement.

"Another plane is arriving soon. We need to be gone before it lands."

This would not be a trip for sightseeing.

Catherine shifted the vehicle into a higher gear. "I need to tell you something, Mary, something I can't confirm. American POWs are routinely transferred here to Luzon Island for work details. I hear rumors that your brother is among them."

Mary's heart skipped a few beats. "I can search for him without compromising my duties, Catherine. I know I can." She hated the desperation in her tone that made her sound like a whiny two-year-old.

Catherine shook her head. "You need to focus and do your job, Mary. I'm only telling you about the rumors so you won't be surprised and blow your cover if you happen to see Daniel somewhere."

Much as Mary wanted to find her brother, Catherine was right. She relaxed and told herself to wait. When the first opportunity arose, she'd search for him. Until then, she'd keep her mouth shut and carry out her orders.

Mary had come to accept the constant secrecy that being a spy entailed. Had it not been for the Brandons' meticulously organized scheme and the secrecy involved, they might never have exposed Morton. His name tasted like bitter vinegar on her tongue and made her want to spit.

She pushed the unwelcome thoughts from her mind and focused on the road ahead of her.

Potholes filled with muddy water dotted the deserted one-lane road. The vehicle bounced through them, splashing water almost into the vehicle. A large pothole sent them careening toward the brush. Mary clung to the dashboard, braced for impact.

The Jeep jostled sideways. Catherine shifted gears and steered them back on course.

Mary blew out a deep, relief-filled sigh.

"S-sorry," Catherine stammered.

"All's well that ends well." Mary didn't shy from manual labor, even in the rain, but she would have hated to push the stuck vehicle from the mud.

Though it was the middle of winter, thick green foliage lined the path that grew skinnier with each mile. Several times, Mary had to duck to keep from being swiped by the overhanging branches and brush.

Later, a large stone monastery, far in the distance, came into view. Behind the structure, the ocean lapped at the beach. Thoughts of John invaded her mind. Had he come looking for her by now? If so, had Mrs. Drake given him her note? Would he understand that she hadn't deserted him?

She clenched her small bag of belongings in her hands. As soon as they had the enemy licked, she'd find him.

Her eyes closed, and she imagined their last walk along with beach. His smooth voice, telling her about the moon, echoed in her ears. She missed him already. She placed her fingers to her lips, once again remembering their kiss.

Catherine stopped the Jeep in front of the convent.

Mary lurched forward.

Catherine hopped from the vehicle and turned a slow circle. She seemed to study the area surrounding them. Mary glanced behind her, then at the convent. If any enemy were lurking about, she sure couldn't spot them. Her feet hit the ground. Though her legs shook, she grabbed her duffel and ambled forward.

Catherine dragged her through the building's front door.

Inside, the nave was warm and dry. A woman in a white habit approached them. Mary squirmed under the nun's scrutinizing gaze.

"Afternoon, Sister," Catherine said. "This is the woman I told you about. Mary, this is the Mother Superior, Sister Abigail."

She reached for Mary's hand. "You may call me Sister Abigail."

Wrinkles creased the older woman's forehead, and her pale blue eyes beheld wisdom. Crow's feet emerged when she smiled. Every worry fled from Mary, and all tension and anxiety ebbed. Should she nod like she'd seen actresses do in the movies?

She settled for a genuine, "Thank you."

Catherine continued in a low whisper. "Mary speaks a bit of Japanese. Hopefully, she can translate anything any imperial soldiers say in your presence."

"How well do you speak the language?" Sister Abigail asked.

"I studied for almost two months with a Japanese American. He taught me as much as possible with the short time we had."

Catherine turned to Mary. "I need to go. There's a radio in the basement with instructions on how to operate it. Don't use it unless it's absolutely necessary. Remember our code."

"Yes, ma'am," Mary said.

Catherine hurried from the room.

Sister Abigail placed a candle in a holder and lit it. "Come with me. We'll get you dressed in proper clothing, and I'll show you to your room."

Mary followed the woman down a long, semi-dark corridor with high ceilings and stone walls. Sconces, filled with burning candles, hung along the walls. The candles did little to illuminate her damp surroundings. An enchanting floral aroma filled the air, though.

And yet, she shivered. She told herself it was because of the chilly atmosphere, but she wasn't convinced. She was on her own now. There would be no help waiting in the wings like there had been with Morton. A sliver of fear poked her heart and tried to fester.

She thought of John again and wondered how he was faring. He never allowed fear to reign in his heart. His faith was too strong for that. She must find the courage to overcome her fears. Like John did. Lives might depend on it.

Sister Abigail opened a heavy wooden door. "Here we are."

They stepped inside the dark storage closet. The woman handed her a pile of garments without bothering to check sizes. The heavy robe and habit were difficult to wiggle into, but Mary figured it out and was dressed in minutes. She stuffed her civilian clothing into her duffel bag and followed Sister Abigail up a stone staircase.

Twice, Mary stepped on the hem of her garment and stumbled. Would she ever grow accustomed to this clothing? There was no handrail along the staircase, so she hugged the wall and stepped carefully. At the top, the woman led her down a long, dark hallway.

"Here you are." Sister Abigail opened a small door hewn from planks of wood.

Mary peeked inside. A cot with a threadbare blanket occupied one wall. A small table and chair sat in the other corner. Mary blew out a small sigh.

Sparse furnishings.

Much sparser than what the military provided.

"Thank you," Mary said. "I'm beat and looking forward to a nap."

"Oh, it's not rest time yet. I need to show you the basement."

"The basement?"

Sister Abigail eyed her but didn't utter a word.

That's right, the radio.

Mary didn't question, rather she dropped her small bag on the rickety bed. She followed the woman down the flight of stairs to the main floor of the convent. A short walk down another dark hallway led to the kitchen.

In the middle of the room, a large wooden table sat atop a colorful rag rug.

"Help me move this, please." Sister Abigail grabbed one end of the table.

Mary reached for the other end. It was much heavier than she would have guessed it to be. How had this aging nun managed to lift her end? She was obviously stronger than she looked.

Sister Abigail pulled the rug aside, revealing a trap door roughly three feet by three feet square. Then she yanked on the handle and pulled the trap door open.

Mary leaned forward and peered down the opening. A rickety ladder led down into the belly of the convent. Sister Abigail descended into the darkness using nothing but a candle to light her way.

Mary lifted the hem of her robe and managed to follow the woman without slipping off the ladder. Her feet landed on the dirt floor with a thump. Curious, she studied her surroundings.

Jars of canned produce rested on shelves that lined the room. Boxes of potatoes and carrots sat on the floor. She breathed in the earthy aroma, and her lips curved into a smile.

On a small nightstand in one corner sat a shortwave radio. The dials and knobs looked intimidating, but Mary wasn't about to be deterred. If she could change a broken fan belt and repair a leaky radiator, she could operate this contraption.

She reached for the instruction manual and flipped through it. "May I study this for a while and take some time to practice working with this thing?"

"Of course. I'll see if the kitchen has anything for you to eat." The sister climbed back up the ladder with surprising ease, considering the gray wisps of hair that escaped her habit.

Studying the manual with nothing but a candle for light was difficult. It wasn't long before the words swam across the pages. Her eyes and head ached. She dropped the manual on the table and rubbed her temples.

Sister Abigail reappeared and placed a sandwich on the table. "How are you doing?"

"All right, I guess. Can I have another candle for light?"

"Yes, of course. I'll get one."

Mary watched her disappear back up the ladder. Then she wolfed down the sandwich, suddenly realizing how hungry she'd been.

Moments later, Mary spied the hem of a white robe descending into the root cellar. The sister had brought her two candleholders, candles, and a box of matches. She placed them on the table and, with a warm smile, returned to the kitchen.

When Mary finished reading the instructions, she fiddled with the knobs and the headset. Everything seemed to be in working order. She stretched and plopped onto the floor and then leaned against the dirt wall. She was tired. Camp Pendleton was in a different time zone and several hours ahead of where she was now.

She closed her eyes and allowed her mind to drift.

"Are you all right?"

Sister Abigail sounded like she was speaking underwater. Reluctantly, Mary pulled herself from her dreams of John. How long had she been asleep? Her legs shook, and she yawned. "This thing works like a charm."

A smile curved across the woman's face. "That is comforting news to hear, but I must tell you something of vital importance."

Mary was immediately wide awake. Her mind, trying to catch up, swirled with activity. How much did this kind woman know about Mary's work here in the Philippines? How much, if anything, was she allowed to share with her?

Mary swallowed the grit in her throat. "What's of vital importance?"

"This radio must not, under any circumstances, fall into enemy hands. It must be hidden to keep it safe, or destroyed."

"At all costs?" Mary gulped.

Sister Abigail locked eyes with her. "Even if it costs us our lives."

———— ≈ ————

For a week, the ship cut through the waves of the south Pacific Ocean, carrying John and thousands of other Marines farther and farther away from Camp Pendleton, toward Japanese-held islands. The creaking cots, snores, and murmurs of the men droned in his ears, preventing him from sleeping.

Samuel, his head resting on his duffel bag, snored in the cot beside him. Two additions to their radio crew, Corporal Riker and Corporal

Goshen, slumbered in cots nearby. John welcomed the men to his crew, though he suspected their orders were to protect the code and not necessarily him and Samuel.

John turned to his other side and squirmed to get comfortable.

A rosy fragrance ebbed from the envelope in his shirt's front pocket. Mary's note.

Memories of time spent with her paraded through his mind. Where had she been transferred to? Was she out of danger or smack in the middle of it? She was a strong and capable woman who could take care of herself. Yet he hated not being there to look out for her.

"Lord, please keep her safe. Please keep us all safe," he prayed. Exhaustion overtook him, and he closed his eyes. After a moment his overwrought muscles relaxed, and he drifted. Blessed sleep pulled him into a deep slumber.

Shouts and a cacophony of noise erupted from topside.

John bolted upright. The ship ground to a stop. Had they reached their destination already? How long had he been out?

Samuel rolled over in his berth. "Are we there yet?"

"I don't think so." John jumped from his berth and climbed the ladder to reach the top deck. There, he sucked in breaths of fresh morning air. The lush landscape of the Hawaiian Islands sprawled out before him.

"Excuse me, Lieutenant Brandon, sir, why are we stopping here?"

Four small boats loaded with wooden crates approached the ship.

The lieutenant chuckled. "We need to drop off and pick up supplies. Chow for those here on the island and ammo and fuel for soldiers on the front lines."

He immediately thought of Mary. How many times had she told him about the crates of food, mostly Spam, she had delivered to the chow hall at Camp Pendleton?

He raked his fingers through his sweat-streaked hair. His comrades and superior officers counted on him to perform his duties without being distracted. Their lives were at stake. It wouldn't bode well for anyone if he was too preoccupied to do his job. But how could he not worry about her?

John pushed away from the ship's railing. "Lieutenant Brandon, may I go ashore and look around a bit?"

"Sure, but only for a few hours, and stay close. We're only here for a short time, so don't get lost."

John received a pass and then hopped in one of the boats.

He wandered to Wheeler Air Force Base and breathed in the fresh, clean tropical air. Sunlight had crept over the eastern horizon and illuminated the sky with ribbons of pink and orange. Palm trees swayed in the breeze as if they were waving to the heavens. Torn pieces of airplane wreckage blemished the side of the airstrip like festering wounds on flawless porcelain skin. The juxtaposition was a stark reminder of the attack on Pearl Harbor.

In spite of the wreckage around him, this place was a paradise. If he was headed somewhere half as beautiful as this, he'd count himself lucky.

Though Pearl Harbor had happened more than two years ago, the emotional remnants of the attack were evident in the eyes of the men around him. Sailors were buried forever in the depths of the *Arizona*. Flames of righteous indignation burned within him. He clenched his fists and swore to give the enemy a good swift kicking. The United States *must* prevail, for justice for these sailors and for all those lost since then.

Once the enemy was defeated, he could return to Camp Pendleton and find Mary.

Would she go back to living in the same apartment? Or would she return to her reservation in Washington State? How had he neglected to obtain that information before they were separated?

They had talked about walking along the beach again, barefoot by the Seaside Palace, but hadn't set a specific date or time. Once the war ended, he hoped to find her quickly and without difficulty.

There he went. Thinking about her again.

He placed a fist to his forehead and tried to focus.

Grunts worked feverishly, loading cargo into the hold of a Flying Fortress named the *San Jose Honey*. He was certain he'd heard that name and seen this aircraft before, perhaps near Camp Pendleton? Though weary to his bones, he walked over and assisted them. The sooner the supplies were loaded, the sooner the aircraft could be on its way.

Too soon, it was time to go back to the ship. John climbed up the cargo net and then down into the ship's belly. He found Samuel wide awake.

"I'm hungry." His friend yawned. "They got any breakfast for us?"

John slapped his friend's shoulder and laughed. "I stopped by the mess hall and got two tins of tuna, dried applesauce, and a D ration chocolate bar."

In spite of a full meal last night, he was famished. He voiced a quick but sufficient prayer of thanks and tore open the package of crackers. Samuel used his P-38 to open the tuna.

Not a single Navajo marine, within earshot, complained about the meager meal.

The anchor was raised and the ship's engines roared to life. Soon, they were cutting through the waves once again. He and Samuel devoured their breakfast. The food settled well in his stomach. The men seemed to have gotten used to the pitching and rolling of the ship and weren't as seasick. For that he was also grateful.

Belly full, John leaned back against his duffel bag. His fellow Marines closed their eyes, and he followed suit. It would be several hours before they reached their destination. A group of men played a lively game of cards. John tuned out the racket and closed his eyes to sleep.

One thought meandered through his mind like a rattler stalking its prey. When he woke, he'd be that much closer to Japanese-held territory.

⧉ CHAPTER 18 ⧉

It was late afternoon, and a tropical storm was blowing in. The ship rocked like a baby in a cradle. John pushed his still dozing friend out of the way so a green-faced soldier could pass them and reach topside before being sick. He felt sorry for the poor guy.

He closed his eyes and remembered the night he and his comrades had left Camp Pendleton.

Mary had been on his mind that night. His fingers instinctively went to his front pocket where he kept her letter. Had she been on that plane? Was she headed somewhere safe? Or had she landed smack in the middle of danger? The ship pitched hard to port. His stomach roiled, and he wondered if he might be joining the seasick soldier topside.

Difficult as it was, he shifted his focus away from the gal he loved and to what lay ahead.

"John, John." Samuel shook him by the shoulders.

John rubbed sleep from his eyes. When had he dozed off? At least he'd been able to sleep. The seasick soldier squeezed past them, carrying a tray loaded with food. They must have passed the storm.

Samuel continued. "We just dropped anchor. We're headed to shore soon but not into any fighting yet."

John followed his friend topside for a view of the place they'd call home for at least a while.

Lush green landscape skirted the sandy beaches. Palm tree leaves lost their hold on the tree trunks and blew across the landscape. The wind threatened to blow them off their designated landing spot.

Lieutenant Brandon approached.

John faced the man. "Where are we?"

"Luzon Island, in the Philippines."

The fine hairs on John's arms bristled. Mary had said her brother, Daniel Wishram, was being held POW on these islands. The first chance he had, he'd ask around and see if someone had heard of him. If luck swung his direction, he'd find the guy.

A deep need to help Mary reverberated through him. In a moment of bravery, he turned to Lieutenant Brandon and asked, "Sir, what's the status of the POW camps on the islands?"

The lieutenant folded his arms over his chest. "You and I both know Miss Wishram's brother is interned somewhere over here."

Sweat formed on John's brow. "Sir, I mean no disrespect. I was just asking."

"I hope you're not thinking of doing something stupid, like trying to break the man out."

"No, sir." First, he had to find her brother, and then he'd figure out his next step. Breaking him out of prison wasn't exactly on the agenda. Not yet anyway.

Samuel raised his eyebrows and nudged him in the ribs. If by chance he was able to rescue Mary's brother, could he trust his friend to keep quiet about it? If he found the man, he'd at least ask Lieutenant Brandon to send word to Mary. She filled his thoughts, and for the umpteenth time, he prayed she was safe.

The waves rocked the ship portside again. John clung to the railing.

"Is it time for chow yet?" Samuel had deftly changed the subject.

"Yes," Lieutenant Brandon said. "You'll be joining a Marine division near a small village. They'll feed you the best they can. I bet you're hungry, as usual."

"You guessed right." A grin brightened Samuel's face as he saluted their commanding officer and jogged for the chow hall.

John asked, "How long before we go ashore?"

"Shortly. You best eat and gather your gear."

John saluted and rushed to join his friend for chow.

Afterward, he, Samuel, and Corporals Riker and Goshen grabbed their gear and climbed topside. He descended the cargo net without difficulty and dropped into the rocking small boat waiting to take the men ashore. Rain poured from the cloudy gray sky. Once on the beach, he ducked under the tarp to keep from being soaked. No wonder everything was green. The place received enough precipitation to drench the driest desert on his reservation.

A GMC truck, with bench seats lining the bed, rolled to a stop in front of them. A canvas top covered the back of the vehicle's bed. He breathed a prayer of thanks that he'd stay dry. The men clambered in. He and Samuel took a seat where they could see the landscape behind them.

The vehicle lurched and moved forward. A cool breeze provided a welcome reprieve from the waves of suffocating humidity.

Ten minutes later it stopped at Base Camp, where the other Marines were stationed. Dark green canvas tarps were strung from one splintered tree to another. Men huddled underneath the makeshift shelters playing cards and smoking cigarettes.

John and Samuel hopped down and were pointed to the chow hall, which wasn't much more than a green tent without walls. The toasted bread and gravy were hot, the weak coffee as well. John watched Samuel devour his meal, seemingly unfazed by the stench of the latrine on the opposite side of camp.

After dinner, they were ordered to dig a foxhole.

Digging foxholes hadn't posed a challenge back at Camp Pendleton, but the dirt had been dry. Scooping enough mud to create a hole three feet in diameter presented an entirely new challenge. How were they were to sleep in a mudhole for the night?

Corporals Riker and Goshen dug small foxholes several yards apart. Then they helped dig a large foxhole in between the two smaller ones.

Goshen said, "I'm going to find some cans we can string up."

"Good idea," Samuel said. "Bring some cans of food, and then we can string them up after we eat the contents."

John laughed and tried to shore up the inside of their foxhole. He feared they'd be swallowed by the muck while they slept. He thanked the Lord that the radio and headsets were waterproof. The thin crescent-shaped moon slid across the sky and did little to illuminate his surroundings. The gray clouds did a fantastic job of hiding the stars.

It was going to be a long night.

Two days later, God turned off the water faucet and the sun emerged from the dark gray clouds. John clambered from his mudhole and pointed his face to the warm orb shining in the clear azure sky.

"Time to shed these wet clothes and let them dry while we have sunlight." John peeled off his soaked socks. His feet resembled giant raisins. "I sure hope neither of us gets jungle rot."

Samuel squeezed the excess water from his socks and draped them over a clothesline strung between two trees. John prayed they'd dry before too long. Jungle rot was an ever-present threat to the soldiers inhabiting the island. Every time Lieutenant Brandon made the rounds, he urged them to keep their socks dry and allow the sun to beat down on their bare feet.

Men sank halfway to their knees when they tried to walk through camp. John and Samuel helped break apart ammo crates. Other Marines laid the slabs of wood on the ground between the chow hall, latrine, and commanding officers' quarters.

Later, Goshen and Riker met with Lieutenant Brandon. The rest of men played baseball. There hadn't been enough wood slabs to create a baseball diamond, so the men played in mud that was ankle deep. John sat penning a letter to Mary. He had asked Lieutenant Brandon how to mail it, since he had no address for her. To his chagrin, the man didn't have an answer.

"I'll just write a letter to Mrs. Drake instead. If nothing else, it'll brighten her day," John mumbled to himself. The woman was nice enough. He didn't mind writing to her. It gave him something to do since boredom had proved to be as nerve-wracking as hand-to-hand combat.

Cheers echoed around him. He looked up and saw Samuel wading most ungracefully through the muck toward home base and then scoring a point.

"Gives a whole new meaning to the phrase 'sliding into home base,' huh?" Samuel laughed and wiped clods of mud from his body.

John chuckled. "You need a bath."

"Later. Now, it's lunchtime." Samuel poured rainwater from his helmet onto his hands to wash away some of the grime. "You want to go with me to get something to eat? I'm starved."

"Yeah, sure." He stuck his notepaper in his duffel bag and followed his friend.

"Lieutenant Brandon said we might see action tonight. You ready for it?"

A lead weight seemed to land at the bottom of John's stomach with a silent thud. He nearly doubled over and gasped. If the situation arose, could he look another human being in the eye and shoot him dead? Even to save his friends and family back home? He gulped. "Ready as I'll ever be, I guess."

Base Camp had not dried by the time the swaths of gold and purple colored the western horizon. John checked his socks and turned them inside out to help them dry faster. He did the same with his friend's socks and prayed the rain wouldn't start again. At least they had plenty of fresh drinking water and enough for showers too.

After lunch he finished his letter to Mrs. Drake while Samuel penned one to Susanna. John didn't know how long it would take for the missives to find the mainland, but he prayed they reached their destination.

Later, Samuel took John's mess kit to the chow hall to get dinner.

John turned his gaze to the foxhole, dreading another night there.

Samuel strode toward him carrying two mess kits containing small portions of rice and fish. He'd even scrounged a tin can of peaches. The aroma wafted in the air and smelled like heaven. Compared to the boarding school he had attended, the chow was good, hot, and plentiful. How could the tough Marines complain?

Samuel dropped into the foxhole and handed John his food. John prayed and then devoured his meal. As he started to go back for a second helping, a noise snagged his attention.

The whine of an airplane cut through the crisp night air. John listened intently. The noise didn't resemble that of a US bomber, Corsair, or transport plane. He shaded his eyes with his hand and squinted into the fading sunlight.

"Take cover!" The frenzied scream rent the peaceful atmosphere.

John dropped his tray and dived into his foxhole. He landed practically on top of his yelping friend. A hail of bullets slapped into the mud around them.

Chaos erupted.

Officers shouted orders to their men.

Artillery shells whistled through the air and exploded with deafening booms.

Hot bullets streaked through the atmosphere and thwacked against trees, tents, tanks, and men. Their screams sent waves of helplessness cascading over him.

A runner ducked his head into the foxhole. He shoved a piece of paper at them.

"Time to go to work." Samuel cranked the radio's handle.

John donned the headset. "Arizona, Arizona, *de-he-tih-hi*. . . *jay-sho*. . ."

Minutes later a host of fighter planes flew across the sky to help protect a bomber from enemy artillery fire. For the next two hours they transmitted messages from the battlefield to the artillery crew in the rear and destroyer ships in the harbor and then back to the front lines.

When John's arm grew weary of cranking the radio handle, he and Samuel switched places. Then John transmitted while Samuel cranked. At times the enemy was so close he heard a Japanese officer shouting orders to his men. For a terrifying moment he wondered if he'd join Mary's brother in a POW camp.

At one point during the long night, a runner brought them cold Spam sandwiches. John cranked the radio handle with one hand while gobbling food with the other.

By the time the moon had drifted halfway across the night sky, they were exhausted. The gunfire ceased.

John's hands shook. He tried to tell himself it was from fatigue, but he knew better.

Lieutenant Brandon appeared, seemingly from nowhere, sporting a helmet with a ding in the left side. "Good job, men."

"Thank you, sir." John pulled off his helmet and inspected it for dings. Though he found none, he did discover a tear in his left sleeve. A small gash cut across his bicep. How had he not noticed it earlier? "Sir, have the wounded been cared for?"

"Yes, they have. And you have done your country proud."

Warmth radiated in John's chest. He'd struck a blow for his country, for his people. He slapped Samuel on the back, hoping his friend felt as good as he did.

Lieutenant Brandon rubbed his chin, fixed his gaze on the ground for a quiet moment.

"What is it, Lieutenant?" Samuel groaned, his shoulders sagging.

Uneasiness rippled through John.

"A few of the men are headed to Australia for rest and recreation. You boys are being transferred to the other side of the island. Your services are needed there."

———— ≈ ————

Mary pulled her hands away from her ears. Had it been an hour since the last bomb exploded? She listened for friendly voices. Hearing nothing, she crawled from under the table and clambered up the rickety ladder. Though her knees shook, she shoved the trap door open.

Thankfully, Mother Superior had helped Mary rig the table and rug in such a way that she could come and go quickly and easily while still concealing the trap door.

Once through the trap door, she hurried to the sanctuary to check on the nuns. That was where they congregated during the bombings, to pray.

She entered the sanctuary, skidded to a stop, and hollered, "Is everyone all right?"

Sister Abigail raised her head and glared at her. Mary bit her lip. After more than a week there, her untamed demeanor would gain her another scolding from those in charge. Being quiet and subdued had never been her strong suit.

"My apologies." She folded her hands and ducked her head. "I was just concerned for everyone's safety."

Sister Abigail lifted her eyes toward the bell tower above and then bowed her head.

Mary took that as her cue to leave. She walked to her room, pulled out her notebook, and plopped onto her bed. She had been instructed to record the goings-on but had neglected to scribe every little thing. Certainly the US government didn't care if she had rice and soup for lunch.

She groaned and dropped her head into her hands.

Almost two weeks had passed without a single opportunity to search for Daniel. Today, she vowed, she'd find a way.

That afternoon, she found herself in Sister Abigail's office. She asked, "Are we sure that radio is working all right? I heard transmissions, but they weren't English. Well, except for the word *Arizona*."

The woman pursed her lips into a tight bow. "I didn't hear the transmissions so I can't say what they were."

Mary assumed as much, but still, she was curious. "I may not be fluent in Japanese, but I understand enough to know it wasn't Japanese flowing across the airwaves last night."

Sister Abigail closed her eyes a moment before opening them again. "Should you be worrying about such things?"

Mary squirmed at the truth and changed course. "Are there any POW camps around here? Perhaps we can take them supplies. I have minimal training as a nurse. I'd be happy to try to help the imprisoned men."

Sister Abigail eyed her with suspicion written on her face. "A mission like that could be very dangerous."

"Yes, I know, but I need to do what I can to help." Mary didn't reveal that her brother could be among the POWs. If Sister Abigail suspected that Mary would cause trouble, she wouldn't allow her to go. She'd caused enough trouble already.

As if reading her thoughts, Sister Abigail replied, "You could be killed, especially if you tried anything. . .inappropriate."

Mary stood straighter and lifted her chin. "As a nun, I could visit the camp on a charitable mission. I'd also ask the soldiers questions and maybe hear something important that I could relay to HQ."

"And because you speak some Japanese, you could listen to enemy conversations and relay *that* information to HQ as well." A smile curved across the woman's face, an unspoken camaraderie between the two.

Mary exhaled with relief and hope. "Will you please draw me a map to the camp?"

Sister Abigail nodded. "I'll even have the sisters pack the Red Cross boxes we've received into the truck. I've been told you know how to drive?"

"Yes. Let me change into my robe, and I'll be ready shortly."

"You're excused," Sister Abigail said.

Mary stood and bounded out of the room. Today, she hoped to find her brother. She raced upstairs and changed quickly. To her way of thinking, the garment provided a measure of safety. She couldn't imagine the enemy, cruel as they were, executing an unarmed nun.

Or would they?

She shivered.

Lifting the hem of her robe, she hurried down the stone staircase. She'd learned to move about without tripping over the lengths of cloth. She proceeded to the courtyard, where three nuns lifted wooden crates marked with bright red crosses into the back of a battered GMC truck. Just where these nuns had obtained a vehicle she didn't know, but she wouldn't be surprised if Catherine Brandon had something to do with it.

Excitement at the possibility of finding her brother hummed through her. Today, she might be standing before him, giving him food and hope. What if she found her brother and the Japanese guards discovered they were related? Would they allow her to see him? She'd cross that bridge if and when she reached it.

"I'm ready to go as soon as the truck is packed." She reached for the last crate and tucked it among the others in the back of the vehicle.

"There's one more thing," Sister Abigail said.

Mary clutched the truck's cold tailgate. An uneasy feeling swarmed in her middle. If this woman tried to stop her when she was so close to finding her brother, she didn't know what she'd do.

She swallowed hard. "Yes, Sister Abigail?"

The woman stood tall and squared her thin shoulders. "I'm going with you."

⊒ CHAPTER 19 ⊒

"But Sister Abigail, please." If Mary thought it would help her brother's situation, she'd throw herself at the woman's feet. She'd explained the unclassified details of Daniel's situation. It had gotten her nowhere. She gritted her teeth, unwilling to give up.

Catherine Brandon had ordered her not to search for Daniel, so she really *shouldn't* have told Mother Superior of her plans to find him. The sister might go to Catherine Brandon with the information. Mary hoped that wouldn't happen. At the very least, Catherine would yank her off the island, and then what?

If her brother was not at the camp they were visiting today, she'd ask the other nuns about other camps on the islands. If that didn't yield results, she'd widen her search.

Next time Sister Abigail took a nap, perhaps Mary could sneak into her office and search for maps. Stealth was paramount. Her spy training would be useful.

Until then, she would do as she'd been told. Mary and Sister Abigail climbed into the truck. She started the engine and shifted into gear. They bumped along the road, dodging potholes to the best of her ability. Only once did the truck slide along the rain-soaked path. Fields of shorter grasses gave way to taller and thicker brush.

"Turn left up here." Sister Abigail pointed to a set of worn tire tracks that veered into a dense thicket of jungle.

Mary struggled to turn. She steered too wide, running over a series of bushes, but soon bumped along the right direction.

"Have you been here before?" Mary hoped the woman could offer insight as to what they were walking into. Perhaps the sister had met Daniel.

"I used to come every week, until the new Japanese commander told me to stay away. I heard recently that he's been replaced. Still, we don't know what we'll find."

Mary sat higher in her seat. "I won't be turned back without giving these supplies to the detainees."

"That's brave of you, but even if the commander allows us inside, you must prepare yourself for the worst. These men are emaciated. They have no access to soap and water, so don't be put off by the lice, fleas, and disease. The last nun who delivered medicine nearly vomited upon seeing several of the sickest and most seriously wounded."

Mary gripped the steering wheel. Though squeamish, she was determined to keep her lunch where it belonged. Thinking of her brother, she muttered, "I won't be deterred."

Mary rehearsed in her mind what she'd say if Daniel recognized her. After so much time apart, she'd be tempted to embrace him, but she rapidly decided against it. Doing so would raise suspicions with the guards and reap a myriad of repercussions.

Her brother would understand and not do anything that would jeopardize his safety. He'd have sense enough to refrain from spreading around camp that she was his sister. Not only would that blow her cover as a spy, but it might put them all in danger.

Images of being waterboarded, bamboo under her fingernails, and a variety of other tortures flooded her mind. She squeaked without meaning to. A shudder rolled through her.

Sister Abigail shot her a look then turned her gaze back to the road.

Silence stretched between them. If Daniel was there, how could she go off and leave him? Could she arrange an escape? Did she have a choice? She didn't have the answers but was certain the questions would haunt her when her head hit the pillow that night.

Mary smelled the camp before she saw it. The stench permeated the air.

Body odor.

Excrement.

Despair.

Her soul seemed to wrench in two imagining the horrors she was about to witness. Tears smarted in her eyes. Her stomach ached. She swallowed the bile climbing up her throat. Heaven help her.

Heaven help these men!

Sister Abigail pulled a jar of Vicks VapoRub from her pocket and smeared a blob under her nose. "Here. You'll want to do the same."

Mary stopped the truck and did as the head nun ordered. She handed the jar back, and they proceeded toward the camp.

Rows of bamboo huts came into view. Men stared at her. They weren't much more than walking skeletons as they ambled toward the barbed wire fence and stopped three feet from it. Tattered rags hung from their bony frames.

When she pulled to the front gate, she was already breathing through her mouth. She tried to reconcile the Takahashi family in the Manzanar War Internment Camp with these scowling brutes who shouted threats and curses at the soldiers who dared approach the truck. As bad as the Takahashis' conditions were, this was so much worse.

She didn't speak Japanese fluently, but she knew enough to recognize choice words and phrases the guards screamed at her and Sister Abigail. Like Mary, the woman was fairly versed in Japanese, though the foul language didn't seem to bother her.

Mary stepped on the brake and the vehicle rolled to a stop.

"The guards here know me. I'll do the talking." Sister Abigail slid down from her seat and approached the guards. In broken and halting Japanese, the woman said, "Good morning, gentlemen, I wish to speak with the commanding officer."

The voices were not difficult to distinguish. The guards yelled, spat, and brandished their bayonets. Mary leaned out the window, listening, hoping to pick up a tidbit of information she could relay to a reconnaissance team. The radio in the convent's basement hadn't been used yet, but she was itching to give it a whirl.

A short guard aimed his weapon at the sister.

Indignation streaked through Mary. She killed the engine and climbed down from the truck. If one of these brutes harmed this good woman... She stormed protectively over to where the sister stood.

The camp's commander approached. "What are you doing here?" His English was thickly laced with a Japanese accent.

"The Lord has sent us," Sister Abigail said. "We have humanitarian supplies. Red Cross care packages for the men."

Mary studied the officer. Average height, not heavily muscled. For a moment she thought she and Sister Abigail could overpower him. What they lacked in size and strength they made up for in gumption.

A sideways glance revealed several guards, three poised in watch towers, aiming their rifles at her. She quickly abandoned her thoughts of tackling the man.

Overpowering the commander would only hasten her demise. The scowling guards, eyes blazing with hatred, reinforced that truth. They despised her, and she could do nothing but appear meek and obedient under their scrutinizing gaze. She gritted her teeth and clenched her fists.

Helplessness and impotent fury struck her a humiliating blow. Her life, and those around her, depended on her remaining meek and obedient. Her stomach and emotions churned as she unclenched her fists and bowed her head.

How had these prisoners coped with such torment?

She gazed at the prisoners. Several stared into space. If they were rescued that moment, she feared it would take years for them to recover. The need to rescue Daniel burned within her like hot coals, even more so now.

After a few minutes of conversation, the commander relented and waved his guards forward. The guards frisked Mary and the sister for weapons and contraband. Mary blushed crimson and nearly fainted when the guards groped her through her habit.

Next, the guards broke open the Red Cross boxes and rifled through the contents. Almost every guard brazenly stuffed their pockets with items meant for the prisoners. Mary stifled the comments that likely would have gotten her shot.

Finally, after no contraband had been found, they were allowed into the camp.

The POWs stumbled forward. A tall, unshaven man in a dirty, but whole, uniform shook hands with her and Sister Abigail.

"Afternoon ladies, thank you for coming. I'm Captain Robert Greene, United States Marine Corps. I'm a four-year med student. I dropped out and joined the service. I'm as close to a doctor as they have here."

Hearing the officer's rank and branch of service, she stifled a gasp.

It was struggle enough imagining her brother in a place like this. Fresh waves of anguish cascaded over her at the thought of John in one too. She prayed it never happened.

Four additional officers in tattered uniforms reached to shake hands with her. She tried not to stare at their torsos, which reminded her of her grandmother's washboard for doing laundry. Even under such harsh conditions, the men behaved gallantly.

"Thank you," Sister Abigail said. "But that won't be necessary."

Mary noted a blush on the woman's cheeks. Could it be the way the men fussed about her and complimented her bravery in coming to such a place? Two men appeared and placed chairs, rickety ones, under a palm tree.

These soldiers were gentlemen in every sense of the word. Their families back home would be proud. The least she could do was remember their names and send word back home to their families. Catherine Brandon wouldn't have a problem with that. She hoped.

Rather than sit, Sister Abigail directed the supplies to where they should go.

Captain Greene offered Mary his elbow. "I'll show you to Sick Bay." Two stronger-looking prisoners followed them with the medical supplies.

Sick Bay was nothing more than a thatched roof shack. Though Mary had limited nursing skills, she was not eager to enter the quarters. But those were the ones who needed her most. Mustering her courage, she strode that direction.

The smell rolled over her like a torrential wave. Still, she proceeded and introduced herself to the sick and wounded.

She helped Captain Greene bandage two soldiers with head wounds. The missing pieces of skull bones were gruesome beyond anything she'd imagined. Somehow, she managed it without screaming, vomiting, or fainting.

To Captain Greene she said, "Will you excuse me a moment, please?"

He nodded, as if he understood. She stepped from the shack, placed her hands on her hips, and pointed her face at the sun. Mary wished she could avoid the hospital altogether. The sight of human beings suffering under such brutal conditions brought tears of frustration.

In the distance she spotted Sister Abigail handing out the few blankets the nuns at the convent had procured.

Two men gasped for breath as they lugged a pot of food from the makeshift kitchen toward the hospital. Mary rushed to assist them, taking a ten-pound oblong can of Spam from the skinniest one. The other joked about eating like kings that night.

A pudgy, snarling guard followed them without offering to help. She bit her lower lip to keep from scolding the man.

They entered the hospital and served the food. The Japanese guard wandered out of earshot. Mary took the opportunity to lean close to Captain Greene and whisper, "Is Private Daniel Wishram here?"

The captain shook his head. "Sorry, I just got here a week ago. That's why I'm doing the brunt of the work. I'm not weakened like those who've been here for years."

Years?

Moisture pooled in her eyes. An hour here sapped her hope and dignity. How had these men endured it for years? Where was God in all this mess? How could He turn a blind eye to such torment? If John were here to witness such inhumane conditions, would he still cling to his faith like a buoy in stormy waters?

Probably!

Indignation welled in her. The P-38 can opener was clumsy in her hands. She yanked the lid off the Spam with more force than she intended. The sharp metal edge sliced into her palm.

"Ow!" She reached for a rag on a nearby table.

"Here, let me help." Captain Greene placed a cloth over the wound. Though he kept his head still, Mary noted his gaze darting from one guard to another.

He whispered, "I'll ask around, see if anyone has heard of your brother. Douse your hand with hydrogen peroxide. Don't let it get infected."

She willed the tear in the corner of her eye into submission. The soldiers here were surrounded with enough misery. She didn't need to add to it by sobbing like a child. "Thank you. I'll wait until I'm back at the convent. I'm not using anything here that's intended for men who need it more."

"You're very brave," he said.

His gaze once again scanned the compound. "I'm a fighter pilot from Independence, Kansas. Please let my family know I'm here, and that I'm all right."

"Yes, of course." It was the least she could do, especially if he found her brother.

Together they worked side by side, feeding and caring for those in need of medical assistance. The captain was a talented medical student. When the war ended and he hung up his fighter pilot wings, he could hightail it out of Independence and land a job at the most prestigious hospital of his choice.

When the men in the makeshift kitchen finished cooking, the soldiers lined up with flat pieces of metal as plates, their cutlery whittled from scrap wood. Her heart lurched at the primitive conditions.

"I need to go. Sister Abigail is waiting for me." She didn't care how much her stomach knotted with hunger, she refused to consume food meant for starving soldiers who had given so much to defend freedom.

"Try to come back, if you can," Captain Greene said.

"Yes, of course," Mary replied.

Sister Abigail stood near the truck, conversing with the camp's commanding officer when Mary approached.

"I'm ready to leave when you are." Mary hopped into the driver's seat. The sister groaned as she climbed in on the passenger side. Minutes later, they were bumping down the road. Ideas on how to inform Captain Greene's family of his whereabouts filled her mind. Could she get away with contacting them? She should ask Catherine Brandon.

She turned the vehicle toward the convent, disappointment rattling through her. She had learned nothing about her brother or any pertinent information to send the Allies. Silence once again stretched between her and the head nun.

The sun had almost edged over the western horizon when she steered the vehicle into the convent's courtyard. It had been a long day and her body ached, but her mind was a whirlwind of activity.

Once inside Sister Abigail said, "I'll arrange another trip. I want you to go along."

"Okay. I'd love to go." That would yield another opportunity to speak with Captain Greene, to see if he'd heard anything about Daniel. It would be nice if she had news from the captain's family next time they met.

Her heartbeat lurched to a halt. Catherine Brandon's training bubbled to the surface in her mind.

She was a spy.

She couldn't do anything that put the soldiers' lives at risk, no matter how much the families craved news of their loved ones. She understood the importance of keeping secrets. And it weighed heavy on her heart.

———————≈———————

John cranked the radio's handle. Samuel relayed the message to the battleship fifteen miles out to sea. Shelling had lasted for hours, and they were exhausted. When his right arm felt like it would fall out of its socket, he switched and cranked with his left.

Another deafening boom as shells exploded. Bits of splintered palm trees and sand rained down on them. He instinctively used his body to cover the radio. If the radio became unusable, countless Marines would be in peril. Dying to protect the contraption would save lives.

When that barrage ended, he straightened and resumed cranking. For the next hour, runners slid into the foxhole with scraps of paper scribbled with quadrants, calls for more ammo, and orders to move left or right.

His left arm went numb. He switched places with Samuel and quickly donned the headset. He relayed so many messages his throat became raw and parched. How many bottles of ice-cold Coke had he drunk while stationed at Camp Pendleton? What he'd give for one now.

Boom!

Another explosion.

Palm leaves and coconuts crashed onto the top of the foxhole.

One coconut came clear through, narrowly missing him and Samuel.

Samuel kept cranking.

John relayed the message to the commander at the front lines. An additional ten boxes of ammo were on the way.

Minutes dragged.

Darkness deepened.

The shelling continued. Somewhere in the melee they switched places again. Weariness crept over him. His eyes stung from lack of sleep. He flinched at every mortar shell that exploded and caused his ears to ring.

Then, blessedly, the sounds of gunfire grew further and further apart. His ears perked like a bloodhound's, straining to identify every small noise he heard. His hair stood at attention.

Waiting.

The palm leaves that had fallen over the foxhole rustled.

John and Samuel reached for their rifles.

A runner, his face blacked with soot, slid inside. "The Japanese have fallen back."

The runner slipped back into the darkness, as if he'd been nothing more than an apparition.

Samuel whipped off the headset and tossed it at him. "I'm done transmitting for the night. Any more messages come in before dawn, you can translate them."

"No problem." He tried to stretch his leg in the cramped, damp foxhole. Their rain ponchos covered the top to help shield them from the downpour, but they didn't work well.

Samuel stood, his knees bent to keep from hitting his head on the "roof" of their shelter. "I'm going to see if I can find some chow. You hungry?"

"Sure."

His friend slipped and slid from their little hovel and disappeared into the night. John closed his eyes and thought of Mary. Where was she? Somewhere safe? If only the war would end. How many more men had to die before Japan surrendered?

Samuel reappeared with cold Spam sandwiches. "I traded the cigarettes from our K rations for these two pickles. One for each of us."

John gave thanks and chomped on the spicy dill. The abundance of food that tasted good was always something to be thankful for. Good thing neither he nor Samuel smoked.

"Plenty more where this came from." Samuel stuffed a bite into his mouth.

"Good for you, I suppose." John rubbed his full stomach.

"Hey, man," Samuel said between bites, "I saw Lieutenant Brandon."

"What did he have to say?"

Samuel stuffed the last bite in his mouth. "We got a mission tomorrow. Translating for some Army guys, or something like that. Said he'd fill us in at dawn."

A heavy rock settled in John's chest.

"I'm going for more. You want some too?" Samuel asked.

"No, I'm going to try to sleep." He emitted a long, deep yawn that he thought would dislocate his jaw.

"Suit yourself." Samuel's splashy footsteps died away.

John closed his eyes. What did the Army want with him and Samuel? Normally the branches of service didn't mingle well, but when the need arose, they put their differences aside to do the job. In his mind there wasn't much difference between the branches. They were all on the same side as far as he was concerned.

Rain cascaded from the sky like waterfalls from heaven. More palm leaves now covered the top of the foxhole. It leaked less than usual. Raindrops plopped onto an empty oil drum. The *tappety-tap-tap* reminded him of the drumbeats back home.

Home. How he missed his mother and little sisters. They had to miss him as much as he missed them. Exhausted, he asked God to watch over them.

He listened for the sound of the tin cans strung on trip wire surrounding the perimeter. The wind rattled the wire but not enough to clang the cans together.

Would an encroaching enemy be wise enough to step over the trip wire? If so, they could sneak into camp and shoot his comrades before they had the chance to reach for their rifles.

Snakes and rats weren't tall enough to trip the wire. Rats ran amok through camp. Their bites could give him rabies or Lord only knew what other kinds of diseases. Instinctively, he curled his toes and curled his body into a tight ball.

John tried to remember who was on patrol. Any replacements? If so, he hoped they were paired with someone with experience. He prayed that the guards would stay awake and be alert to any enemy advancements.

It was a terrible thing to go to sleep, knowing that he could wake up fighting for his life. His muscles rebelled at being scrunched into a fetal position for so long. He stretched his legs and bumped into Samuel, who groaned, then snored. He turned his thoughts to his family and his flocks of livestock that roamed the wide-open spaces of his reservation.

Blessed sleep beckoned him, and his muscles relaxed. The raindrops pattering to earth played a tune that echoed in his dreams. Only, the beats seemed off-key somehow.

Had the trip wire jangled?

Strange voices yanked him from slumber.

He slapped his helmet on.

"What the—" John reached for his rifle.

Shouting erupted outside. He locked eyes with Samuel. His friend was likely thinking the same thing he was. Which one of them would poke their head out to see what was happening?

Voices drew closer. The louder one sounded familiar.

John shoved aside dead palm leaves and a coconut and wiggled out into the cool air.

When had dawn arrived?

Ribbons of pink and gold stretched from one end of the horizon to the other. The sky was a glorious sight, though the sun wasn't all the way up yet. The beach around him yielded painful images of destruction. He craned his neck, taking in the sight. Someone approached. In the glare of the cresting sun, he couldn't tell who.

"You boys ready to go?"

"Lieutenant Brandon," John squawked. "Sir, fancy meeting you here, I guess."

Like a curious prairie dog, Samuel stuck his head up from the ground.

"Grab that radio and follow me. You too, Goshen and Riker."

John did as he was ordered. He and Samuel followed behind the lieutenant, stepping over downed trees and dodging craters big enough to swallow a car. Waves lapped the beach, sending the aroma of salt water into the atmosphere.

The smell reminded him of Camp Pendleton.

He followed the lieutenant and a handful of Marines onto a pontoon boat that took them into deeper waters where a transport ship waited. They were being taken into danger, he was certain.

CHAPTER 20

Mary thought of Captain Greene as she steered the truck toward the POW camp. A larger load of Red Cross boxes for the imprisoned soldiers filled the back of the vehicle. Even more precious than the crates of food and medicine was the secret treasure she carried. Tucked into her brassiere was a small square of paper and a short pencil.

She hadn't informed Sister Abigail of her daring plan. One thing she learned from the fiasco with Major Morton—a mission's success depended on secrecy. She'd have Captain Greene scribble a quick note to his family. Then she'd include it in a letter to Catherine Brandon. Mrs. Brandon could then send the letter on to the captain's family in Kansas.

The chances of this plan succeeding weren't great, but somewhere in Independence, a family waited, prayed, for a shred of news indicating their loved one still lived. Considering what she'd endured regarding her brother, she had to at least try to give this family hope.

"Do you remember how to get there?" Sister Abigail asked.

"Yes." Hauling supplies all over Camp Pendleton and beyond, she'd developed an excellent sense of direction—one she was quite proud of. Given the opportunity, she was sure she'd learn her way around the rest of the island. Knowledge of the area would help her locate her brother.

"Good," Sister Abigail said. "Because the next time, you're on your own."

If she thought Mary would tremble at the news, she was mistaken. Mary smiled. This gave her more opportunity to collect messages from Captain Greene and maybe a few others. If that went well, she'd send those messages to Catherine Brandon as well.

The turn in the road approached. She rounded the corner without difficulty. Sister Abigail looked pleased. The accomplishment warmed Mary.

As the camp came into view, she braked and the truck rolled to a stop. The guards met them at the gate, sporting their customary sneers.

A muscled guard carrying a bamboo club stepped forward and quickly frisked her for contraband. Heat enflamed her cheeks. She closed her eyes, silently praying the items she carried wouldn't be discovered.

"Enter!" He pointed his club at the open gate.

She tamped down her fears and followed Sister Abigail inside.

The commander strolled toward them. Mary's heart leaped into her throat. A bead of sweat meandered down her temple. If the man had any inkling of her plans, would he torture her first and then kill her? Or would he just kill her?

Was this crazy idea was worth the risk?

Yes!

She adjusted her robe, listening for a rustling of paper hidden in her undergarments. Hearing nothing, she grinned, her fears temporarily assuaged.

She and the commander exchanged small talk for a few minutes. The man might have thought she was smiling at him. She wasn't. Her grin deepened at the notion of pulling the wool over his eyes.

The short, pudgy guard who'd followed her and Captain Greene on the last visit stepped forward to inspect the Red Cross boxes. He didn't step away until his pockets were bulging and his arms were laden with clothing, blankets, and food meant for the soldiers.

Meek and obedient.

She must remain meek and obedient, or she and the POWs would be killed. She kept her hands to her sides, gripped in the folds of her robe, and bowed her head.

Finally, the guards finished pilfering. The commander, seemingly satisfied, granted her permission to bring the boxes inside and distribute them. She strode out the front gate and to the truck and gathered as many supplies as she could carry.

The soldiers waited inside the fence. Did any of them think of sprinting out the gate? Or had the guards tortured them so much they were terrified of taking such a risk?

Captain Greene directed the men to take the supplies to the

appropriate locations. His cheeks had a touch of color in them that hadn't been there last week. These care packages had made a difference. Satisfaction ran through her.

When all the crates were brought in, she hurried to the medical tent. Captain Greene dispensed aspirin to a man writhing with malaria-induced fever.

Her pulse raced like a jackrabbit. She unloaded a box of cough syrup and cod liver oil. When finished, she sucked in a breath, held it, and then released it slowly.

Captain Greene hummed a tune she didn't recognize. He placed additional bottles onto a shelf. As nonchalantly as possible, she stepped close to him.

She whispered, "Don't look up. Keep working without drawing attention."

He stopped for a fraction of a second then resumed, with the good sense not to ask questions or gawk at her. She opened a box of bandages.

Keeping her voice to a whisper, Mary said, "I'll drop these. When we squat to pick them up, I'll hand you paper and pencil. Scribble a note to your family. Hand it back, fast."

The bandages fell silently to the dirt at her feet. He emitted a deep sigh. To his credit, he carried on as if she hadn't just dropped a weighty matter onto him.

Mary could hardly blame him for showing emotion at sending word to his family. His life, and the lives of others, depended on him remaining calm. But he obviously loved his family very much and wanted them to have proof he lived. His mind must be careening.

A lump formed in her throat. No family waited for her at home. She had only Daniel, and he was in a POW camp. . .somewhere.

Using her peripheral vision, she cast sideways glances around the camp. Sister Abigail stood inside the kitchen helping the cooks prepare soup, doing a good job of keeping them preoccupied.

Captain Greene's reply sounded ominously nervous. "Let me help you pick those up."

The hair on her arms prickled at the way he said the words. Taking his clue, she squatted to retrieve the bandages. Quickly she slipped the paper and pencil into his hands. She lifted a section of her robe and brushed the dust from it, helping to conceal the captain's actions.

Seconds crawled by with all the speed given to the average snail. She brushed, and brushed, and brushed, until she was sure the guards would notice.

Don't attract unwanted attention. She kept her head down and slowly picked up a roll of gauze. But she couldn't stand yet.

How long did it take to scribble a few sentences?

Finally, he handed her the note. She turned her back to the guards and quickly stuffed it into her clothing. They gathered the bandages and stood.

Captain Greene whispered, "I'll put the pencil in the box of bandages. I'll try to write more. If you come back, I'll hand you another message."

"Okay." Using her peripheral vision, she glanced at the guards who had moved to just inside the front gate. If any of them decided to wander into the medical tent. . .she dropped the bandages again. This time they rolled in every direction, and she inadvertently stepped on two of them.

"Oh," she groaned. She couldn't afford to waste supplies these men needed. She chastised herself for focusing too much attention on the guards and not on the task before her.

"Just scoop them into the box. The men won't care. Most of our supplies are filthy anyway." Captain Greene placed his hands on his hips, studying the crates as if taking inventory.

Guilt seeped into her. She shouldn't ignore the other men who needed care. She moved from bed to bed, checking with each soldier, committing their names and hometowns to memory. When she returned to the convent, she'd find a way to contact Catherine Brandon with the information.

A noise drew her attention.

Her heart leaped into her throat and refused to return to its rightful place. Sister Abigail approached. Her eyebrows scrunched together, her lips set in a thin line.

A sense of cold and dark foreboding surrounded her. The sister wouldn't have such a gloomy countenance unless something was terribly wrong. Had someone witnessed Captain Greene? She placed a hand on her chest. The paper lay cool against her skin, but the corner of the folded note poked her rib. She prayed a bayonet wouldn't soon be doing the same.

"We need to leave, now." Sister Abigail grasped Mary's elbow and dragged her toward the front gate.

"What's wrong?" Mary whispered. She hustled past the barbed wire, an ache in her middle for those who weren't allowed the luxury. She glanced behind her, fearing for those she was leaving behind. Jolts of fear hummed through her.

"Get in the truck," Sister Abigail ordered as she climbed into the passenger seat with speed and ease Mary didn't expect from someone advanced in years.

Mary hoisted herself into the driver's seat, revved the engine, and drove away, thinking of the men. Fear for them blurred her vision.

"What's wrong?" Mary turned onto the main road leading to the convent.

Sister Abigail released a long sigh. "One of the POWs was caught scribbling in a homemade journal. The man may have wanted us to smuggle it out of the camp."

Mary's heart hammered against her ribs. The note from Captain Greene burned a hole in her chest. What if they had been caught?

Heavy shudders tore through her. The truck left the road and ran over a bush before she could steer it back onto the road. "Wha–what will happen to him?"

The sister eyed her suspiciously and cleared her throat. "I only know what I overheard. We had to leave before the commanding officer suspected us of something."

"Oh," Mary said. It took all her strength to keep from rubbing the spot where Captain Greene's precious note lay. She calmed herself enough to ask, "How was this discovered?"

"The short, pudgy guard had been spying on the man and caught him. The guard beat the poor soul and dragged him to a hole in the jungle. Only the Lord knows if he will live through the experience."

But for the grace of John's God, that could have been her. Or worse, Captain Greene. Would any of the other POWs suffer due to the discovery of the journal?

Catherine Brandon had extolled the importance of keeping things secret. She finally understood the ramifications when that order wasn't followed. She gulped and blew out a sigh. Thankfully Mother Superior didn't ask questions.

Silence hung in the air between her and the head nun. When they arrived at the convent, Mary killed the engine. Sister Abigail jumped down from the truck and stormed into the abbey.

The sister demanded a meeting in the sanctuary. Mary dragged her leaden feet that direction and dropped into an empty pew in the rear.

Sister Abigail wrung her hands. "I want you all to know that we must be careful not to smuggle items in or out of the POW camp. This will do nothing but break the trust between us and the commanding officer of the camp."

Mary's stomach churned like a whirlpool. Had the woman suspected Mary had done something nefarious? How could she have been so foolish? She swallowed for the umpteenth time, hoping to choke down the lump stuck in her throat.

Mother Superior's lips formed a hard line. She stared at each nun, her eyes blazing with anger. "The poor soul who thought he could smuggle out a journal detailing war crimes is now spending the week in a hole without food or water. He likely won't survive."

———— ≈ ————

Three days after John, Samuel, Goshen, and Riker had returned from a recon mission, John tried unsuccessfully to sleep. He treasured his friend Samuel, but such close quarters tried the patience of a saint. The guy drove him crazy.

Samuel hummed a love song while writing his umpteenth letter to Susanna. Between bites of cold Spam and crackers, he droned on about the girl's beauty and poise and his undying love for her.

John envied the man's ability to communicate with the gal he loved.

Maybe that was what really bothered him. Samuel knew where his girl was. He could not only write to her but receive letters from her too.

And she was safe.

John climbed from the foxhole and headed for Lieutenant Brandon's quarters.

He stepped inside and saluted. "Excuse me, sir, may I speak with you?"

The lieutenant shuffled a stack of maps on his desk and looked up. "What is it?"

John yanked his hat from his head and crumpled it in his hands. "I'm sorry to bother you, sir, but can we find a way to mail a letter to my girl, Mary?"

Lieutenant Brandon chewed his lower lip. "I don't know, John. Let me see what I can do."

He gripped his cap so hard his fingers ached. "Sir, can you tell me if she's safe?"

"I can't tell you that."

"Sir," John pleaded. "Please. I don't need to know where she is or what kind of secret operation she's involved in. I just need to know if she's okay." He gulped. "Will I even be told if anything happens to her?"

"As you know, her brother is her next of kin, but he's in a POW camp. So, if *you're* listed as her next of kin, you'll receive a telegram if she's MIA or KIA."

Killed in action.

John swayed backward as if he'd been struck in the chest. "Thank you, sir. May I be excused?"

The lieutenant waved him out. John stormed to his foxhole. Thankfully, his friend was too busy writing to engage in conversation. John dug his Bible from his duffel bag and tried to read. His thoughts drifted.

Each island they wrestled from the enemy moved them that much closer to Japan, that much closer to ending the war. Why couldn't the Japanese just surrender? Every Japanese soldier was willing to die to take as many GIs as possible with them into the grave. It was a concept John had difficulty understanding.

He clambered from the foxhole and strode toward the beach. Then, remembering Mary and their last night at Camp Pendleton, he did an about-face and poked his head into the foxhole.

Samuel asked, "Do you have any envelopes to spare?"

"Sorry, I used all mine sending money home to my family." John pulled his knife from his duffel bag and then headed deeper into the island jungle for solitude.

Snakes of all sizes and colors slithered among the thick greenery. If one reared its ugly head, John was ready to use his knife. He chuckled, remembering that Mary was terrified of snakes. He tried to reconcile in his mind the sweet, brave girl he loved with one who would scream and faint at the sight of a reptile.

He had to be careful not to wander too far. Japanese booby traps were everywhere.

The sound of rushing water drew him to a small waterfall that cascaded over a tall, rocky outcrop and settled into a pool at his feet. The sun glinted off it, creating prisms and rainbows. The beauty took his breath away. He yanked off his boots and dipped his feet into the cool pond.

There weren't places like this near where he lived on the Navajo Reservation. He wanted to find a photojournalist with a camera and ask him to take a few snapshots for him. His family would love to see photographs of where he'd been.

He missed nights on the reservation, standing outside his hogan, staring at the vast sky filled with stars and the moon. He couldn't loiter outside his foxhole at night here, because that's when the Japanese hit the hardest.

Assurance settled over him. He didn't need to stare at the moon to know God was with him. God was everywhere, even in that tiny foxhole with him and Samuel.

After a few moments of quiet reflection, he realized he was wrong to be jealous of his friend, no matter how much he missed his girl. He and Samuel had grown closer the past few months, and love wasn't something to be hindered in a world where hate had taken too strong a hold.

Not ready to don his boots, he grabbed them from the water's edge and strolled toward camp. Ever mindful of snakes.

Shouting drew him from his daydreams.

The high-pitched whine of airplanes reverberated across the sky.

Two Zeros at 0400 high.

Panic welled in his middle. He sprinted back to camp, jumping over downed trees and mud puddles along the way.

He dived into the foxhole. Samuel cranked the radio. John jammed on the headset as a runner rushed over and shoved a scrap of paper at them.

John kept his voice steady as he relayed the information. He turned to his friend. "Why are the Japs attacking now? They usually wait until dark."

"How should I know?" Samuel paused to stuff his letter into his duffel bag.

Another runner scrambled into the foxhole, handed them a message, and then scrambled out. Samuel cranked the radio.

"Arizona, Arizona," John relayed the message.

Rounds of enemy fire cut across the beach, spewing sand and debris. Soldiers on the beach returned fire. The first Zero burst into a ball of orange flames and spiraled into the ocean.

John pulled his hands away from his head and listened. Was the second plane's engine growing quieter or louder?

Louder!

The Zero must have turned.

It flew closer, the noise echoing in his ears.

Bullets pinged off the top of the foxhole. John dived over the radio. When the firing ceased, he peeked over the edge of the sandbags. To his horror, the fighter plane banked hard to the left and came around for another pass.

Lieutenant Brandon shouted at the artillery crew. "Blast that thing out of the sky."

The marines aimed their artillery guns into the air and opened fire. The fourth shot hit the aircraft. It exploded into a bright orange-and-red fireball. Pieces of burning metal hissed and steamed as they smacked into the frigid ocean.

Men rose from the ground and cheered.

"We got him, Samuel." John waved his hat in the air and cheered.

Lieutenant Brandon bellowed, "We've got wounded."

Three corpsmen hurried to the injured.

"Be right back, Sam." John began to climb from the foxhole but stopped. His friend hadn't answered. He turned.

Blood soaked the front of his buddy's uniform.

☰ CHAPTER 21 ☰

Mortars erupted when they hit the area surrounding the convent. In the basement with the radio, the walls shook. Mary covered her ears. The convent's occupants—nuns, two priests, and a doctor who'd recently arrived—had been lucky so far. No bombs or mortars had directly hit the structure.

For what seemed like hours, she hovered over the radio, wondering if she should send out a distress call. When she and John were becoming friends, before they'd fallen in love, he'd said something about being a radio operator. What she'd give to have him by her side at that moment. Not just because he knew radios.

The booms grew farther apart and, to her relief, finally ceased. Though her knees wobbled, she stood, clambered up the ladder, and flung the trap door open.

Inside the kitchen, she checked for damage. Finding none, she sprinted to the sanctuary as fast as her bulky robe allowed. She skidded to a stop. The nuns kneeled before the altar, praying as if the whole structure wasn't about to come down around their ears.

How could they remain so calm? She was frightened out of her wits. She leaned against the wall, sucking air into her oxygen-starved lungs. Her mind swirled around one thought—the men fighting on the front lines.

John.

Susanna's love, Samuel.

"Lord, please keep them safe." She tried to convince herself that she was praying because she was frightened, but she knew better. In the weeks since she'd come to the convent, her heart was slowly softening, healing from wounds, coming to grips with the possibility that John's God was indeed real.

She pushed away from the wall and paced the center aisle of the sanctuary. Confusion wafted through her soul as she thought that maybe John's God really did care.

Sister Abigail stood and hurried to her side. "Are you all right, Mary?"

"I'm not sure." She wrung her hands. Did she want to believe in a God who would take her family from her, who would allow such evil to run rampant? It was too difficult to reconcile the loving and compassionate God, whom John and every nun in this place worshipped, with an almighty higher power who allowed such wicked evil to go unchecked.

The sister placed a hand at the small of Mary's back. "Would you like to talk?"

Mary shook her head. "No, but thank you. I think I'll head to my room."

Without giving the woman time to reply, she rushed up the staircase. She entered her room and shut the door harder than she meant to.

She dropped onto her bed and tried to nap, but her mind was a whirl of activity. Images of John popped into her mind every time she rolled over and fluffed her thin pillow. She wanted so much to believe that his God would keep him safe and bring him back to her. And that He would keep her brother safe as well.

The dinner bell rang, indicating that she'd slept at least a short time. Her stomach rumbled with hunger. In all the melee of bombs going off, she'd missed lunch. She didn't even know if the noon meal had been prepared.

She hefted herself off the bed, stretched, and straightened her wrinkled robe and habit the best she could. She walked slowly down the stairs and to the kitchen. Mechanically, she chewed down the plate of rice and chicken and polished off a glass of water.

Memories of drinking Cokes at Christmas with John at the Brandons' house slipped into her mind. What a beautiful day that had been. What would the next Christmas be like? Would the war be over by then?

She tried to imagine John, Daniel, Samuel, Susanna, the rest of John's family, and even the Takahashi family gathered around a Christmas tree. She had agreed to meet John at their special place on the beach at Camp Pendleton once the war ended. Would he be waiting for her? Or would she be waiting for him?

But what if he and Daniel were destined to die? Leaving her all alone?

She gritted her teeth at the frightening possibility.

First, the war must end.

Careful to avoid Sister Abigail and a priest who had worried about her, she slipped upstairs to her room. The Bible on the small table seemed to beckon her. Dare she open it?

No, she couldn't. Not yet.

She changed out of her habit and into her itchy, long, flannel night-gown and shivered as she slid under the chilly coverlet. She rolled left and right, trying to find a comfortable position.

"Lord, if You are there, please help me find a way to stop this evil. Show me what I can do to keep the madness from tearing this world apart."

When sleep finally claimed her, she dreamed of running, dodging rifle fire and bombs raining from the sky. She hid behind trees and stumbled through gullies and rivers, and still, the bullets whizzed around her like a tornado of terror.

She sat straight up in bed, gasping.

She steadied her breathing. "Just a nightmare."

A horrifying realization hit her. For the soldiers on the front lines and thousands of innocent civilians in ravaged war zones, this was reality.

She untangled herself from the sweat-soaked sheets. She drew in a slow, deep breath and told herself to relax.

Dawn had just begun to color the sky. It pierced the darkness that had shrouded her room. She padded to her window and peeked outside. A streak of gold stretched across the horizon.

Her tribe believed in a Creator of heaven and earth. Witnessing magnificent handiwork like this strengthened her belief in a higher power. She opened the window and stuck her head outside. Cool air caressed her cheeks like angel wings. Breathing deeply exhilarated her.

Then a near-deafening boom rent the glorious peace.

A terrible crash followed.

Debris of some sort rained down from the ceiling.

Screams echoed from downstairs.

Terror shot through her. She wanted to slap her hands over her ears and crawl under the bed. Instead, she whipped off her nightgown and yanked on her robe. She scrambled down the stairs, nearly tumbling end over end.

Before her feet hit the last step, a cacophony of chaos rose to meet her. Two nuns rushed toward the sanctuary, their arms laden with a stack of sheets.

"Sister Abigail, what is it? Has the convent been hit?"

"The bell tower was hit and badly damaged, but we can't worry about that. The convent is becoming a field hospital."

That explained the noise she'd just heard in her room. Sister Abigail was right. No time to worry about the bell tower. They had work to do.

She remembered what Catherine Brandon had said about sticking close to enemy wounded. If she overheard anything that could help the Allies, she'd have to sneak into the basement and send a coded message over the radio. Was this an answer to prayer or a nightmare come true?

Two nuns and the priest brushed past her. She stood as if the soles of her feet had rooted into the cold stone floor.

"Come." Sister Abigail motioned her to follow. "Wounded soldiers are arriving. You need to help us with them."

Mary grabbed an armload of linens and bandages, lifted the hem of her robe with her free hand, and followed the head nun. "Will there be any Japanese among them?"

"I don't know," the woman called over her shoulder as they hurried down the hallway to the sanctuary. She dropped the items on the floor and spread a sheet over a wooden pew. "If there are enemy soldiers, we'll need to put them somewhere away from the Allies."

Mary understood why. She could very well imagine the reaction of American Marines being forced to share a room with the enemy.

Marines.

Would John be among them?

Two medics carried a litter holding a bleeding Japanese soldier. The man looked as close to death as anyone she'd ever seen.

---◈---

Though needed on the front lines, Lieutenant Brandon had ordered John to help with the wounded. The lieutenant ordered Goshen and Riker to stay and help fight. John and Samuel were headed to a secured area anyway and wouldn't necessarily need their comrades' protection.

John and Samuel had spent a long night at an aid station waiting for another field hospital to open before his friend could be transported.

Thankfully Samuel was alive and talking, but he'd lost so much blood. At least, it looked like a lot of blood to John. But what did he know of medicine?

John helped load Samuel into a waiting ambulance. Then he loaded the rest of wounded men dropped at the aid station. He insisted on going with Samuel, and the driver didn't object. He climbed into the back of the ambulance and gazed at the wounded men. One was missing part of his foot, another had suffered a head wound, and one's chest pumped enough blood to cover the vehicle's floor.

The ambulance bounced over rutted roads. The men cried out in obvious agony. He'd helped butcher animals on the Navajo Reservation and had seen his share of blood, but the sights and sounds around him curdled the contents of his stomach.

He bowed his head and prayed for his friend, for these suffering men, that God would let them live. He pleaded with God that there would be doctors at this new field hospital who could save them.

While there, if at all possible, he'd donate blood. Judging by the amount pouring from these wounded men, the hospital could use it.

"Hang in there, Sam. We'll be there soon."

The vehicle swung a wide loop and parked in front of a large stone convent. One side of the bell tower had taken a direct hit. The bell hung precariously from a wooden beam that looked ready to collapse in a brisk wind.

At last, they arrived, and the wounded still lived. This convent wrapped solace around his weary soul. He'd seek spiritual guidance and maybe attend Mass while here.

A doctor rushed outside and barked orders at two medics and several nuns standing nearby. They pulled the litters from the vehicle and hurried inside. The medics hurried and thus weren't as gentle as they could have been. The men groaned at the rough treatment.

John followed them inside, holding his friend's hand. A nun rushed from wall sconce to wall sconce lighting candles. The sanctuary grew brighter. More wounded poured into the building.

Cries of anguish echoed through the room. Men lay on pews and makeshift tables. John had never seen anything like this. He used to think he had a strong stomach, until now. Two medics placed a screaming, mangled man with missing limbs onto an operating table.

John slapped a hand over his mouth, rushed outside, and lost his meager K rations among a row of shrubs. Minutes later, his stomach thoroughly emptied, the heaves subsided. He straightened and wiped his mouth and face with his sleeve.

He bowed his head and begged God to give him strength. The scriptures declared that he could do all things through Christ who gave him strength.

The rumble of more ambulances echoed in the distance. John steeled his resolve. The vehicles rolled to a stop in front of the building. He rushed to help carry the wounded inside.

Gently as possible, he pulled the litter from the back of the ambulance. The injured soldier's smooth cheeks didn't look like they had ever seen a razor.

John gasped. So young.

A man with a white armband bearing a red cross and blood-coated fatigues leaped from the vehicle. Together, he and the driver carried the boy inside.

John asked, "What's your name, soldier? Where you from?"

The kid winced and held his blood-soaked sleeve. "Private Greene, from Independence, Kansas. I got a brother somewhere on this island."

They entered the sanctuary. John replied, "Would you like me to find him?"

The private shook his head. "No, you don't understand."

The ambulance driver and John placed him on one of the few empty pews.

Private Greene clutched the bottom of John's shirt. "Please, sir, he's—"

The driver pulled John away from the wounded soldier. "C'mon, there are more wounded to carry in."

"Wait a sec," John grumbled at the impatient driver. He turned to Private Greene. "I'll be back soon. Okay?"

The boy nodded. John followed the driver to the courtyard. Four ambulances waited to be unloaded. Three more barreled toward the convent. John prayed he'd find time to finish his conversation with Private Greene, but it would likely be a while.

For the next hour John hauled wounded men—more than twenty Americans, two Japanese, and four Australians—into the convent. His back ached and sweat poured from his temples in the humid atmosphere. A light drizzle fell by the time the last ambulance arrived.

He trudged into the sanctuary and found Samuel lying on the floor in the back, awake and pale but seemingly recovering without incident. A wrinkled-faced nun with glasses fed him a bowl of hot soup.

"Hey, buddy." John knelt beside his friend. "You're looking better."

"Yeah, Doc dug out a piece of shrapnel. Said I'm lucky. Everything else is fine. I might even go back in a couple of days."

The nun held the spoon in front of Samuel's face but locked eyes with John. "Your friend must eat and rest before he goes anywhere."

"Right." John nodded at the nun. "I'll come back to say goodbye before I go."

She smiled and spooned soup into Samuel's mouth.

John stood and gazed about the sanctuary, searching for Private Greene. He spotted the boy among the sea of suffering humanity crowding the room. He hurried toward him.

"Hello, Private, remember me?"

A smile curved across the boy's features, and his blue eyes gleamed. He reached his bandaged hand out to John. "Hey, thanks for finding me."

"How are you feeling?" John shook the boy's hand and noted his other arm in a sling. He almost kicked himself, realizing he'd asked a stupid question.

"Doc says it's just a flesh wound. A small crack in the bone. I'll be outta here soon. Can you please find out what happened to my brother?"

"Sure, what outfit is he with?"

The boy shook his head. "Ma got a telegram. Said he's in a POW camp."

Steel bands seemed to wrap themselves around John's heart and squeezed until his chest ached. He'd heard stories about Camp O'Donnell. If that's where this kid's brother was, he felt sorry for the guy. To keep from frightening the kid, John refrained from sharing horror stories about the camp.

His throat dried up like a desert. "I'll see what I can do."

The boy closed his eyes. "Thank you."

John glanced across the room. The nun was still feeding Samuel. Might as well kill two birds with one stone. First, check on his friend. Then ask to see the head nun so he could ask her about Private Greene's brother.

Wounded soldiers covered every available space on the floor. He had to perform a few intricate dance maneuvers to step around them. These courageous men were wounded enough. They didn't need the weight of his two hundred pounds causing additional injuries.

John squatted next to his friend. "Don't go flirting with this nice lady. Susanna will be jealous."

Color bloomed on the nun's cheeks. Her lips curved into a small grin.

Samuel let out a hearty laugh and then clutched his wound and grimaced.

John bit his lower lip. "Sorry for making you laugh."

Samuel guffawed. "No, you're not, but don't tell Susanna. She's a great gal, but you're right. She is jealous." He grinned at the nun and winked.

"Mercy," the woman cried. "I'm through here." She handed Samuel the bowl and moved to assist another soldier.

"Catch you later, buddy." He patted Samuel's shoulder and turned to the nun. "Excuse me, ma'am, where might I find the Mother Superior?"

"In the kitchen."

"Thank you, and may the Lord bless you." He winked at her. She slapped her fingers over her lips.

On his way to the kitchen, John heard Japanese voices, hushed whispers coming from a large storage room. He peeked inside.

An enemy soldier, his arm in a sling, crouched by the cots of two other wounded Japanese. The enemy soldier stopped talking the moment John locked eyes with him. The man then climbed into his own cot. He fixed his eyes on John and then looked away.

Uneasiness skittered along John's spine.

These men sounded like they were planning something nefarious. He didn't understand a bit of the conversation. Still, judging by their tone and their body language, the situation warranted further scrutiny.

John found the head nun in the kitchen stirring a large vat of steaming broth. His stomach growled audibly. Nerves? Or hunger? Both?

She aimed a sly smile at him. "Would you like a bowl?"

"Yes, please, and. . ." He scanned the room to ensure that they were the only two people in there. He then stepped closer and whispered, "The group of enemy soldiers in that big closet down the hallway, I don't know what they're saying, but it can't be good."

The woman's face blanched. Her eyes grew round and wide as cannonballs. She stared at the table in the center of the room, glanced at her feet, and abruptly turned back to the stove. She continued to stir the broth.

She finally said, "You needn't worry. HQ is being made aware of the situation."

John sputtered. "But how?"

"Please, sir. Let it be." She dumped a ladleful of broth into a bowl.

He placed his hands on his hips, not wanting to argue with her, but this was important. "I mean no disrespect, ma'am, but my commanding officer needs to know if these enemy combatants are planning anything nefarious. I'm happy to relay the info, if you'll point me to a radio so I—"

She dropped the bowl.

It clattered to the floor.

Her eyebrows scrunched together in a stern frown.

John sensed she was hiding something. Was she siding with the enemy?

≡ CHAPTER 22 ≡

From her seat in the basement next to the shortwave radio, Mary heard voices through the floor above her. She couldn't distinguish them, but gooseflesh prickled on her arms at the tone. What excuse could she give if she were discovered?

The enemy—and heaven only knew who else—listened in on radio communications. She couldn't allow any ole schmuck, especially the enemy, to overhear her sending classified information across the airwaves. Catherine Brandon had ordered her to be very careful about that. Someone might take it the wrong way, wantonly share it with others, twist the facts, or worse, commit treason and divulge the information to the enemy.

And if the Japanese discovered her position and the radio? A shiver washed over her. She couldn't let that happen.

Her thoughts spun like a child's toy top. Nothing plausible coalesced in her mind. Her gaze flew to the radio.

The voices stopped. Heavy footsteps shook the floorboards enough to send dust and dirt cascading down on her. A sneeze tickled in her nose.

She slapped a hand over her mouth.

Squeezed her eyes shut.

Willed the sensation to pass.

Second by slow second, the feeling ebbed. She sucked in a quiet breath.

Silence surrounded her for several tense moments. No clocks hung on the basement walls, and she didn't own a watch. There was no way to tell how much time had passed.

The radio's instruction manual sat on the table. She entertained herself by playing tic-tac-toe on the back cover for a few minutes.

Had enough time passed so that it was safe to send messages?

It no longer mattered. Devotion to her country shoved her fears into submission. She needed to send the information without wasting another second.

She yanked the headset from the contraption. She and Catherine Brandon had created their own secret code for sending messages. Without any hiccups, she sent the information to their middleman, who would then transcribe it and hand it to Catherine personally.

Her legs shook as she climbed the ladder. Thankfully, Sister Abigail had moved the table and rug. Mary pushed open the trap door leading into the kitchen. Darkness shrouded the room. The stove was cold. Thankfully, no one watched her. She climbed the last step and shut the trap door.

She needed to locate Sister Abigail fast and find out what had happened. First, she checked on the Japanese soldiers. They were sleeping and, thankfully, not cooking up more ideas on how to overcome the Allies.

She found the sister in the sanctuary, conversing with the doctor. The woman locked eyes with her and moved away from the doctor toward Mary.

Sister Abigail grabbed Mary's sleeve and dragged her back to the kitchen.

Once there, she whispered, "There was an American soldier here not long ago, causing trouble. I asked him to leave."

"Was that the ruckus I heard a little while ago?"

She nodded. "He saw the Japanese soldiers and figured they were up to no good. He asked for a radio, and well, I didn't know what to tell him."

An image of John flashed in Mary's mind. What were the odds of him being on the same island as her? She blew out a sigh, discarding the possibility from her mind.

"We'll have to be more careful. I'll relay information faster to limit my time in the basement."

Sister Abigail's head bobbed again. "That would be helpful, especially while we have so many soldiers here."

"Speaking of soldiers, I think I'll check on them. I know it's late and they're probably sleeping, but I'm too wound up to sleep myself."

"Well, I'm not." She chuckled. "If you don't mind, I'm going to bed."

"Good night." Mary excused herself and headed to the sanctuary. The first soldier she checked had lost his left foot. He stirred in his sleep. She placed her hand on his chest and spoke softly to him, hoping to quell his apparent uneasiness. They would have to watch him closely and continue checking him for fever.

The next soldier asked her to dictate a letter to his sweetheart. She obliged, then located an envelope for the missive and promised to mail it. His eyes glistened when he thanked her.

She proceeded along the row of suffering soldiers.

The last soldier she reached stirred empathy in her. His pink cheeks dimpled when he smiled.

"Evening, ma'am," the kid said.

"Evening, soldier, where you from?" Mary knelt beside him.

"Name's Private Greene. I'm from Independence, Kansas."

Mary gulped, stammered. "Is that so?" This kid had to be related to Captain Greene in the POW camp.

Private Greene continued. "I got a letter from Ma. She said she got a telegram that my brother's in a POW camp. I wish I could sneak out of here and go look for him."

Mary blew out a sigh. So, this kid and Captain Greene *were* brothers. How well she understood Private Greene's plight. She needed to contact Catherine Brandon about this. She wanted to let this kid know his brother was safe, the last time she'd seen him, anyway. But she didn't know if Catherine Brandon would approve.

She took the kid's hands in hers. "Let me ask around. I'll find out what I can and get back with you."

"Okay." Private Greene yawned and closed his eyes.

She patted the kid's shoulder and moved on. She stood and glanced around the room.

There, in the back, she saw John's friend Samuel, sleeping. Desire to find out anything she could about John burned within her. Samuel's wounds were evident by his ashen complexion and the number of bandages covering his chest. Reluctant to wake him, she chose to visit later.

Perhaps she could write a letter and have Samuel deliver it, providing he knew John's location.

Catherine Brandon would blow a gasket if she knew what Mary had plotted with Captain Greene, but regret didn't cross her mind. She did what she had to do to get word to the families of loved ones. She didn't mind the risks she was taking, as long as she wasn't risking the lives of innocent soldiers or any operatives.

Uneasiness wiggled through her. She needed to be mindful of all the many secrets she was keeping, before they ushered in life-threatening trouble.

John rode to the front lines in an empty ambulance. The trip was a stark contrast to the chaotic ride to the convent. Night birds called from their perches in the trees overhead. The smell of rain hung in the air. It was almost peaceful, tranquil, if bombs had not marred the landscape.

He leaned his head out the door to see the moon.

There it was.

A sliver of crescent-shaped light nestled among the stars. God was still with him, with Samuel, with Private Greene, and with Mary, wherever she might be. He bowed his head and prayed that Samuel and Private Greene would recover quickly. He hoped the young boy would find his brother alive and as well as he could be in a POW camp.

He prayed for wisdom. What should he do with the information he overheard from the wounded Japanese soldiers? Doubt plagued him. He knew only a few words, and he couldn't be sure exactly what the men said, but their tone and behavior spoke of something ominous.

The head nun had told him to let it be, but that didn't sit well. He didn't want to think she'd keep information from the Allies, but enemies of the Allies took many forms.

John decided to say something to Lieutenant Brandon specifically, if the opportunity presented itself.

When the vehicle rolled to a stop near the front lines, he hopped down and looked up at the moon again. Peace settled over him. Amid the chaos in the world, he felt peace that God was in control.

He stumbled through the dark toward his foxhole, keenly aware of his friend's absence. Loneliness jabbed him. He pushed the feeling aside. Samuel would return soon. Until then, and always, he had Jesus as his friend and companion.

John hoped the enemy would decide against attacking tonight and give the Allies a much-needed break. Maybe tomorrow he could find a way back to the convent. He could visit Samuel and Private Greene and see if he could overhear anything else from the Japanese POWs.

A metal box of ammo thudded onto the sand by his foxhole.

Lieutenant Brandon said, "How's Samuel? Recovering fast, I hope. We need him here. One code talker won't do us much good."

"You can't find me a temporary replacement, sir?"

"Sorry." Lieutenant Brandon shrugged. "Don't think so, but I'm trying."

This didn't lend John any comfort. Could he crank the handle and man the headset at the same time? Never mind about returning fire. Big help the box of ammo was. "Can I go see him tomorrow? I'll ask Doc when he can return."

"Sounds good. I'll arrange a transport. We have a delivery scheduled anyway. You can ride with them."

Lieutenant Brandon turned to leave.

"Sir, one more thing." John informed him of the Japanese soldiers at the convent. Grim lines covered his commanding officer's face.

"Thank you, John. I'll take care of things," Lieutenant Brandon said.

This helped soothe John's anxiety. Tomorrow he could visit his friend and Private Greene. It also gave him the opportunity to eavesdrop on the Japanese soldiers. His mind whirled with ideas on how to move close to them and listen in. Perhaps he could speak with the head nun again, maybe squeeze her for information.

"Sleep tight." The lieutenant sighed, stepped away, and called over his shoulder. "I have work to do. Find me tomorrow if you still need to talk."

"All right, good night, sir," John replied. He stretched out the best he could in the cramped quarters and closed his eyes. If he was lucky, he'd sleep tonight without having to pick up his rifle and fire it.

Best keep listening for the clanging of cans on the trip wire around the perimeter.

Gunshot shattered the tranquil night air.

The racket of clanging cans cut through the air, as did Japanese voices.

Bullets pinged off the case of ammo sitting beside his foxhole.

He slapped on the radio's headset and cranked the handle until his forearm ached. If a runner handed him a message, he wouldn't have much choice but to relay the information the best he could.

Footsteps slapped the ground above him.

Panic engulfed him. Should he pick up his rifle, in case this was the enemy? Or was a runner delivering a complicated message for him to send? On his own?

A figure dived into the foxhole. He heard a few choice words in English. Thank the Lord, this wasn't a Japanese soldier. This person hadn't shoved a slip of paper at him, so he couldn't be a runner. Who was he?

The figure pulled off his helmet and grinned.

"Hello there, I'm Private Soaring Eagle. I just got ordered to help you."

John blew out a relief-filled sigh. "I remember you from class. Here, crank the radio."

Private Soaring Eagle took the proffered radio and cranked the handle with vigor. A smile creased the man's face, and his eyes twinkled with excitement. John remembered when he'd been so green, ready to take on the whole Japanese Army by himself. He wondered if this was the new recruit's first battle.

Voices cut through the night air, and a runner dived into the now-crowded foxhole. He handed John a slip of paper. Coordinates for bombing a cave filled with enemy soldiers.

The roar of US bomber planes filled the air.

Bombs whistled as they dropped onto their target. Flashes of light illuminated the inky black sky. A deafening boom reverberated through the air. The ground shook.

The runner said, "I was told they were close. Sounds like we got 'em."

Goose bumps prickled over John. How close had they advanced toward the enemy while he was at the convent? Perhaps he shouldn't go back tomorrow. The runner wiggled out of the foxhole and sprinted into the night.

An hour later the booms ceased, but the deafening sounds echoed in John's mind long afterward.

⫶CHAPTER 23⫶

In the convent's kitchen with Sister Abigail, Mary helped prepare breakfast for the wounded in their care. She told her about John and his thoughts regarding his God and the moon. Sister Abigail smiled and said John was a wise man.

"Excuse me a moment, please."

Mary ran from the convent and out into the courtyard. She stared up at the pre-dawn canvas above her and turned until she spied the moon. She found the shining orb in the far reaches of the horizon, about to kiss the world good night and disappear over the edge of the earth. It wouldn't rise again until the sun had scooted across the sky from east to west.

She remembered the night, not so long ago, when she and John had walked along the Southern California beach. She tried to imagine his God, the Creator of the universe, being with her always, even in the darkness.

Ambivalence flipped her emotions from one side to the other and back again, like a pancake on a hot griddle.

If God was real, then how could He allow such suffering in the world? Why had He allowed her people to be nearly decimated? Weren't they made in His image too? And thereby just as precious as any other human being? One couldn't tell by the way the Indians were discriminated against. At least that's what Sister Abigail said.

Mary had taken the time to write a long letter to John. She'd gone into great detail about her feelings about God. When finished, she'd given the missive to Samuel to give to John. She prayed the letter reached him all right, and that he'd understand.

"Lord, if You are really there, if You really care, then show me." The stars shone a bit brighter, twinkled for maybe a second or two, and then lapsed back to their original shine. Was this God's way of shining on her? Or had she imagined it? Maybe there was a celestial explanation, like shooting stars or something like that.

No matter. There was work to do. She hurried into the convent, determined to do everything in her power to alleviate as much suffering as possible. She headed to the sanctuary, intent on telling Private Greene that she'd met his brother in a POW camp. Handwritten notes might be too risky, but she could carry verbal messages between the two.

"There you are, Mary." Sister Abigail grinned, as if she knew the goings-on in Mary's head and what she was secretly planning. "Private Greene is asking for you."

Mary could hardly contain her excitement. "Yes, Mother."

"And, Mary," she continued, "when you are finished tending to the private, please check on the Japanese POWs. They seemed restless and need to be cared for too." She raised her eyebrows and dipped her chin in a slight nod.

Mary's cheeks heated. Compassion and caring filled this woman, and she expected Mary's behavior to reflect the same. "Yes, of course."

She filled a cart with medical supplies and pushed it to Private Greene's bed. She angled the cart so it created a barrier that others couldn't see around. One of the nuns might imply that it hinted at scandal, but that wouldn't bother her. Two brothers desperately needed to be in communication with each other, and she intended to facilitate the process.

"So"—Mary leaned close to the private—"I heard you asked for me. First, I need to tell you something, but you must keep it a secret. Do you understand?" She reached for his hand and unwound his old bandage, never taking her gaze from his.

Private Greene's eyes widened. He slowly nodded.

Mary peeked over the cart and glanced around the room. Most everyone in the sanctuary lay sleeping. She whispered, "I know where your brother is."

Private Greene yelped.

She slapped her hand over his mouth.

Again, she checked the room to see if they were being watched.

Thankfully, painkillers induced drowsiness. Everyone remained asleep. She leaned close to Private Greene and placed her index finger to her lips. "Shhh."

Private Greene clamped his lips together and nodded.

Mary whispered. "He's in a POW camp close to here. He's tending the wounded and seems to be in good health. Last time I was there, he wrote a note to your mother, and I smuggled it out for him."

Private Greene squeezed her hand. His eyes glistened with unshed tears. He swiped a hand over his face. "Thank you. Do you have the note? Can I see it?"

"Yes. I haven't been able to mail it. There's a war going on, you know."

The soldier grinned. "Yeah, there is. I wrote to Ma. I can put his note in with my letter."

"I think that's a splendid idea. I'll get it right now." She excused herself and bolted up the stairs to her room.

She pulled the note from her Bible, and an extra piece of paper from her notebook, and grabbed the pencil from her desk. She paused a moment, thinking maybe God had just answered her prayers. He had provided a way for her to get this precious bit of information into the hands of this man's family.

Warmth radiated through her, along with a joy she hadn't felt in a long time. She practically skipped down the stairs, and without tripping. Careful to avoid Sister Abigail, she slipped into the sanctuary.

Private Greene nearly yanked the scrap of paper from her fingers. His eyes seemed to devour the information scribbled there. A sob escaped from his lips. He kissed the paper then hugged it to his chest.

Happiness washed over Mary. She was truly joyous for Private Greene, but this moment also exacerbated the ache in her middle. How she longed for news of her brother.

Private Greene tucked the note in his pocket. "Thank you, Sister. I promise to guard this information. I won't tell a soul where I got this note."

"Thank you." She placed the blank sheet of notebook paper in his hand. "Here, write a note to your brother. I might not be able to hand it to him, but I can at least tell him what it says."

He took the paper and pencil. "When will you be going back to the camp?"

"I don't know. With the convent being used as a field hospital, we nuns are kind of needed here, but I'll do my best to get your note to him, and another one from him too."

"I understand. Thank you again. I'll let you know when I finish this."

Mary stood and patted his shoulder. "I must go now. I have other wounded soldiers to check on, and I need to help the sisters prepare breakfast."

Private Greene chuckled. "I'll have steak and eggs, please."

A soldier across the room stirred. "Did someone say we're having steak for breakfast? I want mine well done, please."

In the next bed, Samuel propped himself up on his elbows, his hair all askew. "Are we having steaks?"

Mary stifled a laugh. She didn't wish to wake those who needed their rest. Of all the things to rouse a man from deep slumber, it would be food.

"Sorry, fellas," she soothed. "We're not having steaks for breakfast, but there is an abundance of powdered eggs and Spam."

Groans reverberated through the room. One soldier placed a pillow over his head and turned over to face the far wall. Many men complained about the food the military served, but at least it kept them from starving.

She left the sanctuary and spent an hour treating the enemy soldiers. They spoke freely, but she was careful not to reply to their questions. If they knew she understood them, they wouldn't speak as freely about military matters. She smiled and nodded, hoping that helped them feel at ease.

She spoke soothingly as she changed their bandages and refilled the water pitcher on the nearby nightstand. Her ala's favorite hymn popped into her mind, and she hummed the tune because she couldn't remember the words.

She wished these men would speak about their commanding officers or where their troops were stationed.

Instead, they discussed their families in Japan.

Her heart dropped into her stomach. It was all she could do to keep her face stoic. When one of them reached for her hand and looked into her eyes, waves of compassion rolled through her. He spoke his name and patted his chest. Then he pointed a finger at her and asked her name.

She patted her chest. "I'm Mary."

He put his hands together in praying fashion, nodded, and said the words "Thank you."

In that moment they became more human to her and no longer enemy. He then pulled a picture of his family from his front pocket and showed her. She smiled at him and ran her fingers through his hair. How she could betray them?

Guilt pricked her spirit.

She struggled to tamp it down. As soon as the war was over, the dying would cease. She used hand gestures to indicate that she would return with food.

In halting English, another one of them said, "Thank you."

The needle of guilt drove itself deeper into her soul.

Catherine Brandon had trained her well, but she hadn't been prepared for this. She strode outside, thinking of John.

Dawn was breaking along with her heart. The promise of a new day was at hand. So were the impossible choices before her.

———————— ≈ ————————

John dug the remaining bits of Spam from the tin and shoved them into his mouth. The salty stuff wasn't too bad. He polished off the crackers and took a swig from his canteen. He dropped the wrappings in a garbage can. How long before the rats feasted on the crumbs?

He tried not to think about rats while sitting in a chair under a tent, staring at the landscape. Spring in the South Pacific meant relentless rain. Sure, everything was a lovely shade of green. He'd spotted several wildflowers he'd never seen before blooming in bright colors. But it didn't take long for his helmet to fill with rainwater during a torrential downpour.

Vehicles sank up to the axles in the mire. Canvas tents sagged under the weight of all the water and eventually collapsed. Rain slickers were nothing more than a feeble attempt at staying dry. Men waded through mud that reached their knees. Boots rotted and fell to pieces. Jungle rot was claiming more toes and heels than he cared to think about.

Did the Japanese soldiers have the same trouble with the mud? There hadn't been an assault for two whole days and nights. He almost hoped the underground caves flooded.

Regardless of the reason, he welcomed the break in the action.

The transport Lieutenant Brandon had scheduled wasn't able to return to the convent. It couldn't be helped. The roads had turned to rivers of brown quagmire, and no rigs moved. He missed seeing Samuel and Private Greene.

The lack of combat gave him extra time to study his Bible. He spent the morning putting his friends in God's hands. By placing the top of a crate atop two five-gallon gas cans, he'd created a makeshift table. Not the most comfortable desk, but it worked well enough to write a letter to his family. He wondered how often they thought of him. Ma had to be busy running the farm alone while his sisters were in school.

His letters to the reservation had to be censored, but hopefully not too much or his mother would worry even more than usual.

"Hey, Painted Horse, did you miss me?" Samuel ducked into the tent. He moved slower and his face lacked its usual color, but the smile gleaming in his eyes said he was glad to return.

John dropped his pencil and hugged his friend. "Yeah, I missed you."

Their laughter filled the air. John dropped into his chair. "We only had one skirmish while you were gone. Lieutenant Brandon found me a temporary replacement while you were gone, but that was two nights ago. We haven't seen any action since."

Samuel said, "Don't lose your cool when I tell you this, but Mary is at the convent. She asked me to give you this letter."

John yanked the missive from his friend's hands and tore the envelope open. The aroma of her perfume wafted up to greet his nose. He devoured the words on the pages. She was close by and relatively safe. It was enough for him for now, but first chance he had, he was headed back to the convent to see her.

Samuel dropped onto his cot. "I'll be glad to sleep aboveground and not in a foxhole tonight. I was worried about that on the way here. With all the rain we've had, it'd be like sleeping in a swimming pool."

"The only thing we're fighting now is boredom," John added.

"While I was at the convent, I heard that the Allies are advancing closer and closer to Berlin. We might have victory in Europe before we know it."

A mix of relief and hope coursed through John. If only things looked as optimistic in the Philippines as they did in France.

"Let's find Lieutenant Brandon and ask for an update on things here in the South Pacific." John tucked the letter to his family into his duffel bag.

"Nah, you go ahead." Samuel rubbed his stomach. "When will chow be ready? I'm starved."

"You must be fully recovered to be thinking of food again." John laughed. "Getting to the mess tent is a chore."

They stood and walked along boards that served as trails from company headquarters to the chow hall.

"It hasn't rained all morning. Maybe things will dry out a bit. The truck that brought me back managed all right." Samuel loped along, holding his stomach.

John slowed his pace. He'd have to continue praying for his friend.

The sound of arguing echoed from the officers' quarters.

"What on earth?" John couldn't distinguish what was being said, but the tone and the shouting indicated something terribly awry.

Several men stopped and stared at the direction of the commotion. More shouting, along with a string of curses, ensued.

Then he recognized the rough voice.

His Spam and crackers threatened to come up.

He walked forward for a better view of the officers' tent.

Emerging from the premises was Second Lieutenant Morton.

⟁CHAPTER 24⟁

Mary broke from her duties at the convent to deliver a truckload of supplies to the POW camp. She shifted the gears and steered around the corner without running over the green foliage. She was grateful to have learned to navigate her way around the island without getting lost.

Finding her way there didn't bother her, but the secret note tucked into her clothing gave her pause. If she was caught smuggling information in and out of the camp, the Japanese commander would execute her, nun's habit and robe or not. She shoved her fears aside. Connecting the two Greene brothers was worth the risk. Would she want someone to take such risks for her and Daniel? Uncertainty wound through her. Of course she wanted information about her brother, but if someone attempted to smuggle information about him and was caught and executed, it would haunt her for the rest of her days.

Barbed wire appeared ahead. Her pulse revved into high gear. She sucked in a breath and steadied her racing heartbeat. It shouldn't take more than an hour for the guards to check the supplies for contraband and for the prisoners to unload the supplies. The transfer of notes would take only seconds.

The truck rolled to a stop in front of the gates. She shut the engine off and climbed out. The camp's doors swung open. The commander greeted her.

The stench of uncared-for human beings and hopelessness wafted out to greet her as well. To her chagrin, she was becoming accustomed to the smell. She cringed. Never had she wished to become immune to such smells.

The men didn't seem as emaciated as they did on her first trip. For that she thanked God.

Wait. Was that considered a prayer? She had been thinking more and more about God in the last few days. Her heart reacted with a tiny buzz of joy.

She moved to the back of the truck, undid the latch, and lowered the tailgate. The short, pudgy guard met her there. He cracked open the boxes and fished through the contents. His pockets soon bulged with food, as well as a number of other things.

A sinister grin replaced his sneer.

Mary ducked her head to keep him from noticing her scowl. With resignation, she carried in a large crate filled with bottles of medicine.

Captain Greene approached. "Afternoon, Miss Wishram. It's good to see you." He looked better fed, healthier. His cheeks held more color than the last time she'd visited.

Once inside the medical hut, she whispered, "My convent has become a field hospital. Your brother is there, but he's fine." She handed the captain the letter from his brother. He shoved it into his pocket.

The pudgy guard marched into the area carrying a ten-pound bag of raisins. He dropped it onto the counter. He glared at the captain then turned his gaze on her. She forced another smile to her lips. Heaven help her if she said or did something that triggered suspicion.

The man fiddled with the handle of his sheathed bayonet and then strode toward the truck. She exhaled a shaky breath. Only then did she notice that Captain Greene had carried on as usual.

A moment later, the captain pulled a bottle from the shelf. He sat on the edge of a cot where an unconscious man lay. "Will you hold this soldier's head up so I can give him this, please?"

"Sure." Mary sat on the other side and lifted the slumbering man's head from the pillow.

"Does he know I'm here?"

"Yes." Mary glanced at the guards at the front gate. She dared not look at the ones in the high towers. It was difficult ensuring that no one watched them.

"Does he know that you're smuggling information?"

"Yes." It took every ounce of strength to keep from gawking at the guards stationed around the camp. Instead, she used her peripheral vision.

"Did you bring paper for me to send another note?"

"Yes." She dropped a package of tongue depressors on the floor. Captain Greene stooped to help her retrieve them. In the process, she smuggled him the paper.

They stood. She didn't scrutinize his movements but wondered where he'd hidden the paper she'd just handed him.

The pudgy guard strolled back inside the hut. Mary smiled, hoping it hid the anxiety cascading through her. Should she flirt with the man, to distract him or hopefully put him at ease? Or would he see through her charade and become more suspicious?

The guard reached for a handful of the raisins and popped them in his mouth. He eyed the captain. Mary squirmed as he studied her from the bottom of her boots to the top of the braid piled on her head in a bun.

"Hello," she said. Her cheeks heated.

He mumbled something in Japanese, glared at the captain, and sauntered outside.

Breath whooshed from Mary's lungs.

Captain Greene brushed against her, tucking his note into her hand. "Are you all right?"

She placed a hand to her chest, adjusted her robe, and tucked the note into her underclothing. "Yes, I'm fine. Thank you. I'll feel a whole lot better once I'm out of the camp and back at the convent where it's safe."

His mouth formed a thin line before he turned away. "That makes two of us."

How could Mary have been so flippant about her ability to leave the camp when the soldiers here didn't have that option? She could have kicked herself.

"I'm sorry," she mumbled. She joined the captain in sponging off the fevered soldiers' foreheads with a cool cloth.

"Don't worry about it." He drew near her again. "I need you to do us a favor if possible. Can you smuggle in a copy of *Stars and Stripes*?"

"Yes, I can. The ambulance drivers left several copies at the convent. The papers might be a few weeks old, but they're still news."

"Good." He nodded. "And in return, I'll find out what happened to your brother. I haven't heard anything yet, but I'll dig deeper. Deal?"

"Deal." She dared not shake his hand to seal the agreement or ask what means he'd use. He was a man of his word, and she trusted that he would get the job done without endangering his life or others.

The thought of finding Daniel planted hope in her soul and brought a smile to her face. Her mind whirled. Once the captain discovered which camp her brother was in, she'd approach Sister Abigail about taking supplies there. Once inside, she'd find her brother, and a way to rescue him!

She was one step closer to being with him. A small laugh escaped from her lips before she could rein it in.

"What are you two doing?"

Mary glanced up.

The pudgy guard stood in the doorway.

He spoke English?

Every hair on her body stood at attention. Had this man overheard anything between her and the captain?

A feline-like grin spread across the guard's face. "You are surprised I speak English, yes?"

Mary had lost her voice. Apparently, so had Captain Greene. She glanced at him. His mouth clamped shut, his jaw muscles twitched.

The guard burst into laughter. "You lovebirds, don't worry. Your secret is safe with me."

This guard thought she and the captain were romantically involved? Horror coursed through her. For the guard to think she'd carry on with someone she didn't know well, especially in a setting such as this, revolted her.

Had she somehow given the guard the wrong impression? Should she enlighten him about the misunderstanding? Would it anger him to be proven wrong?

The guard laughed and ambled from the area.

Captain Greene was beside her in an instant. "I know you're not that kind of girl, but I think this could work in our favor. If this clown thinks we like each other, he might afford us a few minutes of privacy."

"Excuse me?" Anger bubbled in her. She hadn't expected such behavior from this man. A snake like Morton, yes, but Captain Greene? Never.

The captain stepped back and shook his head. "I'm sorry, I didn't mean it like that."

"What *did* you mean?" He stepped so close, she smelled his perspiration.

"Privacy gives us opportunity to smuggle information, and possibly goods."

Yes, it did. At the risk of their lives. Was that a chance she was willing to take? If she refused, how could she sleep peacefully at night?

"I understand." He was right, of course. But that didn't mean she liked it. If he took dangerous risks to find her brother how could she not help him and these men in camp?

What if rumors circulated that she was sweet on this guy and John found out? It would break his heart. Though he was a man of faith, she could hardly believe he'd forgive her.

Could she risk his love, his heart, for a reunion with her brother? Could she risk losing John to gain Daniel's freedom?

She rubbed her thumb and index finger over her aching temples. Captain Greene dunked the ragged cloth into the bowl of water and continued to sponge off the fevered soldiers. He locked eyes with her, beseeching an answer.

"Okay, okay, but make sure nobody finds out."

"Don't worry." He held his hands up. "I can't have my wife back home thinking I've been unfaithful to her."

Knowing he had a wife eased her discomfort. He was risking the relationship with someone he loved, just as she was.

For the next hour she helped him serve the sick and wounded soldiers their dinner. The pudgy guard looked at her often and laughed every time. To continue fooling the guard, she stayed close to Captain Greene. They told jokes to each other to keep the mood light.

It was growing dark when she left camp. She'd been gone much longer than she anticipated. Sister Abigail might be angry. It was one of the many worries that tangled in her knotted stomach.

Anger boiled in John as he shoved his belongings into a knapsack. He handed Samuel the letters to his family and Mrs. Drake to mail in case he didn't return.

Mailing them himself would be best, providing he returned from this recon mission without being injured, or worse, captured. Neither of which looked like a good prospect considering the team leader.

Second Lieutenant Morton.

How could God send him directly into contact with that vile man again? How could any sane officer put this man in charge of anything, let alone a dangerous mission? John believed the man had insisted on taking the lead and requested John go along. What sort of revenge had Morton plotted?

He gritted his teeth as he painted black camouflage paint onto his face. Someone needed to operate the radio in case the Japanese attacked. Samuel and Private Soaring Eagle were staying behind. A small mercy.

Heavy footsteps and the clanking of weapons sounded outside his tent.

John paused, his senses heightened.

"Ready to go, Loverboy?" Morton snorted.

The man had the stealth of a charging buffalo.

John laced his tone with disdain. "Ready, sir." He reached for his rifle and unlocked the safety. To his satisfaction, the cocky grin on the second lieutenant's face fell. John stormed from the tent and glanced over his shoulder. Samuel gazed at him, concern emanating from his eyes. If John died, it would be tough on his friend.

John fell into line with Corporal Goshen. His heart did a belly flop into his middle. There were so many things that could go wrong. Lives were at stake.

John growled, "Let's get this over with."

Morton smirked and stuffed a cigar in his mouth. "Right this way."

Goshen and John followed the swaggering peacock to the debriefing tent.

Goshen paused, anxiety etched in his face. "Stay close to me, and if we run into any problems, do what I say."

"I will." John gulped. Each man knew what was expected of him, and each other. Though neither of them had spoken the government orders aloud, they both understood what was expected. Corporal Goshen was a compassionate man of God. John wondered if the man could follow through if faced with such a terrible choice.

They strode into the room and up to a table spread with maps. John studied everything closely, committing as much as possible to memory.

John hoped for a moment with Lieutenant Brandon, to check the validity of this mission, but he was nowhere to be seen. He shook his head and focused on the intelligence before him. Perhaps he'd be along shortly. Until then he needed to prepare for this operative.

He snuck glances at Corporal Goshen. Was he absorbing all of this? Too soon, the meeting adjourned.

"Where's Lieutenant Brandon?" John asked.

Morton stuffed another stogie between his lips. "On rest and recreation."

"Then let me speak to whoever is in charge." John gritted his teeth. He hated being polite, but he didn't want to be sent to the brig, or court-martialed, for being snarky either.

The second lieutenant stepped closer, his face an inch from John's nose. "He's away too, as if that's any of your concern."

John blew his breath between his teeth. Morton had planned this perfectly. Who knew what this deranged man had reported to the commanding officers above Lieutenant Brandon?

"Look, Morton," he said. "If you have something against me then so be it, but Goshen here doesn't deserve to die."

Morton turned the air blue with profanity. "Don't you tell me, how to execute a recon mission, or I'll have you court-martialed. Unlike your attempt on *me*, I can make the one against *you* stick."

John gritted his teeth. There was no arguing with this man. He focused his attention on performing his duties and praying he'd return to the base camp.

The second lieutenant strutted to the edge of the jungle. John followed. Trying to keep his voice low, he said to Corporal Goshen, "Stay close. We need each other."

The corporal's eyes smoldered with anger. "Roger that."

Blood drained from John's face. He fought against lightheadedness.

"I promise to do my best to bring you back alive." Goshen nodded.

John's faith prevented him from wishing harm on people, but if anything happened to their leader, they stood a better chance of returning unharmed.

When he turned, he faced Second Lieutenant Morton. The man stood directly in front of him, so close he smelled the stench of the half-chewed cigar hanging from his half-open mouth.

"Just so you know, you cocky wagon-burner, it won't break my heart one bit if you get captured by the Japs. I hear they got a POW camp not far from here. From what I hear, the place is almost as grand as the Ritz." The second lieutenant laughed loud enough to be heard in Tokyo.

"Let's just get this done." Although he and Goshen were much stronger, much more solid than Morton, he didn't dare start a fight, or this time he would be the one court-martialed. They left the base camp and traipsed deeper into the jungle.

John prayed and focused on scriptures that reminded him that fear was not of the Lord. It was from the enemy of his soul. He never expected to find such a formidable enemy in his own ranks, walking ten paces ahead of him.

John believed the man's mind was unhinged, but he wasn't the only danger surrounding them. Snakes and Japanese soldiers lurked about, waiting, probably hoping, to send them to their deaths.

Twenty paces later, they stepped into a clearing. John gazed at the sky, dotted with sparkling stars. There, directly above him and shining like a polished gemstone, the moon lit up the darkness.

God was, indeed, with him.

And he, indeed, needed God.

⩔CHAPTER 25⩔

Bombs exploded. The sound of crumbling stone filled Mary's ears. She bolted upright in bed, fear chasing her from her romantic dreams of John. She raced to the window, opened it, and stuck her head outside.

A mortar whistled through the air, followed by the sound of a palm tree splintering to bits. Pieces of trees, rocks, and coconuts rained down on the convent.

Screams echoing from the floor below ascended the stairs and sailed into her room.

The wounded soldiers. Private Greene. They must be terrified.

With a shudder, she threw on her robe and hurried downstairs to help.

Mother Superior stood in the foyer, barking orders and directing a group of medics to the sanctuary. She faced Mary.

"Another battle has commenced. More wounded are coming in."

Mary straightened her collar. "Shall I help the medics?"

"No. I need you in the basement running the radio. Relay our position to the Allies' commanding officers."

"Yes, ma'am. What of the wounded Japanese?"

"The MPs have already taken them. Now go, before we're blown to smithereens."

Mary raced into the kitchen. She pushed her weight against the table to move it, pulled up the rug, and then threw open the trap door. Quickly, she descended into darkness. Her hands shook so much it took three tries to light the candle. The flame pushed back the darkness. Relief flooded through her.

She cranked the handle on the radio and turned the knobs. In the secret code she'd created with Catherine Brandon, she relayed the convent's position, the number of bombs that had hit the structure, and the request for assistance.

The structure shuddered at the impact of another bomb.

Determined to be brave, she stifled her cries.

Bits of dirt and small rocks fell from above. A rat leaped from behind a wooden crate and darted into a small hole in the corner of the room.

More debris rained down. Several large rocks dropped from above and slammed into the radio. She grabbed it, not knowing if it had been rendered useless, and dove under the table. The rickety piece of furniture wouldn't do much to protect her, but it was something.

"Oh God," she cried, "if You are real, please keep us safe."

Minutes later, the bombing ceased. She waited. Her shaky breaths were the only sounds. She set the radio down, clambered from under the table, scaled the ladder, and emerged into the kitchen. Broken dishes and spilled food covered the floor.

She bolted into the sanctuary and bumped smack into a tall Marine. Her breath caught in her throat until she realized this man was not her John.

Her John.

He likely faced dangers such as this every day. That knowledge stirred an agonizing pain in her soul. She'd like to dwell on wonderful memories of him, but she had duties to fulfill.

She stopped a corpsman in the hallway. "Where is Sister Abigail?" she gasped.

"Not sure, miss. I'm busy evacuating the place."

"What?" Mary shuddered. They were leaving? Where was Private Greene? She had to find him! Pushing past, she raced into the sanctuary and into utter chaos.

Everyone who could walk assisted the gravely wounded on a mass exodus toward the ambulances outside. Shouts and pain-filled groans filled the air.

Mary reached for a nearby pew to steady herself. Then she stood on her toes and scanned the room.

In the melee of nuns and corpsmen rushing past her in a near panic, she saw Private Greene. He pushed a wheelchair holding an amputee toward the front door.

Mary caught up with him. "Give me the most recent note you scribbled to your brother. I'll find a way to get it to him. I promise."

His eyes were wide. He nodded and pulled several pages from his breast pocket.

Her head swam. This was a much longer letter than she'd anticipated. It wouldn't be easy smuggling a missive of this size.

Seconds later, the medics assisted the man in the wheelchair along with Private Greene into a waiting ambulance.

He waved. "Goodbye, Miss Wishram. I'll never forget you."

She returned the gesture and offered words of comfort. Had he even heard them? She had no way of knowing.

She assisted in the evacuation.

Then, as quick as the chaos had begun, it ended.

Afterward, a hush fell over the sanctuary. She turned a complete circle, twice. The room was empty. Had arrangement been made for her safe evacuation? Or had everyone gone off and left her? Should she run into the woods and hope the enemy didn't find her?

Sister Abigail popped into the sanctuary.

Mary's heart jerked and then beat again. She placed a hand to her chest, inhaling a deep breath. "I'm glad to see you.

"Get the radio. Meet me outside."

"Here, in case I don't make it." Mary handed Private Greene's letter to the woman.

"Hurry!" Sister Abigail turned and raced toward the front entrance.

Mary lifted her skirts to an unlady-like height and sprinted to the kitchen. She scrambled down the ladder and yanked the radio from under the table.

High-pitched whistling noises cut through the air.

More bombs?

A deafening explosion shook the convent. The structure groaned, as if it were in terrible pain. A cacophony of splintering wood, crashes, and rumbling echoed from above.

The place was about to come down around her ears.

She dove under the table and clutched the radio to her chest like a frightened child.

Chunks of dirt, rocks, and debris descended around her. The

basement's ceiling gave way.

"Oh God, please save me!"

———— ≈ ————

John crouched in the hole where he and Corporal Goshen hid. This mission was far from over, but at least they were still alive.

Deep in enemy territory, they needed to return to Base Camp before being discovered. The artillery and the fighter pilots needed the coordinates of where the enemy's caves were and how many big guns they had.

Goshen emerged and whistled a signal for John to come out, and then Goshen held his rifle at the ready and used his body as a shield for John.

"Follow me," the corporal whispered.

Second Lieutenant Morton had disappeared. John somehow felt safer. Reaching Base Camp without being killed or captured was his main concern. Goshen shouldn't be forced to kill someone, or be killed himself, because the second lieutenant wanted revenge.

The Japanese would use any means or method to extract the code from him. He didn't know how much torture he could withstand without cracking.

The two of them snuck through the brush. The saw grass sliced his uniform. Thankfully, not his skin. He feared leaving a trail of blood so obvious that Hansel and Gretel could follow.

He glanced around, comforted that Goshen was still with him. How much farther until they reached friendly territory?

He pulled his compass from his pocket, but the darkness was so deep he couldn't see the numbers on the face. He swiped the drops of sweat pooling at his temples. Humidity hung thick in the air.

He faced the heavens, searching for the moon. There was no sign of the shining orb. The North Star proved to be just as elusive. Gray clouds shrouded the entire canvas above him.

He closed his eyes and bowed his head. He refused to believe that God had abandoned him. That fact needed to remain at the forefront of his mind if they had any hope of staying alive.

Goshen crept forward. John nearly stepped on the man's heels.

The silence scrubbed roughly against his nerves.

"Goshen, where are you from?" he whispered.

"Nebraska."

"Any family?"

"My folks and two little sisters."

Warmth radiated from John's middle to his limbs. This man had family, a home, a life waiting for him, much like himself. He sure needed to reach Base Camp before anything tragic happened.

What seemed like hours later, they were still traipsing through the thick jungle grass. At least, he thought hours had elapsed. He couldn't know for sure since he couldn't see the numbers on his pocket watch.

How much longer before the sun came up?

A snake coiled around his boot. Without a sound, he pulled his knife from his belt and removed the creature's head. Goshen gasped and turned greener than the foliage.

"Don't worry. I killed a number of rattlers on my reservation." He sheathed his knife.

Then he froze.

Voices ahead.

Second Lieutenant Morton.

And Japanese.

CHAPTER 26

Mary slid her eyes open. Darkness wrapped itself around her like tentacles. She sucked in a gritty breath. At least she could still breathe. But for how long? Panic reached out and grabbed her by the ankles. She fought desperately for her sanity.

Where was she?

The memories clamped down on her. The ceiling had caved in. She was buried alive. Had Sister Abigail given her up for dead and fled the convent?

The poor woman probably thought Mary was dead. Nobody was coming to find her. She had to free herself before she ran out of air. She moved her arms, slowly at first to make sure they weren't broken. Feeling no pain, she wiggled her toes and tried to straighten her legs. She could only move so far before the debris around her shifted and threatened to bury her even deeper.

Could she call for help? Where was the radio?

Underneath her. Somehow, she managed to wiggle it free and donned the headset. The handle was bent. The contraption rotated a half revolution before getting stuck. Rocks had damaged it before the cave-in so it likely wouldn't work anyway.

Once again panic reached for her. The desire to live grew stronger with each breath. She shifted her focus from terror to climbing out from under the debris.

Mary laid her head against the broken table leg and thought of John. She couldn't allow herself to think she'd never see him again. She thought of the God he loved and worshipped. Would He hear her now?

"God," she prayed, "I'm sorry for being mad at You. I'm sorry for all my mistakes. Please forgive me. Please help me."

She breathed deeper, somehow. Peace enveloped her and her muscles relaxed.

Was that a shift in the debris around her?

Yes! The ground beneath her seemed to tremble a bit. She could move both her legs now without causing additional showers of dirt and rock. She managed to shove the broken table off her torso and sit partway up. Perhaps there wasn't much debris covering her.

Droplets of hope seeped into her soul.

Maybe John's God really had heard her prayers. Or was the earth's shifting a coincidence? Should she call out to Him again? What if she did and He didn't answer?

She had to try.

"God," she hollered, waiting and hoping. "I need You."

Peace like a cool, refreshing stream flowed into her. "If You help me get out of this, I promise to serve You all the rest of my days."

The earth rumbled again. Debris rained down. She used the table's top as a shield. Strangely, she felt no more panic. If she were to die, she sensed that she'd be with God and that He'd take care of John, her brother, and everyone else she loved.

A bomb whistled toward its target. Once again, the ground shook. More debris shifted. Dust settled, and then a gentle breeze blew into her surroundings. The earth's surface must not be too far above her. Could she dig her way out?

She lowered her tabletop shield, set it at her feet, and used both hands to scoop large handfuls of dirt and debris from above her. Then she placed it under her feet and tamped it down. Her mind hummed with the scriptures John had quoted during their last night together on the beach. "Jesus, You are the same, yesterday, today, and forever. Even if I can't see You, I trust that You are still with me, even in this dark place."

She continually placed the dirt, rocks, and splintered pieces of wood beneath her feet. Her hands were coated with grime. The cuts on her fingertips bled and created a slick, oozing mud as she clawed her way to the surface.

She refused to give up.

Before long, she could stand up straight. The breeze above her was stronger now. A large piece of concrete, likely part of the convent's wall, fell at her feet. Smaller pieces fell around her. One piece conked her on the head.

"Ouch!" She rubbed her aching temple. Her hand was sticky with blood when she pulled it away. That would not stop her. The tabletop shield proved useful again while pulling at the debris. A small mound formed at her feet. She stood atop it and kept working until she could hoist herself up a bit.

"Please help me, Lord Jesus." She shoved her toes into the dirt and climbed up another few inches. She reached above her head, grabbed a splintered beam, and pulled herself up another few inches.

Fresh air seeped into her surroundings, though it smelled like sulfur. Likely from exploding mortars.

Almost to the surface! She saw pieces of broken concrete through a small opening above her. The post where the convent's bell once hung still stood. Was the bell still standing? She couldn't see it yet to know for sure.

She pushed at the debris above her. Cold wind blew over her hand.

Frenzied and desperate, she scrambled upward faster. The small hole above her grew wider. She stuck both her hands through the opening and lifted herself up. She groaned, unable to fit her whole body through.

Frantically, she pulled at the dirt and rocks. Her hands and forearms were scraped and bloodied all the way to her elbows. Numb to the pain, she kept working at the opening.

The hole was finally big enough for her to climb through. She placed both hands on the earth's surface and hoisted herself up. She then flopped onto the surface and pulled her feet out of the hole. She closed her eyes and sucked in deep gulps of fresh air.

Blessed freedom.

Tears spilled onto her dirty cheeks.

"Thank You, God. Thank You," she cried.

She opened her eyes.

And saw moonlight.

———— ≈ ————

John didn't fight the Japanese soldier tying his wrists behind his back. Corporal Goshen lay sprawled on the ground, bleeding, likely near death. John clamped his jaw tightly shut. This was a nightmare created by Second Lieutenant Morton.

Fury colored his vision, but he couldn't fight back. Not yet. Fighting back would get him killed. He'd best pray and wait for an opportunity to escape.

If he remained in captivity, horrific torture was sure to come.

Unless he escaped. His chances were greater if he stayed calm and focused.

He gazed at the shining orb in the sky.

As far as he could tell, these were two Japanese scouts on patrol. They were likely on a recon mission, much like he'd been with the corporal and the second lieutenant. If these enemy soldiers believed Goshen was still alive, they'd run their bayonets through him.

Therefore John looked everywhere but at his former bodyguard. He prayed for the man who had become a friend to him, that he would live and be found by the Allies.

One combatant barked orders through clenched teeth. John locked eyes with him. The man shouted and motioned for him to stand. It wasn't easy with his wrists tied. John's head ached where they'd hit him.

The man prodded John in the back with a bayonet. Sweat coated his forehead, but he stumbled forward.

The man's chest heaved, and the hard lines of his jaw were evident. He shouted at a very young soldier who didn't look old enough to pass grammar school. The kid mumbled something John didn't understand. The infuriated officer then beat the kid with a bamboo stick.

John ducked his head. *God, if I die, please take care of my family.* He almost wished he had Mary by his side. She could make sense of what these men were saying.

They traipsed deeper into the jungle. John silently asked God to give him strength to endure whatever lay ahead. As they marched forward, he did his best to leave footprints and traces that someone could follow. Twice, he intentionally fell to the ground, breaking as much brush as possible.

He kept this up until the officer jabbed him with his bayonet. John winced. A small circle of blood created a wet circle on his shirt. He'd have to be more subtle about leaving a trail.

Gunfire erupted.

He dove to the ground and rolled under a thicket of brush.

The cruel Japanese man dropped to the ground as blood gushed from his chest. More gunfire cut through the air. The young soldier fell. Blood gushed from his stomach. He curled into a ball.

John scooted deeper under the brush.

His shoulder scraped against a sharp rock. He stifled a cry of agony and seized the opportunity. Though pain radiating through him, he rubbed his bindings against the stone's edge. The rope fell off.

In the chaos, John was lucky to escape injury. It was a miracle he wasn't shot.

A group of camouflaged soldiers sprang from the brush on the hill next to John. They tugged him up the hill and into the bushes.

One soldier spoke with an Australian accent. "Come this way."

This had to be the resistance group.

The Australian sheathed his knife and scrambled into the bushes where there was no trail. Several Filipino soldiers, with leaves and branches tucked into their helmets and clothing, joined them.

"Where are we going?" John whispered.

The Australian shushed him and then pointed north. They continued until they reached a clearing. A group of men sat around a fire burning in the base of a hollowed-out tree trunk. The smoke drifted up through the hollowed-out tree and lingered among the branches.

Smart thinking, John thought. This tactic helped prevent the enemy soldiers from detecting them.

The smell of food wafted in the air. John's stomach growled. How long had it been since he'd last had a meal? He was handed a bowl of stew and sat down to eat.

An American officer sat beside him. Bruises covered the man's face, and rope burns circled his wrists. *But for the grace of God. . .* John shook the thoughts from his mind.

"I'm Captain Greene." The officer handed him a sandwich. "I was held captive in a POW camp until it was liberated by the Australians."

"Thank you for rescuing me. I don't know how much longer I could have survived." John bit into stale bread spread with a thin layer of sauce he didn't recognize and a slice of meat that definitely wasn't Spam.

"Me either. I've been unable to reach the Allies, so I joined the resistance."

"I might be able to get us back to my unit," John said. At least, he hoped he could reach his unit.

"I hoped you'd say that."

"As long as I have a map and a compass, I should be okay."

Captain Greene said, "I'm going with you."

That sounded good to John. He missed Corporal Goshen already. A second set of eyes and a smart mind would aid his efforts to reach the Allies. And help protect him from enemy soldiers.

Captain Greene eyed him warily. "Those two would have tortured you to see what you know about strange messages humming across the radio waves."

John swallowed his bite of food. It didn't go down easy, but he thanked God for it all the same. "How did you guys find me?"

The man chuckled. "A man stumbled into our camp claiming he was lost. A real blowhard. Says his name is Morton."

John emitted a weary sigh. So that was what had happened to him. At least he hadn't been captured by the enemy. Morton wouldn't have thought twice before ratting out John and the code. He ought to be charged with treason.

The captain continued. "We let him talk. Learned where you were headed. We got to you as soon as we could."

John shivered. "Thank you, again."

Captain Greene grinned. "We didn't mind taking out a few enemy soldiers."

Everyone laughed at the joke. Relief flowed through John, thankful to be spared the horrors of a POW camp.

Captain Greene's expression turned serious. "We can't let the enemy capture you."

John nodded and took another bite. The more he chewed, the more time he had to formulate a response. He couldn't say much, but he had to say something. He swallowed and wiped his hands on his pants. "I am privy to classified information. I can't share it. You understand, right?"

A smile curved across the man's tanned features. He placed a hand on John's shoulder and squeezed. "I sure do."

"Good," John replied. "So you understand that, yes, I cannot get captured."

"Which is why we rescued you. Now let's find our way to your unit. How good are you at traveling by the moon and the stars?"

"I think I can do all right. How many soldiers are there?"

"Oh, we're not all going with you. Most of them would rather stay in the brush and fight guerilla warfare–style. We thwarted the enemy's supply chain twice last week." Captain Greene pointed at the ragtag group of men. They grinned and waved.

John understood. "That's probably best. I don't think I could lead the whole lot of you through the brush. We'd leave a trail a mile wide right to Base Camp."

A pain-filled groan cut through the air. He flinched. "What was that?"

Captain Greene emitted a deep sigh. "We found him locked in a hole, badly beaten, starved, and talking to himself."

"The poor man. Sounds like he needs a doctor." John cringed.

"I am a doctor." Captain Greene looked indignant.

John continued. "I'd love to take him with us, but there are risks to that."

An injured soldier might slow them down, increasing their chances of being recaptured.

But how could he go off and leave an American soldier stuck in the midst of danger?

"I know what you're thinking, but we're taking him with us. I owe it to his family—or what he's got left of his family."

Captain Greene had almost called him a coward, and that didn't sit easy. He squared his shoulders and sat straighter. "Why do you owe this guy? Did he save your life?"

"I said I owed his family. He's going with us, and that's an order."

John was shocked to see the man pull rank but thought better of arguing. He figured the wounded guy must be really important, like maybe a general's kid. "What's this guy's name, anyhow?"

Captain Greene stood and nodded his head at a small brush-covered tent. "Said his name is Wishram."

⧱CHAPTER 27⧱

Mary gazed at the Japanese boots on the ground in front of her. She had barely escaped being buried alive, suffocating, and starving to death. Now she was being captured by enemy soldiers?

The two men shouted at each other. She had never claimed to know Japanese fluently, but in this case, it didn't matter. These men spoke so fast her mind couldn't keep up.

She snuck glances at them. They were so animated she almost wanted to laugh had she not thought they'd shoot her.

The lone officer in the bunch grabbed hold of the ripped and filthy habit she wore and hoisted her to her feet. The few words she was able to understand sent shivers running the length of her spine. The officer wanted to take her to his commanding officer as a prize.

The next part of the conversation became civilized. The young one said no good could come from harming an innocent woman of faith.

Mary kept her head down—meek and subservient, just like in the POW camp. She couldn't allow these men to know she understood parts of what they said.

The officer jabbed her in the back with the butt of his gun.

The air flew from her lungs, and pain reverberated through her rib cage.

Helplessness washed over her, followed closely by anger. What she'd give for a weapon right then. She'd show these cruel enemy soldiers what she was made of.

And probably get shot for it.

The officer grunted in English, "Walk."

She did as she was ordered but not before aiming her fiercest scowl at him. As she stumbled forward she made so much noise she hoped people heard all the way to Manila.

Minutes later, sweat beaded on her forehead at the exertion, wetting the hair at her temples and forehead. She slowed her pace, praying the officer wouldn't be angry with her. Perhaps he'd think she was simply savoring her last moments of freedom. At least, the last bits of freedom she'd enjoy for a while.

She allowed herself to reflect on her fate.

Maybe it wouldn't be so bad to enter a POW camp, especially if Daniel were there. It would make for a bittersweet scenario. At one point, she'd sworn she'd stop at nothing to find him, rescue him, and bring him home safe. She'd always dreamed of a joyous reunion, but not one that had her imprisoned as well.

The Allies were gaining ground every day. How much longer could the war go on? She bucked up her chin. If necessary, she could survive a few months in a POW camp. All she had to do was keep her head down, obey orders, and refrain from foolish activity. She refused to contemplate which torture would be worse, the physical or the emotional and mental.

She shifted her gaze to the still shimmering moon in the heavens and focused on more hopeful topics. Could she be headed to the same camp with Captain Greene? Or Daniel?

Maybe she wouldn't be imprisoned at all.

Lost in thought, she stumbled on her hems and fell. The officer cursed at her. She hopped to her feet and continued, though it wasn't easy in her long, heavy garment.

It wasn't like she could remove the thing. She had underclothing on but cringed at the thought of traipsing through the jungle like that. Heaven only knew what kinds of bugs and mosquitoes would feast on her flesh without the protection of her robe.

She tried not to be frustrated with her encumbering clothing. The heavy robe would keep her warm that night. It was difficult, though, to remain optimistic considering her circumstances.

In desperation, she prayed. "God, be with me and please help me."

"Silent!" the officer ordered.

Mary clamped her mouth closed. All those trips up and down the convent's stairs proved beneficial. Her legs were in excellent shape, and she kept up with her captors without difficulty.

But how much farther did they have to go?

The sun was creeping over the eastern horizon. She dared to pause and admire God's handiwork. The moon had long since slipped below the western sky. There would be no more sign of it until twilight, but she wasn't dismayed. She didn't need to see it to be reminded of the Lord's presence.

They stopped for breakfast. She plopped onto the ground. The officer built a small fire and glared at her as if he wished to drop her into the cooking pot along with the rice. She wished she could shrink in size and disappear underground like the mess of ants crawling nearby.

The officer stalked into the brush. One of the kinder enemy soldiers tended to the fire and the pot of rice.

Seeing the human side of him reminded her of the wounded Japanese she'd cared for at the convent. What had become of them? Memories of the Takahashi family drifted into her mind. Because of them, she understood that not all Japanese were the enemy. If only the United States government would come to believe the same and release them from the internment camps.

Her thoughts jumbled, and her head ached. Blowing out a deep breath, she closed her eyes and leaned against a palm tree trunk.

The smell of cooked rice drifted into the air. The commanding officer returned and scooped a small portion onto a dirty plate and handed it to her. She bowed her head and gave God thanks for the meal, meager though it was.

When she raised her head she noted the guard scowling at her. She sat straighter, refusing to allow his disdain to keep her from reaching out to God.

The rice was bland. She ate because she needed sustenance. What she didn't need was to faint from hunger. The prisoners at her future residence would need her to be strong. She thought about the different kinds of things she'd share with them, about life in the States, music, movies, and how the Allies were advancing.

Her heart fluttered in her chest when she thought about her time in the States. She remembered her time at Camp Pendleton with John. That walk on the beach on New Year's Eve, had that really been only a few short months ago?

When she finished eating, they resumed their trek. They hadn't been on the trail for more than a few minutes when she heard a rustling in the bushes alongside her.

She paused, listening, but heard nothing more.

Was the noise simply her heart hammering in her chest? A figment of her imagination? Or was she about to be rescued? Perhaps it was something more sinister, like additional enemy soldiers to contend with—ones who were even more ruthless and unscrupulous.

The officer struck her in the ribs again. This time more forcefully. She cried in pain and fell to the ground again. "Please, God, don't forsake me."

The officer roared, "Silent!"

She rose to her feet with what little dignity she had left.

Hours later, they were still walking. Her tattered footwear wouldn't last much longer. If the things fell to pieces, what would happen to her feet? She silently prayed they'd reach their destination soon. Her legs were beginning to ache anyway, and hunger knotted in her stomach.

The sun dipped into the horizon, casting eerie shadows through the jungle. The moon would appear soon, a peaceful reminder of God's presence. Dizziness swept over her in spite of that knowledge.

Once again, she fell to the ground.

The officer roared at her and slammed his weapon into her ribs for the third time that day.

She cried out in agony as tears swam in her eyes. How much more must she endure?

"Get up!" the man shouted.

She slowly rose to her blistered feet and focused on a scripture John had once mentioned.

"Be strong and courageous."

Lifting the hem of her robe and her chin, she stepped forward into a fate known only to God.

John stared at Mary's brother, hardly believing it. He had spent the day talking to him, explaining what his sister had been doing before he had been shipped out. He didn't have any updates on her.

Daniel's dark eyes mirrored Mary's. How overjoyed she would be to know he lived and no longer resided in a POW camp. If only he had a way to reach her with the news.

John wished he could have relaxed under the trees all day, but he had to lead this ragtag crew to safety. Once they reached Base Camp, he'd find Lieutenant Brandon. Then they'd find a way to alert Mary. If he had paper and a pencil, he'd write the letter that moment and find a way to send it to the convent. Of course, Daniel would want to write to her and see her soon too. He contemplated sending a letter to Mrs. Drake and updating her on the situation.

He raked his fingers through his grimy hair. So much of what transpired was classified information. Lieutenant Brandon would have to decide what could be shared with whom.

"Lord, I miss her," he grumbled.

Mrs. Drake had proved good at her word and had sent him two letters. He had to believe she was writing to Mary as well.

The Allies were advancing, but at great cost and far too slowly for his liking. The band of resistance fighters could only do so much, though their mighty hearts brimmed with courage. Captain Greene approached with a bowl of stew made from a wild pig they had slaughtered early that morning. The men would eat well for a few days, at least.

John sat near the fire, gave thanks for his meal, and ate. The food was tasteless on his palate. He needed his strength, so he finished it. Though his stomach craved additional sustenance, he sought privacy to pray.

For the next hour he sat on a boulder, praying and waiting for the sun to sink into the western horizon. The atmosphere grew darker. The moon peeked over the eastern skyline. There was no sense in delaying the inevitable. He headed toward the other men.

"Time to go." He checked his gear to ensure he had enough water to last a few days. Captain Greene did the same. Then, they helped Daniel with his gear.

Daniel appeared much stronger than yesterday, in heart, body, and mind. John would bet the guy was as determined to see Mary as she had been to see him.

That was a blessed answer to prayer. John didn't know how long it would take to reach Base Camp, but he needed to be strong in case it took several days.

The men shook hands and were saying their goodbyes when a growly voice cut through the still, quiet night. John's stomach rolled a few somersaults. The chances of leading the men to Base Camp plummeted.

Second Lieutenant Morton emerged from a nearby tent.

John scoffed. "Where has he been this whole time?"

"Sleeping it off." Captain Greene aimed a sneer at the man.

The second lieutenant's face flushed and coated with a layer of sweat.

John smelled the man before he reached them. Even though the blowhard had been demoted, he still outranked John.

There was no way Morton could come along. They didn't trust him. John gazed at Daniel and the captain. Worry etched their features. That didn't seem to matter to the second lieutenant.

Morton marched up to John and jabbed a finger into his chest. "You backstabbing Indian. If you think I'm going to let you take charge of this mission, you're crazy."

Captain Greene stepped between them. "Morton, *I* outrank *you*, so *I'm* in charge of this mission."

The captain obviously understood the importance of getting Daniel Wishram to the hospital for care. John shuddered, imagining the damage Morton would do to Daniel's fragile mind. The second lieutenant puffed out his chest and placed his paws on his ample hips.

Captain Greene didn't waver. He stood his ground, eying the man with a hard glint in his eyes. John almost hoped a fight broke out. Captain Greene would flatten Morton like a pancake.

Morton waved a hand at Captain Greene and snorted. "Fine."

Whispering another prayer, John glanced at the night sky. No sign of the moon. He reminded himself that moon or no moon, he had a job to do.

His stomach rolled again as the party stepped deeper into the brush.

⊒CHAPTER 28⊒

Mary traipsed through the thick brush. Blisters on the soles of her feet popped and bled. Waves of heat beat down on her and her captors as they trod along. The once-white robe now hung filthy and tattered about her frame.

The heavy garment absorbed the heat like a dry sponge after a rainstorm. At times it seemed like the world spun before her. Fearing her captors' rage and their penchant for revenge, she dared not grumble or complain.

Hacking at the thick vines that hung from the trees made for slow progress. Sweat poured from the brow of the enemy soldier in front of her doing the work. The commander walked behind her, his rifle poking her in the back whenever she slowed her pace. She knew deep psychological scars when she saw them, and she sensed one in him. Part of her pitied him.

Later, through her raw and parched throat, she cried, "Water, please." She spoke English so they wouldn't suspect she spoke Japanese.

They stared at her, without moving to assist her. She assumed they didn't understand, so she made motions of drinking and prayed they understood. The kind guard who had shared rice handed her his canteen.

The cool water slid down her throat. She replaced the lid and smiled at the guard as she returned the canteen.

"Thank you," she said.

He merely nodded.

At every house they passed, the commanding officer demanded food from the Filipinos. Many were old and sick. A few had small children in tattered clothing. Most of them were emaciated and frightened. The parents of the children begged for mercy, but the officer ignored their cries.

These were innocent people who hadn't asked the war to visit them. Mary refused to eat food meant for small children and those who were sick, weak, or elderly.

Still, she apologized to those they had taken supplies from. If the officer understood her, she no longer cared what he thought.

Hours later, the sun sank toward the horizon. In the twilight she noted a small village ahead. She hoped they could stop for the night. How nice it would be to sleep in a real bed instead of on the cold, sometimes wet, ground where snakes and bugs abounded.

As they drew closer, she heard the joyous sound of children laughing and playing. She paused to watch the little ones enjoying an afternoon seemingly untouched by the horrors of war. Her heart warmed to see such happiness.

To her horror the officer snarled at the children.

Then he spoke to his men. Mary's blood nearly froze in her veins. He wanted them to open fire on the children!

Her anger escalated to rage. He was cruel for the sheer sport of it. Terror filled her.

"Lord Jesus, please protect these children," she cried.

The officer turned toward her and shouted. She dared not shout back or he would kill her.

A terrifying thought slammed into her.

This man wouldn't just kill her. He would torture her first and enjoy every minute of it, and then he would kill her. If she wanted to live, she must escape. But how?

A clanging bell drew her attention. An elderly woman stared wide-eyed at them and called the kids into a thatched-roof building that resembled a schoolroom, though it could have been a church or an orphanage. It was late in the day for classes, so Mary assumed they were there for other purposes.

The officer shouted at her.

Soon the sound of the children singing wafted out to greet her ears—probably led by the elderly woman as a means to distract the children from fear of the enemy's presence. In spite of Mary's precarious predicament, she enjoyed the music

She would have loved to stand there and listen to the singing, but the officer moved to face her directly, his nose mere inches from hers. His black eyes emitted such rage and loathing her stomach churned.

She held her head high, unwilling to give him the slightest impression that she feared him. She would not allow this man to break her. If he struck her, she'd fight the urge to defend herself, or he'd kill her.

One thing solidified in her mind—escaping was not only the only road to freedom, but the only way to stay alive.

The officer spun on his heel, yanked a grenade from his belt, and waved it in her face.

What on earth?

Was he a suicide bomber? Willing to blow them all up?

He stormed toward the building filled with children.

Was he going to—No!

She had to stop him from throwing that grenade at innocent children. Her gaze flew to the two guards. Their eyes widened with horror, but they did nothing. She couldn't overpower him without a weapon.

A rock the size of a baseball lay at her feet. She picked it up.

He turned to face them, shouted something about the emperor, and pulled the pin.

Smack!

The rock hit him between the eyes.

Unsteady on his feet, he stumbled backward.

His arms flailed in the air.

He fell, dropped the grenade. . .

Her mind screamed.

Run!

John hissed at Morton for the fourth time. "Keep your voice down, you idiot, unless you want to alert every Japanese soldier on the island of our presence."

The ground shook as an explosion thundered through the air. About a half mile away an orange ball of flames lit up the night sky.

Captain Greene yanked Daniel Wishram under a thicket of brush. John squeezed in behind them. Morton tumbled under as well, landing on John in the process. Pain shot through John's ankle. He stifled a yelp.

The clumsy oaf!

With his body pressed to the cold, wet ground, he closed his eyes. The sickly smell of smoke wafted through the atmosphere. He listened intently. Was the enemy near? If so, would they hear them?

Long, slow minutes ticked by.

There were no more explosions or strange voices.

Not a sound. Exercising caution was still necessary, if they wanted to live.

The pain in John's ankle subsided to a dull ache. "Don't make a sound. The Japanese must be close by."

Morton scoffed and rolled his eyes at the pitch-black canvas above. Mary apparently hadn't knocked any sense into him when she bashed him in the head with that cigar box. Captain Greene and Daniel glared at Morton. They had been imprisoned once by the Japanese. They definitely didn't wish to be captured again.

Several tense minutes passed. When John shifted his weight to his ankle, he gritted his teeth in agony. He ignored the pain, but he realized his ankle might be badly injured.

Everything from midcalf down throbbed. It was at least sprained, possibly broken. Leaning against Daniel, he hobbled from the hiding place, doubting his ability to move quickly through the jungle.

Morton grumbled as he crawled from the space. He fell, cursed loud enough to be heard by the enemy, and then rose to his shaky feet. John almost wished he could hand the buffoon over to the Japanese. Not tonight.

Without the stars to guide him, he pulled a compass from his pocket. Captain Greene stepped forward and removed his rain poncho. Careful not to put weight on his leg, John squatted under the garment with his comrade, who clicked on his flashlight.

Once John had his bearings and was able to gain a sense of where they were, he could hardly keep from shouting praise to the Lord. The captain clicked off the flashlight, and he and John emerged from under the poncho. Captain Greene donned it again.

"Good news." John danced about two steps before shooting pain in his ankle reminded him of his injury. Filled with hope, he pointed west. "Base Camp is three miles that way."

Daniel blew out a soft whistle. "We can be there in less than an hour if we hustle."

Captain Greene gazed at John's foot. Hustle wasn't an option tonight. This was a time for slow and steady. John hoped it would be enough. Determination to reach safety superseded his agony.

"Come on, men, let's go." With Captain Greene's assistance, John hobbled along not far behind Morton and Daniel.

With each painful step, the throbbing in John's ankle grew worse. If it was broken and he continued walking, would he injure it further? Enough that he might lose the limb? The possibility frightened him. He pushed it from his mind. What choice did he have? It wasn't like he could sit and wait for the rest of the group to reach camp and send a vehicle for him. He had to keep going, injured or not.

He listened for sounds coming from camp: the hum of a running Jeep, laughter of those engaged in a lively game of cards. The likelihood of hearing anything was slim because, unlike Second Lieutenant Morton, the men were smart enough to keep quiet at night. They probably wouldn't see any lights or signs of life either, until they were much closer. Hope was a powerful force. He chose to look for those signs anyway.

"One mile down, two miles to go." John tucked his compass into his pocket.

They had gone only one mile? He groaned. Not just from the pain. At this slow pace, they wouldn't reach their destination until dawn. The temptation to stay behind and send them ahead warred with his pride and desire to see his friends in camp as soon as possible. Especially Samuel. His friend had to be worried.

But his injury sapped his strength, and his slow plodding placed the whole team in danger of being discovered by the enemy.

How much farther was it anyway?

Second Lieutenant Morton tripped on tin cans tied to the string circling the perimeter. He cursed and thumped to the ground.

Gunfire cut through the darkness.

A smoldering bullet burned into John's injured leg.

⫷CHAPTER 29⫸

Mary jerked awake to the sound of clanging pans. How long had she slept?

Though her senses were on keen alert and her eyes open wide, she couldn't shake the nightmare of the previous night.

The grenade had blown the Japanese officer to smithereens. The young guard had told her to run. She had scrambled through brush and into a creek, which had brought temporary relief to her blistered feet, before scrunching herself under a thicket of brush.

Though her muscles ached, she was safe for the moment.

The aroma of cooking rice wafted through the air.

A pair of enemy soldiers discussed American troops and where they were located. She stayed hidden. And listened.

They mumbled phrases she didn't recognize. Then they spoke of their families. Silence was crucial to keep from alerting them to her presence. If they found her and discovered she knew what they said, they would kill her.

Finally, they finished their meal and sauntered off into the brush.

Mary dared not move. Her muscles cramped at being balled up for so long. When the pain became more than she could stand, she peeked from her hiding spot. She couldn't see a soul in sight. She slowly emerged from hiding.

Dawn was beginning to color the eastern sky with light, though gray clouds loomed in the heavens.

Mary was immediately grateful that God had directed her to hide where she did. Otherwise she wouldn't have overheard information vital to the Allies. Finding the Allied headquarters was even more important now.

Could she reach them without being discovered by the Japanese?

"Thank You, Lord, for hiding me in the shelter of Your wings." How had these scriptures popped into her mind so easily? John had quoted them often, but it amazed her how well she remembered them.

Hunger twisted her stomach into a mass of tangled knots. One small bowl of the rice that she'd had the day before wasn't enough to sustain her. When she pushed herself forward, a bout of dizziness swept over her. The earth seemed to tilt sideways before it righted itself again.

"Lord, give me strength." She leaned against a palm tree and closed her eyes. Blood flowed into her shaky limbs, and she managed to stay upright until the dizziness passed.

The enemy soldiers hadn't returned. If her luck held, they wouldn't.

She needed to find the Allies fast, but she had no idea where she was. The Americans could be within a half mile away, or an entire Japanese battalion could be over the next hill.

Contemplating the matter would do no good. She was determined to deliver this information to the commanding officers for the Allies. Giving up was something she refused to consider. Her resolve strengthened. Catherine Brandon would be proud.

She blew out a breath and took stock of her surroundings.

The sun rising in the east warmed the left side of her face. She reached her left hand toward the sun. So, west was to her right. She lifted her right hand. That meant her back was to the north, and south lay directly in front of her.

The American troops had landed on the south part of the island and were pushing north. If she pushed forward, she'd eventually run into them, providing she didn't run into any enemy soldiers along the way.

She strode forward. "Go with me, Lord. Lead me in the direction You want me to go."

Later, as the sun beat down in sweltering waves, her parched throat cried for water. The knots of hunger in her stomach tied themselves tighter. She needed food and water soon if she were to reach the Allies and give them the information she'd overheard from the Japanese soldiers.

The sun edged toward the west. Though she had no food or water, she plodded on. Her thoughts drifted. She dreamed of cool waterfalls and tables laden with food, like the Brandons' house on Christmas Day. Had that really been only a short time ago?

The sound of rushing water met her ears. She stumbled toward it, though a sick stench filled the air. The smell intensified as she reached the creek's edge. Noting the dead body of a Japanese soldier in the water, she slapped a hand over her mouth to keep from being sick.

This creek offered no relief from her thirst.

Disappointed but undeterred, she placed one blistered foot in front of the other. Her nun's robe hung in tatters over her aching, sweat-coated body. She gritted her teeth and swallowed every few seconds to coat her parched throat. Every time she licked her chapped lips, pain radiated through them. It wouldn't be long before they bled, if they weren't doing so already.

Voices cut through the air.

Her exhausted mind was unable to decipher if they were friendly or not.

She curled under a thicket of bushes.

Her aching legs protested at being pulled into a ball again.

Was she to spend the day scrunched into a small space, like she had the night before? Or was she about to become a POW once again?

———— ≈ ————

Fog surrounded John. He tried to run, but his legs were tangled in sheets. Why were sheets wrapped around his legs? He tried to kick free. Red-hot pain surged through his leg.

The enemy was hot on his tail.

Bullets flew through the misty air.

He screamed.

Sat up in bed.

A bed?

He glanced left then right. No Japanese soldiers surrounded him.

It had been another nightmare.

Sweat ran down his forehead but didn't hamper his vision enough to keep him from seeing that his leg was still attached to his body, although heavy bandages wrapped around it.

"Thank You, Lord." He'd seen plenty of soldiers who weren't as fortunate. Though pain radiated through his limb, he was grateful. It served as a constant reminder that he was very much alive.

When his breathing steadied, he closed his eyes and prayed. "Thank You, Lord, for sparing me and allowing me to keep my leg."

He raked his fingers through his hair, certain that it was a mess. It needed a good scrubbing at least. He glanced about the hospital ward to locate an orderly.

A nun hurried toward him. He recognized her as the head nun from the field hospital where he'd taken Samuel a few weeks ago.

"There, there, Mr. Painted Horse. You are safe now."

"Where am I? And, I'm sorry, but I didn't catch your name last time I saw you."

She smiled. "I'm Sister Abigail. You're in a hospital on the southern part of Luzon. The rest of the men who were with you are safe. Your friend Samuel is a hero." She sat on the edge of his bed and fluffed his pillow.

"How so?" John asked.

She offered him a wan smile. "He snuck out after you and found Corporal Goshen wounded. He brought the man here."

John raised himself up on his elbows. "Is he all right?"

She nodded. "He has a head wound, but he will recover."

He relaxed and laid back. "Thank God for that answer to prayer."

An audible growl resounded from his stomach. How long had it been since he'd eaten? He'd need to regain his strength before he showered.

Sister Abigail spoke soothingly and tucked the cool sheets around him with tender care. His thoughts drifted. Visions of Mary danced in his mind. How happy she'd be to know her brother lived.

"Thank you, Sister." He placed his hand over hers. "Is Mary here? Can I see her? She'll want to know that her brother is alive and that she can see him."

Sister Abigail chewed her lower lip. "Mary isn't here at the moment. That's all I can say for now." She patted his hand. "I imagine you'd like something to eat. I'm afraid all we have is soup."

His stomach clenched, and it had nothing to do with being hungry. Sister Abigail seemed to be hiding something. He wanted to ask a few pointed questions but understood the need for keeping classified information classified. That didn't mean he had to like it.

He shifted his weight to a more comfortable position. His stomach growled again at the prospect of nourishment. "Soup would be fine. Thank you."

He watched her disappear into the rear of the hospital ward. Her movements were quick and spry for a woman with wrinkles creasing her face and gray hair escaping its habit.

It would be a while before he was up and gadding about.

He raked his fingers through his hair again. What would Samuel say at his disheveled appearance? He hoped his friend had heard of his return. Maybe Samuel would come see him. And what of Captain Greene?

He closed his eyes and tried to remember what had happened. As soon as he regained his strength, he'd find Corporal Goshen. The guy had done a good job keeping him safe—so good it almost cost the poor man his life. The least he could do was find the man and see if there was anything he could do for him.

Captain Greene jolted him to the present.

"You're lucky, son. The bullet went in one side of your leg and exited out the other without hitting the bone. You could walk out of here in a matter of days, though I'd advise you to take it easy for a few weeks."

"Thanks, Doc." He glanced at his heavily bandaged leg. Relief washed over him like gentle waves of the ocean.

Fear-filled groans resounded from across the ward. Captain Greene excused himself to tend to his other patient. John prayed for the poor soul. That had been him just minutes ago. If there was one thing he had learned by now, it was how precarious—and precious—life was.

Sister Abigail reappeared with a tray. A savory aroma wafted from the soup. His mouth watered.

Hungry as he was, he still gave thanks for the meal. He had much to be thankful for, but he needed to return to the front lines. Hastening the end of the war was crucial. The thought of shirking his duty hung around his heart like an anchor. No matter how kind the staff was, he wanted no more men sent to this hospital ward.

John had almost finished his soup when shouts echoed through the hospital ward. His meal threatened to climb up his throat.

Second Lieutenant Morton's voice drilled its way into his ears.

☰CHAPTER 30☰

The Japanese patrol had passed by Mary without discovering her.

Had she really spent a second night hidden under the bushes?

Yes.

She climbed from under the brush, groaning with every move. Pain shot up her ankles with each step. She had to find the Allies soon.

She plunked onto a nearby stump and examined her toes. Dirty, raw blisters had burst and oozed, but her feet had escaped serious injury so far. She tore a hank of cloth from her hemline and wrapped it around the remains of her shoes to keep them on her feet.

Her thoughts drifted back to the day she'd found out about Daniel being captured. What she'd give to have that broken pair of shoes right now. They'd provide more protection than the tattered remnants clinging to her feet. She snorted. Life had been so cozy then, and she hadn't realized it. Circumstances likely weren't cozy for her brother.

"Lord, wherever Daniel is, please be with him and keep him safe." Tears formed at the corners of her eyes. She blinked hard. Tears would do her no good right now. She stood on limbs that shook with weariness. She was slowly starving.

She gritted her teeth and pushed herself forward.

One slow, pain-filled step after another. The sun beat down on her. Every so often she glanced at the sky. If storm clouds appeared, she could hope for rain. It might be difficult traipsing through a slippery trail, but at least she'd have water to quench her dust-coated throat.

Just before the sun reached its peak overhead, she halted.

There, in the distance, a road curved around a river. A rushing waterfall lay several hundred yards downstream.

She stumbled toward it.

Her cries of thanks to God sounded more like croaks.

She ducked into the water, relishing the coolness washing over her. Tiny fish darted around her, likely trying to swim away from the strange, squealing giant that probably frightened them silly. She used the bottom portion of her robe as a net to capture a few. Then, she trudged back onto the river's bank, wondering how to cook the creatures.

Later, having eaten the wiggling fish raw and drinking water from the waterfall, she dozed for a few minutes. With food in her belly and her thirst temporarily sated, there was hope of locating the Allies. She resumed her journey.

After two days in bed, John was more than ready for the front lines.

"Hello, friend." Samuel wove around the number of beds crowding the hospital ward and strutted to where John rested. "Sorry I haven't visited sooner. I was in the middle of a battle."

John greeted his friend with a warm embrace. "How are things going?"

"All right, I guess. We're gaining ground every day."

"One small patch at a time, right?" John leaned back on his elbows. "You hear about Goshen?"

"Yeah." Samuel nodded. "They sent him home. At least he's alive and in one piece."

"I'm glad I got to say goodbye." John reached for a notebook under his cot. "I got his address if you want to write to him."

"Thanks, I'd like that. Did you hear Lieutenant Brandon has made Soaring Eagle your temporary replacement? He's not bad, but I'd prefer you. We work well together."

"The doctor said I could to leave day after next. They needed the bed for someone injured worse than me. Help me up so I can take a spin around the place."

Samuel helped him stand. John reached for his crutches. He limped around the perimeter of the crowded hospital ward. As usual, Samuel prattled on about Susanna. Rather than feel envious, John was content to hear his friend so happy.

On the second trip around the ward, his leg throbbed and he was out of breath. He had to sit on his bed for a minute, to rest before he could continue. It surprised him how much strength it took to recover from wounds like his.

"You look beat," Samuel said. "Get some rest. I need to write another letter to Susanna."

John chuckled. "Tell her I said hello."

"Sure thing," Samuel called over his shoulder and exited the ward. John watched his friend leave and then closed his eyes. He could hardly wait to return to active duty. He needed to be more productive and help end this terrible war. So Samuel could return to the woman he loved. So he could find Mary and tell her how much he loved her.

After what seemed like mere seconds, he opened his eyes. Napping like a child stung his pride, but Samuel was right. He needed rest. Maybe he wasn't ready for the front lines after all.

Daniel Wishram approached.

The guy maneuvered around the sea of beds and then plopped onto John's bed and patted John's shoulder. "I want to say thank you for telling me about my sister and bringing me to your camp."

"Of course," John said. "Now that we're back, I need to tell you something." This man had been through so much. How could he tell him that he was in love with his sister? And he had no idea where she was?

Daniel was her brother. He could find her easy enough. John hoped Daniel could relay a message for him. He wanted Mary to know he was all right, that he missed her, and hoped to see her soon.

Sister Abigail called out to them from across the hospital ward. She waved at them as a grim frown darkened her features, and she hurried toward them.

She placed a hand to her chest and breathed heavily, her gaze falling on Daniel. "You are Daniel Wishram, am I correct? I was told you were here visiting Mr. Painted Horse."

Daniel looked confused but said, "Yeah. Why?"

Sister Abigail sighed. She shook her head.

John's stomach flopped like a freshly caught fish. An awful feeling swirled around him.

Several long moments elapsed before the woman found her voice. "There was an Indian girl assigned to the convent. I'm not sure if you're related, but her name was Mary Wishram."

Daniel sprang to his feet.

John leaped from his bed.

Mary? His Mary?

He tried to speak, but his tongue tied itself into a thick knot.

Daniel grasped the woman's shoulders. "She's my sister! Is she all right?"

Sister Abigail glanced at the floor and chewed her lower lip. She looked up and shook her head.

Daniel said, "Please, take me to her. I need to see her."

John was desperate to see her as well, but foreboding swept over him. If Mary was all right, why hadn't she made her way to this field hospital like Sister Abigail had? She would have raced here to see him—and Daniel. For some reason, she hadn't.

Why?

Sister Abigail stammered. Her chin drooped to rest on her chest. She wrung her hands and then met their gaze. "I'm so sorry, gentlemen, but she was in the basement of the convent when a bomb struck."

The air was sucked from the room. John dropped back onto the bed. His lungs gulped for air like a freshly caught fish.

"And?" Daniel's eyes widened, his chest heaved.

John's heart squeezed in his chest. Mary had been so worried about losing her brother, of being left all alone in the world. He had to believe the God he loved and served wouldn't do this to Daniel instead.

Sister Abigail shook her head. "The building collapsed. I'm sorry, I don't think she survived."

⫸ CHAPTER 31 ⫷

Mary stumbled into Manila, grateful to be alive. The city had just been liberated, and finding a United States military base hadn't been difficult. By following a cook dressed in a sailor's uniform, she found her way to the Navy's headquarters.

The cook disappeared inside a large chow hall.

She needed to find a superior officer and tell him what she knew about the Japanese forces. She hurried past a series of green tents before locating the bomb-pocked building. She entered and proceeded to the clerk seated at a desk outside a large office.

The clerk's gaze traveled from her tangled hairline to her tattered footwear. His lower jaw dropped. She must look a fright and smell worse, but there were more important matters at hand. She briefly explained her situation.

The wide-eyed clerk said, "Don't worry, miss. I'll let the colonel know you need to speak with him, urgently."

"Thank you." She stepped aside and waited. There were no chairs available, so she wandered down the hall a short distance. Several clerks passed by. One had the audacity to cover his nose. She happily watched him disappear around a corner.

"Miss Wishram."

She recognized the voice. She pivoted and stared at the smiling face of Colonel Goldman.

"Sir," she sputtered. What was he doing over here? It didn't matter. He was someone she trusted, and she was elated to see him. "How is your family, sir? You have a wife and three daughters, right?"

"They are fine. Thank you for asking." Colonel Goldman escorted her into his private office. "Please, have a seat. What can I do for you?" He motioned to a folding chair.

Mary relayed all the information she'd overheard from the Japanese soldiers. When finished, she blew out a breath.

"That's quite a story. You're lucky to be alive."

He scribbled furiously on a notepad and tore off the sheet of paper. He hollered for his clerk, who hustled through the door. "Pass this information up the chain of command, please."

The clerk grabbed the paper and rushed out the door.

Colonel Goldman folded his hands. "Now, would you like a room to get cleaned up, some fresh clothes, and something to eat?"

"Yes, please," she said. Soaking her sore feet, washing her tangled hair, putting on a soft, clean dress—those things sounded like heaven. Never again would she take them for granted.

"I'll have a bath drawn in the guest bedroom upstairs, and I'll have my cook bring a tray of food to you as soon as she can prepare it."

"Thank you, sir." Mary added, "Also, I need to let my bosses know that I'm all right. Can you help me with that, please?"

"Of course," he replied.

Mary gave the colonel Catherine Brandon's name. From there she was guided to a private room. She stripped off the tattered clothing and stepped into the tub. Nothing felt as good as that hot bath. She plugged her nose and submerged herself in the steaming hot water. Days of dirt, sweat, and tension washed away.

She stayed in the tub until the water was so cold she shivered. Only then did she step out and wrap a soft towel around herself. Though she was clean, bruises circled her wrists and covered her shins and knees. They were tender to the touch but also badges of honor, a small price to pay for helping the Allies.

Once dried off, she slid into a silky dress the housekeeper provided. Mary felt like royalty.

Later that night, she walked around the town. Citizens were rebuilding and jubilant in their newfound freedom. She enjoyed the smiles and laughter of children playing games of hide-and-seek while their parents patched together their damaged homes. The sun was setting by the time she decided to walk back to HQ.

A familiar voice snagged her attention. She spun around. "Private Greene!"

The wounded boy from Independence, Kansas, who had been brought to the convent when it served as a field hospital raced toward her.

The boy embraced her in a friendly hug. "It's good to see you, Mary."

"Thank you, Private. It's good to see you too. I see you've recovered all right." She remembered this kid had a brother she'd seen in a POW camp. "Have you found your brother?"

Private Greene nodded and blew out a breath. "I found him, and yours too."

"What?" Mary gasped. "You found my brother? How? Is he okay?" She squealed and twirled in a circle. Her brother was alive!

Private Greene placed his hands on her shoulders. His face was somber. "The POW camp they were in was liberated. They joined the resistance until they could reach the Americans. Someone, I don't know who, guided them into friendly territory."

"But he has to be all right." To be this close to finding him. . .it nearly undid her sanity. She grabbed Private Greene by the lapels. "You have to take me to him, please!"

Private Greene nodded. "That's why we came to find you. Colonel Goldman has asked me to escort you to a base camp south of here. We can leave in the morning, but, between the damaged roads and dodging the enemy, it might take several days."

———— ≈ ————

Two strokes of luck rolled John's way. The bad luck—Second Lieutenant Morton had requested the bed directly beside him and refused to be quieted about how he'd led Captain Greene and Daniel Wishram to freedom. Most folks didn't believe him, especially when the captain and Daniel stated otherwise.

To John's chagrin, being demoted and injured had not squelched the man's demeaning behavior toward women. If he uttered one more derogatory comment about the nurses, John swore he'd leap from his bed and toss the guy from the hospital ward. And that was if the nurses didn't clobber him first.

The good luck—the papers in his clenched hands, which were his orders to report back to Camp Pendleton. Not exactly discharge papers but a transfer to safer territory. He had a feeling Lieutenant Brandon knew the truth about the botched mission and wanted John out of danger as soon as possible.

There were things he had to do before he left. He had to find Sister Abigail fast and then find someone to drive him to the bombed-out convent. The woman claimed to have returned with two sisters to look for Mary. After digging through the ruins, they'd found evidence of Japanese soldiers. Fearing for their safety, they'd fled.

John refused to give up so easily. The bombing had happened only a few days ago. If Mary had survived being buried under the rubble, there was a chance she still lived, slim though it was. For his peace of mind, he had to at least try to rescue her.

And if she had died. . . A lump formed in his throat. His hands shook. At least her body would be transferred home. Daniel would never recover from the loss, but at least he wouldn't spend the rest of his life wondering what had happened to her. He prayed there'd be a measure of peace with that knowledge.

Early the next morning Captain Greene drove him to the convent with Sister Abigail and Daniel. What would they do if they found her body? Perhaps they should have brought a clergyman along. He thought about Pastor Ephraim at the church near Camp Pendleton. If he lost the woman he loved, he'd need the pastor's guidance to recover.

Following Sister Abigail's directions, Captain Greene found their destination. John sucked in a breath. He hardly recognized the place. The towering structure had been reduced to rubble. He ambled toward a pile of broken rocks that had once been the bell tower. Only the courtyard remained. It looked bereft among the ruins.

"Dear Lord." He sank to his knees.

"Mary!" Daniel hollered. "Mary!"

The man's grief-stricken cries bounced off the ruins and created haunting echoes in the cold, still air. John's own heart seemed to crumble like the shattered structure around him. No one could have survived this.

"The basement was directly over that spot, there." Sister Abigail pointed to the middle of the heap, slightly to the left of the demolished bell tower.

He asked God to help him through the next few hours. Gritting his teeth and steeling his mind, he climbed over the twisted wreckage. A dark hole yawned at him.

He crouched low and poked his head into the darkness. "Mary!" he yelled.

Daniel pushed him aside and shoved his head into the hole. "Mary, it's me, your brother. Holler if you can hear me, please."

Nothing but eerie silence met their ears.

Daniel continued to holler. "Mary, if you can hear me, please make noise, if you can, please."

There was no tapping or clanking. Nothing but a slight breeze that wafted through the trees. Not even the birds returned their cries. No sound broke the eerie quiet.

John's soul snuffed out like a candle flame in a howling wind. That part of his soul would never burn again. In spite of the bright morning sunlight around him, darkness descended upon his whole world and there was no moon to give him comfort.

For an hour he worked alongside Daniel and Captain Greene, slowly, methodically. They could find no sign of her. They dug deep, but no smell of death rose from the earth and no swarms of flies congregated around them.

John supposed she could have climbed out and run away, but what were the chances of that happening? She would have come across someone, Filipino civilians or other soldiers, who would have directed her to Base Camp.

Unless the enemy had captured her.

If the enemy had her, she could be alive yet.

A thousand thoughts swirled in his mind. The gentle breeze again reminded him that there was no smell of a decaying body. That gave him hope.

The sun had traveled the length of the sky and moved farther into the west. They needed to leave before Japanese patrols discovered them. Sister Abigail cried and uttered a somber prayer. She placed a handful of wildflowers on the pile of debris.

John's insides roiled at the real possibility that she was gone forever.

Captain Greene started the Jeep. John assisted Sister Abigail into the passenger seat. Daniel, silent and somber, climbed into the back beside John. It was a quiet ride to the hospital.

The next morning, John awoke to Lieutenant Brandon at his bedside.

"Good morning, John," the lieutenant said.

John hadn't considered it good, not with Mary missing, presumed dead. He mumbled, "Morning, Lieutenant."

"As you know," the lieutenant continued, "we're faced with invading Japan. I won't sugarcoat this. It's going to be bloody, and we need more code talkers."

"Okay." John shrugged. "What's that got to do with me?"

"There's a new class being formed at Camp Pendleton. Since you've been wounded and are not yet ready for active duty, you're the best candidate for teaching this new class."

"Fine." John pulled the blanket up to his chin, hoping it conveyed the fact that he wanted left alone for a while.

"I'll see about transport." Lieutenant Brandon patted John's shoulder and left.

Later, Samuel strode into the hospital and over to John's bed. "Hey friend, I hear they're shipping you home."

"Yeah." Only days ago he'd been happy to see Samuel. Now, the old jealousy returned. Samuel likely wouldn't be grieving the loss of his gal anytime soon. If anything, he might just be in her arms if the Japanese surrendered. Which they might, rather than face the invasion of their country.

"Hey, don't worry. I've got new orders to move out soon, but I'll keep looking for your girl everywhere I can. I promise."

"Thank you." It was a comfort that so many were searching for her—Daniel, Lieutenant Brandon, Sister Abigail.

"I need a favor but only if you're okay with it."

John rotated his ankle that had suddenly throbbed with dull pain.

"Can you please give these letters and mementos to Susanna?"

"Sure." John reached for the bundle.

Samuel said, "Hey, when I get home, I want for us to get together in Tuba City. That's about the halfway point between our hogans, right?"

"Yeah," John said. He wondered if Samuel would bring Susanna along. Much as he liked the girl, he'd feel like a third wheel.

John was almost embarrassed at how choked his voice sounded. It was tough saying goodbye to his buddy. He prayed the Japanese surrendered without the Marines having to invade the country.

"Hey, I gotta go. We'll catch up when I get stateside, whenever this crazy madness is over." Samuel rose and strode from the ward.

John tried to doze, but Morton waddled in.

"Know what I heard over breakfast?" he growled.

John closed his eyes, not caring one whit about what the man had heard.

Morton continued. "I'm being denied a medal for bringing you and the others back to Base Camp. Guess who the Navy decided to give a medal to?"

"Santa Claus," John muttered.

Morton scoffed. "No, you idiot. Captain Greene."

John was happy for the captain. He deserved the recognition. John made a mental note to congratulate him next time he saw him.

"I also heard they're giving you a commendation." Morton spit on the floor. "You, a wild savage, getting a commendation and not me."

John didn't doubt that Morton was being passed over for accolades. He did doubt the validity of Morton's gossip. Uneasiness washed over him. Morton believed it, and that was enough. A foreboding feeling told him to steer clear of the mentally disturbed man.

Not an easy feat considering the man slept right next to him.

Morton leaned close to John and muttered, "I'll get even with you, just wait and see."

John didn't sleep easy that night. The next morning his duffel bag was packed, and he was ready to leave just as the sun crept over the horizon.

Lieutenant Brandon arrived. "You ready to go?"

"Yes, sir." John nodded and hobbled to the waiting Jeep. The Philippine Islands had cut his heart to ribbons. Without Mary, those ribbons couldn't be sewn together again.

Lieutenant Brandon helped him up the rolling staircase and into the cargo plane. Soon the craft roared down the runway, carrying him away from the Philippine Islands, away from Mary, wherever she might be, alive or dead, he didn't know.

⚡CHAPTER 32⚡

Mary hung on tight as Private Greene pushed the Jeep to go faster. It had taken days to procure a vehicle before they could finally be on their way.

Her heart had leaped into her throat when they narrowly escaped a band of rogue Japanese soldiers. God had been with them so far. She hadn't come this close to locating her brother to be deterred now. Heaven help any Japanese soldier who stood in her way.

Only twenty more miles before they reached the base camp, and Daniel. As fast as Private Greene was going, she almost wished he could go faster.

It had been the last week of October when she'd received that terrible telegram stating he'd been taken prisoner. Now here it was the middle of March.

All this time wondering and worrying about him, and now they were so close to a reunion. She'd imagined it a hundred times in her mind. Would it go as she'd planned, with hugs, tears, and sharing of stories?

The camp finally came into view. A handful of armed guards stood sentry on the road that led into the large group of green tents. Private Greene applied the brakes and provided the necessary papers and credentials. After taking a moment to read the documentation, the guards waved them through the checkpoint.

Private Greene pulled up to the company headquarters and shut off the vehicle. "End of the line, Miss Wishram. The commanding officer here should be able to tell you where your brother is. I need to find my brother. Then I'm checking with the commanding officer to see what I missed."

"Thanks for the ride. I'll catch up with you later." She waved at him and hurried up the board walkway toward HQ. She collided with a corporal. When she asked, he informed her that Daniel worked in the kitchen.

"It's away from combat, ma'am. He's relatively safe there." He gave her directions. She sprinted that way, her heart thumping in her chest. Would he look the same after spending months in a POW camp? Images of the emaciated soldiers with wavering minds popped into her head.

No. Daniel would be fine. She'd recognize his face anywhere. If any cloudiness shrouded his mind, her presence would chase those dark clouds away. She burst into the kitchen area.

"Daniel!" She cried and ran toward him.

He looked up from peeling potatoes, aghast, and promptly vomited into the pile of peelings.

What? This wasn't what she expected. Why was he behaving like this? Shouldn't he be happy to see her?

The shock of seeing her must have been too much for him.

"Daniel?" She flew to his side, placed her hands on his cheeks, stared into his eyes. "Daniel, it's me, Mary."

He put his hands on her shoulders and squeezed so hard it hurt, then he pulled her into an embrace. His voice choked with emotion. "Sister, it's really you. You're not dead!"

Dead?

"Daniel, what are you talking about?"

"Mother Superior, a couple of soldiers, and I drove to the convent where you were, and the place was all caved in. We looked for hours and gave you up for dead when we couldn't find your. . .body."

His voice trailed off. How awful it must have been for him to believe she was dead.

She hugged her brother and soothed him. "It's all right now, Daniel. Eventually, I'll tell you the whole story. We can go home now, I hope."

Daniel shook his head. "Not right away. The Marines need every man they have to prepare for the invasion of Japan."

The thought of her brother invading Japan sent waves of terror cascading over her. Not only would he be in physical danger but his mind would be in danger too. Entering a country responsible for committing torturous atrocities would be a lot for anyone. Her mind spun in a thousand directions, searching for ways to keep him from such a fate.

Daniel said, "Maybe you can wait here for me, and we can go home together. I'll have to ride on the ship, though."

Mary chuckled. "I wouldn't mind, but the Marines might. Most importantly, we need to keep you from Japan." Her mind turned to thoughts of the war ending and arriving back on their reservation. What a happy day that would be.

She cleared her throat. "I need to somehow locate my friend, Sister Abigail. I bet she'll be shocked to see that I'm alive."

"Oh yeah," Daniel said. "One of the soldiers who helped look for you at the convent, his name is John Painted Horse. He says he knows you from Camp Pendleton."

She gasped.

John?

Her John? He was here?

"D–Dan–Daniel," she sputtered. "John is here? Where?"

"He was wounded and brought to the hospital here."

Wounded? Her thoughts whirled. "Is he okay? Where is the hospital ward?"

Her brother pointed.

"Thanks," she called over her shoulder. "I'll find you later, and we can have dinner tonight."

Minutes later she burst into a large tent crowded with beds. How was she to find him among all these men? She walked between the rows, searching the faces for the black-haired marine. She scanned the area for a doctor or nurse who could assist her, but the few she saw were busy and couldn't help.

"Well, hello, dearie."

Her feet froze to the floor. Embers of anger ignited in her heart. She spun on her heel.

Second Lieutenant Morton.

She squared her shoulders and held her chin high. This man held no power over her. She refused to let him goad her.

"Good day, sir." She turned her back to him, to walk away.

"I take it you found your brother. He must have told you Loverboy was here."

She gritted her teeth and said a silent prayer. "Yes, I've seen my brother. Now if you'll excuse me, I'm looking for Corporal Painted Horse."

"He ain't here," Morton snarled.

She had no patience for this man. "Where is he?"

The man emitted a sinister chuckle. Nausea rolled through her at the sound.

"He was supposed to be shipped out yesterday morning, but he got really sick beforehand."

"Where is he?" she asked more forcefully this time.

His expression turned somber, and he lowered his voice. "He was burning up with fever. It all happened so quick." He shook his head. "The doctors tried."

"Tried what?" A new medicine? To transfer him to a hospital ship? The tent roof seemed to collapse around her. The muddy floor threatened to drop beneath her feet. It was like being buried alive again, this time with grief.

Her lungs refused to draw air. She resisted the urge to grab the man by his collar and shake him until his teeth rattled.

Morton's voice dripped with what sounded like sympathy. "They tried to save him, but they couldn't. I'm sorry. He's dead."

———— ≈ ————

The gray, cloudy sky dumped buckets of rain onto the airstrip. The plane couldn't depart until the weather cleared. The muggy air was thick with mosquitoes, intent on feasting on the soldiers.

John swatted one from his neck. For hours he'd been holed up in an airplane mechanic's shack waiting for clearance for takeoff. He and Lieutenant Brandon had dozed and then written letters to their families. A myriad of conflicting feelings intertwined in his heart.

Part of him hadn't wanted to leave, not until he found out if Mary lived. . .or not. Besides, his friend Samuel needed him. Private Soaring Eagle didn't know how to operate the radio that well.

The other side of him was glad to be out of harm's way, at least temporarily. In exchange for helping train a new class of code talkers, he was given permission to visit his family. His mother and sisters would be overjoyed to see him.

The lieutenant grumbled. "I'll see if there's any word on when we can leave."

"And I need fresh air," John said.

He emerged from the shack and leaned against a fuel pump. Hunger gnawed at his stomach. He pulled a package of crackers from his duffel bag and forced himself to chew. They tasted like sawdust, but he needed sustenance.

Lieutenant Brandon held a lively conversation with the plane's captain. With the distance between them, John couldn't tell exactly what was being said.

Nearby, a pair of mechanics were up to their elbows working on a Corsair. They conversed in terms that John didn't understand and used tools he hadn't seen before. Few people on his reservation owned cars. Buses didn't go through with any kind of regularity. So, he'd never had the opportunity to learn about engines.

Watching the wrench turners reminded him of Mary. How well she could drive and repair a GMC truck. Exasperation flew from his lips. Everything reminded him of her. He pushed away from the fuel pump and ducked back into the shack.

It took an hour for the clouds to part. By then they had gained permission to depart. Best take advantage of the time between rain showers.

John slung his duffel over his shoulder and climbed aboard the aircraft behind Lieutenant Brandon. He gave the island one last look. Perhaps, someday, he would return.

He dropped into the bench seat beside his commanding officer. The slow island-hopping journey to the States would be a long one, for many reasons.

Cargo planes carried many things, but comfortable beds weren't among them. It didn't matter, though. He was used to sleeping on the hard ground.

Crossing the International Date Line would give him jet lag for days. But what really bothered him was leaving behind so many people he cared about. *Mary.*

He'd said goodbye to Samuel and promised to visit Susanna and give her the bundle of letters and keepsakes from him. The package rested in his duffel bag. His friend had the assurance of knowing where the woman he loved was. Envy tried to wiggle its way into his heart—fighting it was a constant battle.

Still, he could hardly wait to leave and not just because of the bugs.

Memories of Mary were at Camp Pendleton. He also had to inform Mrs. Drake about what happened. The poor woman would be devastated.

And he needed to say goodbye to Mary, let her go, and surrender her to God.

There was a slim hope that she lived. If God saw fit to bring her back to him, he'd be overjoyed, but there was much work to be done on the reservation and no time to dwell on the what-ifs. He had a family to care for.

Sister Abigail had promised to try her best to inform him if Mary was found, alive or dead.

His heart ached. He closed his eyes and leaned against his duffel bag.

Lieutenant Brandon's voice interrupted his thoughts. "Sleep while you can. It'll be a while before we're home." He stretched his legs and yawned.

He swallowed the thick lump clogging his throat. The plane's engines roared to life. The aircraft shuddered as it rolled down the runway, picking up speed. The momentum pushed against his body.

"Sir," John said.

"Yeah."

"Can you ask Catherine to please try to locate Mary?"

"You know I will, as soon as I see her. But we need to be careful. We can't risk sending classified information over the wires. You understand that."

"Yes, I do," John replied. Though he doubted he'd ever be told the whole story.

≣CHAPTER 33≣

For two days, Mary had asked every doctor and nurse who had been assigned to the hospital ward what happened to John Painted Horse.

"I'm sorry, miss, but I don't remember him." A harried nurse rushed to answer a doctor calling for her. Everyone she'd cornered had shaken their heads and told her they had been overwhelmed with patients and couldn't possibly remember them all.

This was crazy. How could anyone not remember the tall, handsome marine with a heart as big and mighty as the Pacific? Morton had said he died suddenly. But was he lying about the whole thing just to torture her? She couldn't find Private Greene or Samuel to ask them. They must have been given new orders elsewhere. Sister Abigail didn't know what had happened to John since she'd last seen him either.

"Why don't you ask those keeping records of the deceased?" a medic suggested. "They might know something."

Mary straightened her spine. "I already have. They didn't have his name listed in their registers, but thank you for your time."

Dejection clouded her weary mind. Communications with Catherine Brandon were coded, and sparse at that. She was wanted back in the States immediately. Mary couldn't stand the thought of leaving without knowing what happened to John.

She turned and walked to her temporary bunk in the tent with the nurses. Her brother had just been located, by the grace of God. Now she worried about John; would he be listed as MIA, fate unknown?

Her thoughts turned to his family in Arizona. Had they received a telegram? If so, how brokenhearted and frightened they must feel. She empathized with them.

She plopped onto her cot and read the two letters from Mrs. Drake. The woman had delivered them to Catherine Brandon who had gotten them to Sister Abigail. She had included the pictures of New Year's Eve. Mary could hardly look at them without feeling tears stinging in her eyes.

After she'd read the letters for the umpteenth time, she reached for her tablet and pencil. She'd write a nice, long letter to Mrs. Drake and thank her for her kindness. Rather than mail it, she'd hand it to her in person, considering how slowly the military moved correspondence.

Daniel found her after dinner. They spent time together that night sharing stories and talking about John. The time was both heart wrenching and healing. Afterward, Daniel gave her trinkets to take home with her.

Just before bed that night, she prayed for John and his family. She laid her head on the pillow, her mind full of thoughts of him.

It seemed she'd just closed her eyes when someone called her name. It sounded like John, but she couldn't tell through the thick fog surrounding Base Camp. She hollered his name twice, but her voice came out in a soft whisper.

"Miss Wishram!"

The voice was louder and clearer this time. It wasn't John. She opened her eyes a crack. Sister Abigail stood over her bed.

Mary bolted upright and rubbed her eyes. "Have you found John?"

Sister Abigail shook his head. "No. I'm here to tell you that you're flying out in twenty minutes."

"What?" Mary leaped from her bed, grateful she'd slept in her day clothing. "I need a minute to say goodbye to my brother."

"Okay, but be quick. I'll tell the Jeep driver to wait."

This was so much like the night she'd left Camp Pendleton. Mary gathered her few belongings and rushed toward the chow hall. Dawn had lightened the sky enough for her to see. So, thankfully, her brother would be up preparing breakfast.

"Daniel," she cried.

He was perched on a stool peeling potatoes. He dropped his hands into his lap, a mask of confusion covering his face. "What are you doing up so early, Sis?"

"I've been ordered stateside. I have orders to leave, now." She gulped, hoping this wouldn't be the last time she'd see him. Emotion thickened her throat. God had been merciful and spared him once. She prayed He'd do so again and bring him home safe.

A horn honked nearby.

"I've got to run."

Daniel offered a shy grin and then ducked his head. He pulled her into a hug and squeezed her hard. "I hope you find John."

"I hope so too." She prayed that she and John would be given a chance for a forever love.

Mary jumped into the Jeep. She was happy to see that her driver was Private Greene. The ride was a bumpy one that included swerving around potholes filled with muddy water. Much like the trip from Manila to Base Camp.

Private Greene said, "I found my brother. He's flying planes again, preparing for the invasion of Japan."

He swerved around a crater in the road and ran off the road for a few feet before righting the vehicle.

"Careful, will you, please?" she asked.

He aimed a scowl at her. "Sorry, but I got orders to get you there ASAP." He slowed for about two miles then sped up again.

He continued. "Anyhow, my brother and I have both written home to Ma. She should have the letters by now."

She imagined how happy their mother would be with the letters. If she received one from John, she'd be elated. More than once, she'd suspected Morton had lied to her. Yet, if he truly had, why hadn't she found proof otherwise?

Minutes later the Jeep rolled to a stop at the airstrip.

"Thank you for the ride." She reached for her bags, her heart aching. Private Greene hugged her. They promised to keep in touch.

Several people were boarding a large plane sitting nearby. She followed the others up the rolling staircase. She turned and gazed at the scenery and bade the island farewell.

She was going home, but what sort of fate awaited her?

Though John had returned from the islands days ago, still his body struggled to adjust to the time difference. At the hospital he'd found Susanna.

She had squealed with delight when he handed her the bundle of letters from Samuel.

As happy as he was at the romance between her and Samuel, he ached for the same opportunity with Mary. Or would he be more at peace letting her go? He still hadn't returned to the beach to say goodbye. He couldn't, not yet.

He finally understood why she'd been desperate to locate her brother. The *not knowing* threatened a person's sanity. His heart rent in two for the mothers who would never know the fate of their sons, wives their husbands, children their fathers.

Lieutenant Brandon had done nothing but hold secret meetings with his wife. Out of patience, John decided to seek information on his own.

After a fitful night's sleep in his old barracks, he located Catherine Brandon's office and paced the hallway. He wished he could shake the head nurse sitting smugly at the front desk who prohibited him from entering. The nurse was just doing her job, but her attitude lent no compassion.

More than that, his heart struggled to process the fact that Mary wasn't at Camp Pendleton with him.

He was desperate to question Mrs. Brandon about Mary. Cutting through the miles of bureaucratic red tape was tougher than hacking through a jungle of thick, twisted saw grass.

While he waited, Susanna passed by, wheeling a food cart. "Would you like some cookies and juice?"

"Thank you." He took the paper cup. "How are you passing the time these days?"

Her face turned pink. "Besides writing to Samuel?"

He groaned. Of course she was writing to Samuel.

"Miss Yates and I have become good friends."

"Miss Yates? Morton's secretary? How did that happen?"

"She's studying to be a nurse. We hang out after her classes. Sorry, Mr. Painted Horse. I need to deliver these snacks." She rolled the cart down the corridor.

Would he still be standing there when breakfast trays were delivered the next morning? He'd gladly wait that long, if it resulted in information about Mary.

Several candy stripers grinned at him as they strolled by. If another one batted her eyelashes at him, he'd pretend to be sleeping.

He twisted his Marines cap into a wrinkled mess. Was the president himself meeting with Mrs. Brandon? How much longer did he have to wait?

He bowed his head. "Please, Lord, open the doors."

He glanced down the corridor, hoping to see someone—anyone— other than flirtatious candy stripers. The uncompassionate nurse rolled her eyes at him. Did he really look that desperate? How did folks deal with this for months and years? He was going nuts, and it had only been a week.

The knob on Mrs. Brandon's door rattled. A nurse emerged and told him to go in.

John entered and faced the woman. "Afternoon, ma'am. Thank you for seeing me."

"I only have a few minutes. Don't thank me until you've heard what I have to say." She shuffled through a stack of papers on her desk.

Now, he was almost at a loss for words. "Please, ma'am, you and your husband know how much Mary and I care for each other. You saw us at Christmas. I need to know what happened."

Mrs. Brandon scrunched her eyebrows and dropped her files on the desk. "Corporal Painted Horse, you know I can't tell you everything. It's classified."

"Yes, I know that. But the military sends telegrams if, uh, the person in question is captured or, uh—" He couldn't bring himself to say the word *deceased*.

"You already know more than you should." Her eyes darkened and her lips pressed together. "I've heard rumors that she's alive. I've tried to contact her brother, but he's sick. I also tried to contact Colonel Gold-man about the rumors, but they're on the front lines."

Frustration heated his blood. He smacked his hat against his thigh. "So, that's it? More waiting?"

"I'm afraid so."

John huffed. "Thank you for your time."

He stormed from her office, allowing the door to slam. He'd be lucky if Lieutenant Brandon didn't knock him down a stripe for being rude to his wife. But the couple had to understand his anguish.

He left the hospital and hailed a cab. He could have walked to Mary's old apartment, but he was in a hurry. Perhaps Mrs. Drake could answer a few of the questions racing through his mind.

The taxi driver, who couldn't have been a day over sixteen, zipped along the roads. John squirmed in his seat. He couldn't get over how young this kid looked, but most men over eighteen were fighting a war, leaving much younger boys to jobs like this. If the war didn't end soon, the kid could trade his cab for a rifle.

The driver reached the destination without crashing. John's heart skidded to a stop. Mary's old apartment was dark, even in the afternoon sunshine. Memories assaulted him from all angles.

Walking her home, barefoot, from the Brandons' house the night they met.

Meeting her here and escorting her to the Brandons' for Christmas. The fry bread that had tasted heavenly.

Had it really been only a few months ago that he'd walked her home that joyous New Year's Eve? He'd kissed her on that very doorstep.

He hung his head with regret. Why hadn't he told her that he loved her? And wanted to spend the rest of his life with her? Even more crucial, he wished he'd shared more of his faith with her. Had he shared enough? Had she cried out to Him in her final moments?

Anguish escaped from his throat.

"You okay, sir?" The cab driver eyed him.

"Yeah," John's cheeks heated with embarrassment. The driver didn't seem to notice, or care, to his relief.

"I got another customer to pick up, if you don't mind."

"Sure." He paid the kid, exited the vehicle, and watched it drive away.

The walk to Mrs. Drake's apartment was a slow one. He knocked on her door once and then twice.

Apparently, she wasn't home.

He sat on the woman's doorstep, prepared to wait until the war ended for the chance to speak to her. According to his watch, ten long minutes passed. He leaned against the door frame and closed his eyes.

A Jeep full of rowdy soldiers raced by. John bolted upright and rubbed his eyes. Had he been asleep? He checked his watch and realized an hour had gone by.

John blew out a frustrated sigh. He scribbled a short note saying he'd return and hooked it to Mrs. Drake's front door. He walked to his old barracks. Dejection hung on him.

If this was an exercise in patience, he wasn't enjoying the lesson.

CHAPTER 34

While waiting for the plane to be repaired at Midway, Mary paced the entire length of the runway, twice! Darkness encroached. The pilot couldn't fly out until morning. Disappointment welled in her middle. She would have to spend the night here.

The pilot bunked with the mechanics in a nearby tool shed. She'd have to sleep in the plane. The lead mechanic told her not to worry. A guard patrolled the airstrip regularly. She would be safe.

Resigned to her fate, she climbed into the aircraft and lay across the bench seat. Visions of John filled her dreams. As the night grew darker, a nightmare of her brother dying on Japan's beaches stole into her sleep.

Clambering footfalls jolted her awake. The pilot entered the aircraft.

"Ready to go?" he asked.

She chuckled. "More than ready."

Dawn lit the eastern horizon, and the sun warmed the air. A cool breeze filtered into the plane. She reached for her new Bible, hoping to gain insight into her new faith. The verses John had rattled off with such ease were sometimes difficult to find. How had so much information been crammed into one book?

After a few minutes, she set it aside. John could help her understand it more, providing God's grace brought him back to her.

The postponed takeoff had put them behind schedule. It was a boring ride to their next destination on the way to the mainland. She chewed on a few crackers but hoped for something more substantial at their next stop. Her body craved sustenance, but her stomach turned somersaults at the relentless worrying.

They were landing in Hawaii to refuel.

She held on to her seat as the plane descended. Hawaii was the last stop before reaching the mainland United States. The length of time to reach Camp Pendleton was maddening.

The aircraft rolled to a stop.

"How long do we have here before takeoff?" she asked the pilot.

He pulled off his headset and Mae West life vest. "Maybe thirty minutes."

"Mind if I look around? If you promise not to leave me here?"

The tall, handsome blond aimed a wink at her. "Go ahead. What kind of gentleman would I be if I left without you?"

Mary placed her hands on her hips and scowled.

He laid his hand on his heart and tilted his head to the side. "I won't leave you behind, I promise. I'll be chatting with the other pilots, making sure the weather is safe for flying."

Her half-hearted smile didn't dampen his charm. According to the gaggle of girls who flocked to servicemen, pilots were the cream of the crop. Perhaps that explained his suave demeanor. Whatever the reason, she wouldn't be swayed from her feelings for John.

They exited the plane, and he helped her down the rolling staircase. She admired his gallantry, but John wasn't far from her thoughts.

She needn't worry about the flirtatious pilot anyway. He strolled across the tarmac and spoke with a group of mechanics loitering by the machine shed. She saw him speaking to the crew, likely about the earlier repairs to the plane, making sure it was safe to fly on to California.

Her next thought was finding food. The muggy heat wasn't as bad as the Philippines, but a cold drink would still be enjoyable.

She walked away from the airstrip to a nearby café. She dropped onto a seat at the counter and requested a burger, fries, and an Orange Crush. The soda jerk hollered the order to the cook and filled a frosty mug with more fanfare than necessary. Then, with grace that had to have been achieved by years of practice, he slid it down the counter where it stopped directly in front of her.

"Well done, sir." She pulled a straw from a nearby holder and stuck it into the frothy drink. The sugary foam wet her lips.

The soda jerk aimed a lopsided grin at her. Minutes later, he placed her order on the counter next to her drink. "Enjoy."

"Thank you." Bing Crosby crooned from the jukebox, and she was immediately taken back to Christmas night at the Brandons' house. She pulled her mouth away from her straw. Touched her fingers to her lips. Remembering John's kiss.

Much as Second Lieutenant Morton had rattled her, she couldn't make herself believe that John was really dead. Not until she heard it directly from either Lieutenant or Catherine Brandon.

And if he really was dead?

Her heart spasmed painfully.

If it were true, she'd locate his family and share her many memories with them. Of course she'd want them to share stories with her. Though they'd share a common heartache, she hoped they would also find solace with each other.

"You all right, ma'am?" The soda jerk raised his eyebrows.

She gulped. "I'm fine, thank you." She silently chastised herself for thinking such negative thoughts. She'd have to be more mindful to keep from slipping into despondency.

"Okay." He smiled and toweled off the counter. "It's just that you looked lost in thought. Lots of folks come in who have a lot on their mind."

"Who doesn't these days?" She finished her meal and hopped off the barstool. Before exiting the café, she left the soda jerk a nice, well-earned tip on the counter.

"Have a pleasant day, ma'am." He ducked into the kitchen.

"Thanks, you too," she called over her shoulder. She needed to hustle back to the plane. Regardless of what the pilot said about not leaving her, he had a schedule to keep.

The gallant pilot waited at the foot of the rolling staircase. He helped her up, and they boarded the plane. She found a seat as he started the engine and taxied to the runway. The engine revved as the plane picked up speed.

Her ears popped at the change in altitude, and she yawned a few times for relief. At the same time, she gazed out the window at the island below. The wreckage from the Pearl Harbor attack still littered the air-fields and clouded the otherwise crystal-clear waters. Would she join the grieving families of the men lost on that terrible day? Not only did she worry about John but her brother too. The thought of him in enemy territory threatened to unravel her sanity.

She pulled her gaze away from the window. So much loss and heartbreak. Trying to comprehend it all hurt too much. Why did God allow such things to happen? Would she ever have answers to these questions?

She steered her mind to more practical things. Would they reach the mainland before dark? If so, where would she sleep?

Her eyelids grew heavy at the hum of the engine.

She laid her head against the side of the plane and closed her eyes. Her overwrought muscles relaxed. She needed sleep. Dreams of a certain handsome marine occupied her mind.

Fragile embers of hope burned a bit brighter.

The next stop, Camp Pendleton.

———— ≈ ————

John gripped the Jeep's seat with one hand and the dashboard with the other. The vehicle roared over the dirt roads in the hills above Camp Pendleton, crashing through bushes and careening exceedingly close to the edge of the cliffs on both sides of the trail.

This was supposed to be a training exercise to hone their skills, not a joyride. John had been captured and then rescued by the Japanese, survived the jungles of the Philippines and a serious gunshot wound. Dying on the rugged roads would be a fate with a tragic twist.

"Take it easy, kid." He scowled at the seventeen-year-old driver, Private Wendell. The new recruit was amiable enough, but he lacked maturity.

Private Wendell claimed he'd driven his father's tractor over more than four hundred acres since he was a child. He had begged to drive the Jeep. John regretted giving the kid a chance to prove himself first.

If only John's injured leg hadn't ached so much, he might have had second thoughts about relinquishing control of the vehicle. Little help hindsight proved to be at the moment.

They should have reached Camp Pendleton hours ago, but one wrong turn after another had them deep in the wilderness with canyons yawning on each side of them. Darkness was fast approaching. Without streetlights or signs to guide them, they could be lost in these hills until tomorrow. Would anyone look for them?

John gritted his teeth. He should have never allowed Private Wendell behind the wheel.

"Look, kid, I've had enough. Stop this thing right now and let me drive."

Private Wendell slowed considerably. "Let me get to the end of this road, and then we can switch places."

"All right, but be careful." Would he ever see his family again? The way this kid drove, John couldn't help but wonder.

As soon as the Marines discharged him, he'd head straight home. His most recent letter from his mother said she and his sisters missed him. He'd tend the goats and sheep and forget about his time in the service. It wasn't like he could shout to the world the classified operations he was a part of. The code talkers were prohibited from talking about their roles in the military. A thread of bitterness coiled around his heart. Medals, awards, and accolades were abundantly awarded to service members all around him. Code talkers received none of this.

"Look out!" John gripped the dashboard.

The Jeep rounded a hairpin turn, spun on a patch of dirt, and tilted sideways. Private Wendell lost his grip on the wheel.

The world seemed suspended in time.

Tires lost traction.

Slid over the edge.

Careened downhill.

Through bushes, over rocks.

Large boulder ahead.

Sickening impact.

Deafening sound of twisting metal.

John's head went straight into the windshield. Pain blinded him. His ears rang. The acrid smell of smoke and the heat of flames licking close to the gas tank jolted him and kept him from losing consciousness.

John thanked God for protecting him. His thoughts turned to his comrade.

Moans and cries for help reached his ears. His eyes cracked open. Several hundred feet below, Private Wendell lay sprawled at the bottom of the canyon, bleeding.

"Hang on, kid." John moved his arm to his aching head. Blinding pain surged through his shoulder. His hand came away sticky with blood. How was he to save the kid and himself? Let alone go for help?

John glanced up toward the road. Had they really fallen that far? An uninjured man couldn't climb that steep cliff. His chances of scaling the terrain were even slimmer with his injured leg not totally healed yet.

Suddenly a sound sent terror tingling down his spine—the scream of a mountain lion, not far away.

He and Private Wendell were in deep trouble.

John cried out to his Savior.

Then his world went black.

⧮ CHAPTER 35 ⧮

The plane landed at Camp Pendleton. Mary breathed deep with relief. Once the aircraft rolled to a stop, she stood and exited via the rolling staircase.

A Jeep waited for her. She climbed in, and the driver drove straight to the hospital for a meeting with Catherine Brandon. Mary gazed at the building. A series of what-ifs nipped at her heels. She kicked the unwelcome thoughts aside, jumped from the vehicle, and hurried inside.

She strode to Catherine Brandon's office. After checking with the secretary, she ducked into the room.

"Good to see you alive and well." Catherine rose from her desk, and Mary leaned into her embrace. She was more than a commanding officer. Mary considered her a friend. One she would always cherish.

"Have a seat." Catherine motioned to a straight-backed chair. "Before I forget, let me return this."

Mary reached for her Ititamat and held it close to her chest, ever grateful to have it back.

Catherine said, "I just received a coded telegram from Colonel Goldman. He apologized for the delayed response, but he was in battle. He said you showed up in Manila. He remembered you from the debacle with Morton. He also said you made a great spy."

"Yes, ma'am," Mary said. "He treated me kindly."

For the next hour, Mary and Catherine covered everything that had transpired while she had been in the Philippines. Her information had helped the Allies locate a set of enemy-held caves in the hills. The Marines, under Colonel Goldman's command, had rooted the Japanese from the caves and put an end to their attacks.

When the meeting drew to a close, Mary shifted topics.

"Mrs. Brandon, my friend John Painted Horse was wounded in the Philippines. I went to see him, and Second Lieutenant Morton told me he died. I don't want to believe the scoundrel, but no one I talked to could tell me otherwise. Please help me find out what happened to him!"

Catherine pursed her lips into a bow. Then she chewed on her lower lip.

A heavy weight settled in Mary's middle. What if it was true? The air froze in her lungs. Panic closed in around her. Had she been reunited with her brother only to lose the man she loved? She shook her head. God couldn't be that cruel. Could He?

A cry escaped from her lips.

Catherine held up her hands. "It's not as bad as you think. John was alive, as of a few days ago."

Air whooshed back into her lungs. "What? You mean he's alive? Oh thank You, Lord." Happy tears filled her eyes. She had suspected Morton had lied. Now, she knew he had.

"But, he..." Catherine hesitated. She licked her lips and became very interested in a pile of paperwork on her desk.

"He...what?" Mary asked, unsure if she wanted the answer.

"He went on a training mission with a new recruit. They failed to return as scheduled, and they are now missing."

Impatience threaded its way through Mary's middle. "We have to go find them, *now!*"

"We already sent out a search party. They found the remnants of the burned-out vehicle smashed against a large boulder. There was no sign of survivors. They're combing through the wreckage searching for bodies—"

"Stop!" Mary leaped from her seat. "They are probably just lost. We have to go look for them." Had she kindled hope and come this close to being in his arms again, only to be told again that he'd died?

Catherine's voice took on a soothing tone. "Corporal Painted Horse is a very valuable asset to the Marines. Believe me, we're doing everything possible to locate him, but it doesn't look good."

Mary bolted from the room. Catherine called to her, but she wanted—needed—to be alone. She ran down the hospital steps and hailed a cab.

"Fastest way to the beach, please."

The driver raised an eyebrow.

"Hurry, please." She gulped.

"Okay, lady." The driver sped toward her destination. She paid the kid and stepped from the vehicle. The sound of the crashing waves met her ears. The smell of salt water once again tickled her nose.

She stripped off her shoes and allowed the waves to wash over her feet as she strolled along. Tears brimmed in her eyes. She hadn't given up on Daniel when things looked bleak. She wouldn't give up on John either.

She spotted the Seaside Palace. Music reverberated from the outside patio. People dined and laughed as if the world hadn't stopped spinning.

Memories of his laughter echoed her ears. The image of his smiling face popped into her mind. As long as he lived in her heart and memory, she couldn't say goodbye. Not yet.

She hailed another cab, asked the driver to take her to her old apartment, and gave him the address. She hated showing up on Mrs. Drake's doorstep so late, but she needed an objective friend right then, one who wasn't involved in top-secret activity.

The driver zipped through the streets, reminding her of the carefree ride she'd taken with John on New Year's Eve. All of them piled into the Jeep. Would it ever be like that again?

That night, she'd known it was only a matter of time before they all shipped out. She knew the risks. Still, that night may have been the last time she saw him alive. The sting of that reality punctured a painful hole in her heart.

The cab stopped in front of her old apartment. Unfamiliar items resting on the windowsill told her someone else was renting the space. Memories sent a pang through her.

She paid the driver and stepped from the vehicle. A chill swept over her when she banged on Mrs. Drake's door.

Mrs. Drake emerged, her hair in a riot of curlers.

Mary blurted, "John's. . .missing."

Her landlady wrapped her arms around her. Tension melted. Somehow, everything seemed all right when Mrs. Drake was near.

"I'm sorry to show up so late. I hope I'm not intruding," Mary said.

"Of course not. Come inside, dear."

Mrs. Drake led her to the sofa. Mary poured out as much of the story as possible without divulging classified information.

"You've both been through quite an ordeal. Don't give up hope. Let me make you a cup of tea." She rose and stepped to the kitchen.

"Thank you for packing my stuff for me." Mary was grateful for such a kind friend. They drank tea, and Mary elaborated on her newfound faith. And they reminisced about John.

"You must be hungry," Mrs. Drake said. "I'll make you something to eat. Do you mind grilled Spam and cheese sandwiches? I have fresh peas from my victory garden."

"That would be fine." Mary glanced out the window. She hadn't noticed how dark it had become, and she hadn't thought about finding a place to sleep for the night.

Mrs. Drake returned to the living room and handed Mary a plate. She chewed her food without tasting it.

"Why don't you stay with me for a few days?" Mrs. Drake asked. "I have a phone, and you can call Mrs. Brandon first thing in the morning to see if there are any updates."

"That would be lovely. Thank you." It would be nice to have this compassionate friend by her side if she found out John had—

She stopped right there. She had to focus and keep hope burning.

Mrs. Drake said, "Give her my number. She can call when they find your man."

Admiration and affection for the dear woman flowed from Mary's heart like a refreshing spring waterfall. She went to bed that night wrapped in a warm quilt on the sofa. Mercifully, exhaustion swept over her, and she slept without being haunted by nightmares of losing John.

The next morning, she woke to the aromas of pancakes and eggs.

"Rise and shine, sleepyhead." Mrs. Drake chuckled in the kitchen. "Call Mrs. Brandon and see if there's any news."

Mary stood, stretched, and slowly walked to the phone. A mix of hope and trepidation hammered in her chest. Her fingers trembled as she dialed the hospital operator, who then patched her through to Catherine Brandon's office.

Catherine picked up after the first ring. "Hello?"

"It's Mary. Has the search party found John yet?" She bit her lower lip. Anyone could detect the uneasiness in her tone.

There was a pause. "No, we haven't, but the search resumed at daybreak. I hope to hear something any time now."

"Please call me at my landlady's house if you hear anything. She said I could stay here for a few days."

"Of course." Compassion filled Catherine's voice.

Mary gave her the number then ended the call. Though pancakes and eggs filled her stomach that morning, life had been drained from her soul, leaving a yawning emptiness. Could God really fill the gaping chasm of loneliness? She sometimes struggled to figure out how faith in Him worked.

She thought of Pastor Ephraim. He had been a great help to John. She should pay him a visit, and hopefully he could help her too. He would want to know John was missing, so he could pray.

After breakfast, she helped Mrs. Drake wash the dishes. She walked to the grocery store but hurried back in case Catherine Brandon called. To her dismay, the phone had remained silent the entire time she had been gone.

She sat on the porch steps. The warm spring sun burned in the sky, casting waves of heat through the air. The noon hour crawled by. Every minute that passed, she expected to hear the phone ring.

It didn't.

Hunger gnawed in her stomach, but she didn't think she could eat.

Anticipation drove her silly. Sitting around doing nothing would push her mind to insanity. "I'm going to the hospital to see Mrs. Brandon," Mary announced.

Mrs. Drake waved her off.

Later, Mary entered the hospital and strode to Catherine's office, full of hope. To her dismay, there was still no word from the search party.

Mary demanded, "I want to know where they are looking so I can go there and help."

Catherine looked ready to cry herself. "In another twenty-four hours they'll call off the search."

Numb with grief, she nodded and returned to Mrs. Drake's apartment.

That night she climbed into bed on the sofa, unsure of what the next day would hold.

The telephone rang.

Mrs. Drake hurried to answer it and then covered the mouthpiece with her hand. "Sorry, dear, but this is my sister from North Carolina. She doesn't understand the time zone difference."

Disappointment swept through Mary. She snuggled under the soft quilt Mrs. Drake had given her. Though her head ached and her eyes burned, she was unable to fall back asleep.

Fretful hours passed, and then sunlight filtered through the thin curtains and spread across the room. Mary gave up on sleep, dressed, and hurried to Catherine's office. There was nothing else to do but wait and pray.

She found a book and read the first chapter. Weariness wrapped itself around her. Twice she nodded off and nearly fell off the straight-backed chair.

"Maybe a walk will help." She placed the book on the chair and strode into the hallway. She paced the hospital's corridors. The blisters on her feet hadn't fully healed yet, and her feet ached. So did her soul.

Pastor Ephraim popped into her mind. She'd forgotten to visit him yesterday. Surely he could answer the questions she had about her faith and help settle the whirling anxieties in her mind too. Yet she hated to leave the hospital when news about John could come in at any moment.

Mary strolled back toward Catherine's office. Nearby, a cranky nurse whispered to several other nurses that there was no need to prepare for the return of the missing Marines. The commanding officers had called off the search.

If they weren't preparing to treat John and his comrades' wounds, they must not have survived the crash.

No! Mary shook her head, as if to shake the terrible possibility from her mind.

Susanna rounded a corner and summoned Mary to Catherine Brandon's office. An ember of hope tried to flicker, but it lacked the strength.

Mary stepped into the room. Catherine sat at her desk. Her shoulders sagged, her hands folded in front of her. Dark circles shadowed her tired eyes. She was flanked by Lieutenant Brandon and an officer she didn't recognize.

They tried to exchange pleasantries but faltered.

"Mary, I'm sorry." Lieutenant Brandon eased forward. His Adam's apple bobbed before he ducked his head. He cleared his throat twice. "We're calling off the search."

"But you can't." Panic swirled in her stomach and tried to force its way up her throat.

"Mary, you don't understand. It appears that animals got ahold of them. We found what's left of—"

"*No!*" The wail wrenched itself from the depths of her soul and erupted with a pain she'd never felt before and prayed she'd never feel again.

The room turned sideways and blurred before her.

She dropped to the floor. Catherine was at her side, trying to console her.

Never in her life had she wept so hard. Strength and hope ebbed from her with every tear that spilled from her eyes. Mary stood and fled from the room.

The beach beckoned her. It was the last place they had been together. She bolted that direction. She'd remember him much more vividly there. Then, maybe he wouldn't really be gone.

And if he was?

Could she ever really say goodbye?

ΞCHAPTER 36Ξ

Darkness had fallen.

Hours later, after wandering aimlessly around Camp Pendleton, Mary dropped onto a tree trunk that had washed ashore. She slipped off her shoes and stockings and pressed her bare toes into the cool sand.

Her thoughts drifted to John's family. How many days before they received a dreaded telegram? That innocuous scrap of paper would shatter their hearts and change their lives forever. Would they accept the fate of the son and brother they loved so dearly? Or would they besiege the brass for answers that might never come?

And what was she to do without the only man she'd ever loved? Gone before they had the chance to build a life for themselves. Her stomach did a series of nauseating somersaults. She stood and padded across the wet sand. A small, foamy wave rolled over her toes.

She lifted her head to the heavens, to ask the Almighty why He allowed such awful things to happen, like war. The words died on her lips as she gazed at the beauty around her.

The sun had long ago kissed the blue sky good night and slid beneath the horizon. Stars studded the inky black canvas above her. A round, full moon had pushed itself up off the eastern horizon and crept higher into the dark sky.

She wandered to the rock she and John had sat on and talked of everything that had come to their minds. Where they had both laughed and spoken of serious things. Tomorrow she would tie a small shell from this beach to her Ititamat to record his death.

In spite of the heartache wrenching her heart in two, there was beauty in life. In a few moments she would push the heavy rock aside and dig out the medicine pouches they had buried on New Year's Eve, but for now she had to cry. Tears streamed down her cheeks with reckless abandon.

Time seemed to suspend itself as she sat grieving the loss of the man she loved.

Gusts of cold wind blew across the beach.

She shivered.

It was time.

She lifted herself off the rock and tried to shove it aside. It refused to budge. She placed her shoulder to the gritty surface and dug her heels into the sand, without success.

Frustration swirled within her. Those medicine pouches couldn't remain buried. The ocean might eventually wash them out to sea where they would be lost forever. Or someone might come along and steal them.

If they hadn't already.

The pouches would have to stay put for the night. Tomorrow she'd bring someone here to help her move the stubborn hunk of granite. Exhausted, she dropped onto the rock and allowed herself a few more minutes to reflect on how different her life would be without John.

Tomorrow.

Tomorrow she'd obtain the only tangible item she could, a reminder of their last night together, and leave Camp Pendleton. She'd visit the Takahashis at the internment camp and explain what she could about why she hadn't visited in so long. Then, she'd go home to her reservation and wait for Daniel to join her.

Strange noises yanked her from her thoughts.

A dark figure approached.

Who would be out this time of night? Thieves? Drunken sailors? Men like Morton? Indignation at being interrupted at such a moment mixed with fear at what could happen to a woman alone at night.

Should she run? Hide in the bushes? She scoffed at such a notion. This was California, not the jungles of enemy-held territory!

The interloper limped from the shadows.

Sparks of recognition ignited.

What was the Lord giving her?

The man she loved?

"John!" she screamed, leaping from her perch and springing to him.

She threw herself into his arms and clung to him with strength she didn't know she had. Mud was caked in his hair. Scrapes and scratches covered his face. His clothing was ripped and dirty, and his hands were coated with blood.

But this was really him. "What happened?" she cried.

"Against my better judgment, I let Private Wendell drive. I guess he had something to prove, after running away from an abusive home and lying about his age to join the military."

"Can't say I blame him for that, but where have you two been these past few days? I was worried sick."

He sucked in a breath. "I'm getting to that. After the crash, he was too wounded to climb the cliff to get out of there, and my leg wasn't healed enough to climb out either. I was able to drag him into a small cave nearby and barricaded the opening with rocks to keep wild animals out. Then, I assessed his wounds, and I knew." He tilted his head to the sky and was quiet for a moment.

"Knew what, John?"

"He was too badly wounded to survive. It was only a matter of time. I knew folks would be worried about me, but I couldn't go off and leave this kid. Not when he was about to face the Almighty—and certainly not with mountain lions nearby."

"Mountain lions?" This ordeal sounded as frightening and dangerous as being on the front lines. She leaned her head on his shoulder.

"Private Wendell talked about the Sunday school he'd gone to as a child, before his pa died and his ma married a drunkard. I reminded him that God had been with him as a child. And God was still with him right there in that canyon."

She gasped. "Jesus Christ the same yesterday, and to day, and for ever Hebrews 13:8."

"Yeah." John cleared his throat. "Private Wendell died last night. I cleared the rocks from the cave entrance and lifted his head so he could see the moon. He understood that even in the darkest of times of his life, God was still with him. Enabling him to escape from the man who drank like a fish and beat him for the sport of it. And leading him to a place where he could meet God in the end."

"Oh John, I'm so sorry." She ached for Private Wendell's poor mother who was about to receive the worst news of her life via a telegram.

So much loss and pain.

"By then my leg had healed enough. I covered Private Wendell's body with rocks to protect it from scavenging animals. Then, I climbed out of the canyon and walked until a Mexican farmer found me. He brought me to the hospital on base."

"And here you are." Mary hugged him so hard he groaned. Even then, she never wanted to let him go. When he gasped, she relaxed her grip, but just a bit.

"I declined medical help and came looking for you. Mrs. Drake kindly suggested I try the beach."

A mirth-filled giggle rolled from her lips. "And you found me."

"Yes, I found you." John squeezed her in a hug. Then he lifted her chin with his finger.

She met his gaze.

"I love you, Mary, and I want to spend the rest of my life with you. Will you marry me?"

"I love you too, John. Yes, of course I'll marry you." She thanked God for being with her in the darkest of times. The war would soon end, and it would be up to the survivors to shine the light of God's love to the far reaches of the world.

John ran his thumb across her wet cheek to wipe away a happy tear. Then he kissed her again, full of promise of their happily ever after, beneath a peaceful moon.

AUTHOR'S NOTE

Dear Readers, thank you for going on this journey with John and Mary and me. It's been an honor to write this book, but that's not to say there weren't challenges. The hours and hours it took me to research, write, and edit this book sometimes made my eyes cross.

Mary is named after my grandmother, a Yakama who endured tragedy due to racism. She died when I was a small child. It saddens me that I didn't get the opportunity to know her more. I hope I don't offend my fellow Yakama tribal members by using the former spelling of our tribal name assigned to us by the US government. That is how our name was spelled at the time this story takes place, and I wanted to be as historically accurate as possible.

The idea of developing the Navajo language into a secret code came from Philip Johnston, the son of missionaries who had been raised near the reservation. The first group of Navajo Code Talkers consisted of twenty-nine members. Sadly, many of the injustices suffered by my native characters also happened to the Navajo and Yakama people in real life. Many of the code talkers had been sent to residential schools where meals were scant, and they often went hungry.

When they came home from WWII, the state of Arizona didn't give them and other Natives in that state the right to vote until 1948.

Finding my way around the Navajo Reservation was a joy. The beauty of the landscape took my breath away. I'd dearly love to return someday and spend more time there.

For more information about the Code Talkers and the Navajo culture, visit the Navajo Interactive Museum in Tuba City, Arizona, and the Navajo Museum, Library and Visitor's Center in Window Rock, Arizona. "Navajo Code Talkers of WWII" is an educational documentary about these brave men. One of the best and most informative books about the code talkers is Code Talker: The first and only memoir by one of the original Navajo code talkers of WWII by Chester Nez; Dutton Caliber; An Imprint of Penguin Random House; 2011.

Debby Lee, a proud member of the Yakama tribe, started writing as a child but never forgets home, the cozy town of Toledo, Washington, and her Native American roots.

A former president of the Olympia chapter of Romance Writers of America, Debby enjoys participating in both Romance Writers of America and the American Christian Writers Association. Her sixth novella collection with Barbour Publishing released in December 2019. She is represented by Tamela Hancock Murray of the Steven Laube Literary Agency.

A self-professed nature lover, Debby feels like a hippie child who wasn't born early enough to attend Woodstock. She wishes she could run barefoot all year long and often does when weather permits. During football season, she cheers for the Seattle Seahawks with other devoted fans. She's also filled with wanderlust and dreams of traveling the world.